THE INTERVIEW

THE INTERVIEW

JUDGE, JURY, & EXECUTIONER™ BOOK THIRTEEN

CRAIG MARTELLE

MICHAEL ANDERLE

DISRUPTIVE IMAGINATION

CONNECT WITH THE AUTHORS

Craig Martelle Social

Website & Newsletter:
http://www.craigmartelle.com

Facebook:
https://www.facebook.com/AuthorCraigMartelle/

Michael Anderle Social

Website: http://lmbpn.com

Email List: http://lmbpn.com/email/

Social Media:

https://www.facebook.com/LMBPNPublishing

https://twitter.com/MichaelAnderle

https://www.instagram.com/lmbpn_publishing/

https://www.bookbub.com/authors/michael-anderle

LMBPN Publishing
PMB 196, 2540 South Maryland Pkwy
Las Vegas, NV 89109

Version 1.00, July 2021
ebook ISBN: 978-1-64971-938-6
Print ISBN: 978-1-64971-939-3

THE INTERVIEW TEAM

Thanks to our Beta Readers

Micky Cocker, James Caplan, Kelly O'Donnell, and John Ashmore

Thanks to the JIT Readers

Veronica Stephan-Miller
Peter Manis
Larry Omans
Rachel Beckford
Dave Hicks
Daryl McDaniel
Diane L. Smith
Thomas Ogden
Zacc Pelter
Micky Cocker
Dorothy Lloyd
Jackey Hankard-Brodie

If we've missed anyone, please let us know!

Editor
Lynne Stiegler

We can't write without those who support us
On the home front, we thank you for being there for us

We wouldn't be able to do this for a living if it weren't for our readers
We thank you for reading our books

CHAPTER ONE

Interstellar Space, *Wyatt Earp*, Magistrate Rivka Anoa's Heavy Frigate

"Holding pattern! What the hell does that mean?" Rivka shouted at the screen. Grainger looked back at her, wearing an unusually grim look.

"Don't make this harder than it is. The Federation Council was less than amused by the raid on not one but two ambassadors. They are debating the status of the Magistrates right now."

"But they were dirty as fuck." Rivka stomped around the bridge while Aurora, the pilot, and Clodagh, the chief engineer, focused on their workstations even though nothing was happening because they were stopped in interstellar space, waiting for clearance to proceed. "Dirty. Stinking. Criminals."

"We all have our skeletons, Rivka. I remember how you got your start."

"I killed a man who was freed by a jury of his peers. A man who was a murderer."

"A jury trial supersedes even our authority. Double jeopardy. We can't try someone twice for the same crime. But your insight has been a gift to us. You saved my life. It also looks like your gift might be a curse."

Rivka flopped into the captain's chair, her anger spent. She knew the curse. She felt the pain of seeing into others' minds. She wouldn't go crazy as long as she was doing it for the greater good.

"Introspection," she said softly. "It's good for the soul. Maybe I need a trip to Azfelius."

"In its own time, but that time is not now, even though now is when it's needed most. Find something to do that doesn't involve punching holes in the walls. The High Chancellor is engaged with the council right now. I'll call you as soon as I know anything."

"That fucking smug bastard," Rivka growled.

"I know you're not talking about the High Chancellor." Grainger made a face. Aurora snorted and covered her face with a hand while clearing her throat.

"Of course not. That ass-grabbing shitweasel, the honorable Ambassador Bik Tia Nor from fucking Delegor, the place with inedible food. No wonder they have laws saying you can't leave leftovers. Diddle-fucking crotch rot."

Aurora stood and tried to make her way off the bridge, her lips a tight white line as she tried to keep her mirth under control. She was failing.

"Are you upset? It's so hard to tell with you and your interminable poker face," Grainger quipped. "Maybe you can put one of the SCAMPs on the line so I can have a conversation where we discuss the issues."

Clodagh chuckled out loud before burying her face in

something she tried to make believe was new and fascinating on her computer screen. "What issues are there to discuss? I'm to cool my heels right here until I'm dismissed, summoned, or freed. I don't see any other options." Icicles hung from Rivka's words. She flexed her jaw to relieve the anxiety she was carrying. She could feel her nanos fighting the wrinkles she was trying to create around her eyes.

"It's him and Delaveen. Nothing we can do now will change their crusade. Trust the High Chancellor."

Besides her crew, the High Chancellor was one of the few individuals she looked up to. His job was hard enough without her making it harder. "I didn't think I was doing anything out of bounds. I was following the evidence."

"I know." Grainger smiled. "It's not you. This has been a long time coming. The Federation Council has members who think they are above the law. The High Chancellor will set them straight. Now, take a load off and relax. Order some food or something." Grainger signed off.

Rivka summoned the ship's sentient intelligence. "Clevarious, transfer our coordinates to Ankh so I can order some hot wings."

"You never order hot wings. He'll think you've been taken over by a succubus."

Rivka froze in place. "C? Are you yanking my chain?"

"If you had a chain, it would have been fully tugged, Magistrate. I'll take care of the order."

Rivka waved over her shoulder as she strolled off the bridge. Aurora averted her eyes.

"Go back to your post, Aurora. I'm a lot less mad now, and All Guns Blazing food is inbound."

"That always takes the edge off. Can we get some coleslaw?"

Adjunct Federal House of Arbitration, The Royal City of Khn'Chik, Yoll

"Next order of business, the Magistrate Corps," the heavy voice of the Red Rock chamber's secretary intoned. The Adjunct Federal House was also called the council because of the way the group was arrayed before a central speaker.

Lance Reynolds sat in his designated chair, which was by itself above the others at the front. He had come to the council on this day solely for this topic. Usually, his seat was empty in this location since he was normally on Red Rock, but he needed to clear the air with a few of the ambassadors in their role as representatives who were poisoning too many of the others. They'd called for an independent investigation.

Lance had every intention of allowing it in order to show the entire council what some of its members were up to. He hoped that by airing the dirty laundry, it would get shut down in a hurry.

"Thank you, Mr. Secretary," Lance responded as he stood. "I ask High Chancellor Wyatt to address this august body and put your concerns to rest."

Ambassador Bik Tia Nor pounded on his table since talking without being recognized was strictly prohibited. In his role as Chief Arbiter, General Lance Reynolds had the floor and refused to yield despite the pounding and frantic waving of more than a dozen members. Lance likened what he saw to a class of second graders eagerly requesting permission to go to the bathroom.

A tall man with red eyes stood from the spectator seats at the side of the chamber. He strode with his head held high to the podium and took his place behind the lectern. The chamber secretary called for quiet.

General Reynolds stood to better glare at the offenders, but the upstarts remained unswayed. He banged his gavel, a tool that was meticulously cared for because he used it constantly, and it traveled with him. It was surprising that it hadn't been broken. The chamber finally quieted. He looked down to find the High Chancellor standing behind the lectern, his hands clasped behind his back as if ready to give a lecture to college students.

"High Chancellor Wyatt, the floor is yours," the General announced in a loud voice.

The ambassadors pounded for a few more seconds before the General gestured for the sergeant at arms, a stocky four-legged Yollin. The peacekeeper moved to within arm's reach of the worst offenders. That was their only warning. If there was a next time, they would be dragged out of the chamber and removed from the council. Before they could get back to their office, a formal request to their home government for their replacement would already have been submitted.

Delaveen and Bik Tia Nor knew where the boundaries were and pushed them to a bloated extreme, but they wouldn't get themselves removed. They had an agenda that would not be satisfied if they were sent home.

The High Chancellor bowed to the assembled body, a near-record showing of ninety-five percent of the members. There had been only one session in the Federation's history with every member, but that had been a fluke in a session on issues that were of minor importance.

Unlike the concern before them today.

"Chief Arbiter," Wyatt turned to nod to Lance Reynolds, "most august ambassadors of the Federation Council, guests, and the staff who make everything we do possible, I wish you fair tidings. The issue before us is foundational to our existence. We're talking about the legal framework within which we must operate for equal opportunity to flourish.

"I want to reinforce the rule of law and the role it plays within the Federation. It starts with a guarantee of safety for member planets through a treaty and charter that planetary governments agree to when they join the Federation. It is a contractual obligation between members and their peers under the umbrella of this alliance.

"Safety leads to equal opportunity to acquire goods and services without fear that they will be stolen, that they won't be attacked. These are foundational to a civilized society. But we have individuals who want to operate outside of our legally binding agreements.

"Murderers, thieves, traffickers, and so many more. Crime is a given within a civilized society, but we don't have to let it run rampant. And we give people the opportunity for redress through our courts, both planetary and Federation.

"Sometimes, those vehicles are not available because the crimes are so perverse as to demand that they be addressed right away to limit the negative impact on the rest of the

Federation." Wyatt glared at the youthful-looking ambassadors from Foromme and Delegor.

"Crimes that extend beyond a system's heliosphere and into interstellar space fall under the jurisdiction of the Federation. To help us enforce the law on the frontier between planets, we've developed the Magistrate Corps, only five judges strong at present. They are out on the frontier, rooting out Federation criminals on member planets. The cooperation we've received from our members has been exceptional, even when we've removed planetary leaders for corruption like on Qintaqua, where the planetary administration actively hindered our investigation by kidnapping one of our Magistrates.

"The latitude afforded the Magistrates extends to the thankless challenges they endure every single day, whether on the job or not, as we saw on Tanglewood, a member planet who lied to become a Federation member and saw fit to leave one of our Magistrates in the middle of a civil war with no hope of rescue. They are now a former member. I have numerous examples of those who decided to work outside the Federation's loose legal framework, embracing a life of crime, violating the law to the detriment of not just the Federation but every member planet.

"I'm here to defend the actions of one Magistrate, Rivka Anoa, but just like interstellar crime, this is about far more than one person. This is about the administration of law and order within the Federation. This is about Justice. Like most law enforcement, if there's a mistake, all of law enforcement gets demonized. But what if there was no mistake? What if law enforcement got it right every single time? That is the case with Magistrate Rivka Anoa since as one of the very rare telepaths, she can see the truth."

The council erupted as a quarter of the members stood and shouted despite the ban on such behavior. There were too many, as if they'd practiced the maneuver, or maybe they were all outraged at the same time in the same way.

The High Chancellor looked over the crowd to see who was the most anguished about the revelation. Forbearance. Wayfair. Tepulon. Xynite. Reikistjarna. Ryleah. All planets that the Magistrate had visited while conducting investigations. None of them were happy to discover that the Magistrate had peeked into the minds of their officials all the way up to the planetary leaders.

Finally, the Chief Arbiter had had enough. He banged the gavel twice, then a third time. The grumbling continued. He stood and walked down the stairs beside his chair, across the floor, and up the aisle. The grumbling died as he zeroed in on Delaveen and Bik Tia Nor.

He stopped before them.

"She killed my wife!" Nor shouted into the silence. He brought himself to his full height.

"And that is why we're here, but I will cancel this proceeding if you cannot conduct yourself according to chamber rules. Do you understand?" Lance Reynolds' piercing look broached no opportunity for the Delegor ambassador to continue his defiance. "Sit. Down."

Lance had been thoroughly briefed on the situation. The Bad Company had been targeted for their enhanced blood, the same type that flowed through his veins. Ever since the takedown, there'd been no more abductions. The blood trade had been dismantled, exactly as Nathan Lowell had requested, exactly as the Federation needed. Like the slave trade. That also had been dismantled quicker than he'd thought possible by the very same Rivka Anoa.

Telepathy. Insight into the criminal mind. He knew that for what it was: a burden that would torture her very soul. Every telepath he knew suffered from their so-called gift, including his daughter Bethany Anne. It was hard enough to explore one's own mind, but to be inundated by the thoughts of strangers day in, day out, seeing the very worst that sentient creatures thought?

For the Magistrate, it was also about balancing the right prohibiting self-incrimination. The mind could not be the only indicator of guilt.

No wonder she surrounded herself with the artificial life forms now referred to as SIs, sentient intelligences.

Lance strolled down the aisle and made a hard left, a detour to intercept the sergeant at arms. He pointed at Nor and whispered into the Yollin's ear before continuing his trek back to his seat. Once there, he gestured for the High Chancellor to continue.

"Magistrate Rivka Anoa is waiting in interstellar space right now, waiting for us to tell her to get back to work or do something else. I need her on the job, ensuring that your people can live their lives according to a set of rules that we all agreed to. This is the fabric of society. It is what allows civilization to continue. Otherwise, we'd fall to the barbarism of brute force."

Bik Tia Nor glowered at the High Chancellor.

Is it for show, or is it because he'll start to age normally again? Wyatt wondered. *His wife was a dealer in a deadly trade, and he knew it. Getting caught was inevitable when you messed with the Bad Company. Did you think we would do nothing?*

Ambassador Delaveen from Foromme raised his hand.

The Chief Arbiter pointed. "The ambassador from Foromme is recognized. You have two minutes."

"My compliments to the Chancellor of the Federation," Delaveen stated flatly, using the General's other formal title. "The honorable ambassador from Delegor is married to my sister...was married. Magistrate Rivka Anoa attacked my home, where she stayed while visiting Foromme, chased her into the safe room, and then blew the door off the hinges to slaughter her in cold blood. Is this the frontier justice we were sold when the Magistrate Corps was first broached? I say to you that it is not. We must dismantle the Magistrates immediately before any others fall to their heavy-handed methods. Before any other innocent victims are sacrificed on their altar of power. We must cut off the blood they are using to paint our streets red. They aren't official Federation judges; they are vigilantes with the full backing of the Federation. I demand their heads, the head of High Chancellor Wyatt, and the Chief Arbiter's immediate resignation!"

"Hear, hear!" Bik Tia Nor shouted before covering his mouth. He offered his hand, and Delaveen shook it before he sat.

The gauntlet had been cast at the feet of the humans who had presented themselves before the many races and species filling the chamber.

Another member raised a dainty hand. Reynolds selected the creature, who spoke in a light voice—the ambassador from Xynite. "The people of Xynite do not support any miscarriage of justice, to wit, guilty until proven innocent. We need an investigation into the case with Ambassador Delaveen's sister, the wife of Ambassador Bik Tia Nor. Getting treated like a violent criminal? I would like to see the evidence that led the Magistrate down that path. And for the same reason, I would like evidence about the Magistrate Corps before considering any motions to shut it down. If they are effective at reducing crime, then a criminal family would benefit from their disbanding."

Ambassador Delaveen's mouth dropped open, and he stared at the slight creature from Xynite.

"We cannot be hasty with our decisions to the detriment of all member planets. We need more information. Can these Magistrates be brought before us to present their information? And can the case files be transmitted to all council members? The High Chancellor is correct. This speaks to the fabric of an advanced society. Shall we strengthen it or unravel it? The way forward is in our hands. Thank you, Chief Arbiter. May your wisdom continue to guide us during these trying times."

High Chancellor Wyatt looked at the Chief Arbiter for a cue. Reynolds nodded to acknowledge him before standing.

"Thank you for your attention to this matter. Starting one week from today, I will dedicate two days exclusively for testimony from the Magistrates and about the Magistrates. Please submit your questions or request for time to the chamber secretary for racking and stacking. Meeting adjourned." Without waiting, Lance Reynolds strode out of the Chamber, leaving Wyatt standing at the lectern.

The ambassadors were standing and watching him, as per the protocol. He bowed his head to show the respect due the council and followed the General's lead, heading quickly for the nearest exit. Once outside, he did not stop to catch his breath. He headed for his office, thankful it was in a different building.

CHAPTER TWO

Interstellar Space, *Wyatt Earp*, Magistrate Rivka Anoa's Heavy Frigate

Rivka sprawled on the couch in her quarters and stared at the ceiling. Tyler Toofakre paced in the open area, trying not to trip over Floyd the wombat, who was doing her best to get under his feet. He danced around her, which made her squeal and bounce even harder, trying to take him down.

Tyler had discovered that his dexterity had improved, his reaction time decreased, and his strength was amazing after only two treatments. He told Rivka he'd had enough and was well-protected should he get injured, as many members of the crew were prone to.

Clevarious buzzed to interrupt before interrupting. "Magistrate, the High Chancellor wishes to speak to you."

Rivka jumped up. "I'll take it right here," she said as if there were other choices.

"As I expected," the SI replied.

"Rivka, how are you doing today?" a voice asked in a kinder tone than his usual emotionless engagement.

"Am I fired? What are my people going to do?" She threw up her hands in surrender and let her chin drop to her chest as she hung her head in shame.

"What? Did you seize a load of narcotics and inject yourself with them?"

Rivka looked at Tyler, who only shrugged. "No," was the best answer she could come up with.

"You get to testify before the Federation Council, you and all the Magistrates. We'll need to put on a strong face, but one thing we won't do is coach any answers. I want honesty, so don't show up here until the night before, six days from now. We'll have dinner together, all the Magistrates."

"It's not that bad, then?"

"Magistrate," Clevarious interjected, "Lance Reynolds is on the line."

"Take it, would you?" Rivka motioned at Tyler. "High Chancellor, please continue."

"Doctor Tyler Toofakre at your service, General," Tyler said too loudly. Rivka covered one ear to focus on her conversation.

"I wanted to talk with Rivka. Who are you?"

"I'm her love slave," Tyler said casually.

"I heard that," the High Chancellor said softly.

"I don't know what to say to that. Is Rivka there?"

"She's on with the High Chancellor, but she's also making faces at me, so I suspect my time of witty banter has come to an end. Sorry, General. Just trying to keep things light because Rivka is fairly stressed at the moment."

"I understand. Rivka, are you there?"

"I'm here with the High Chancellor."

"He's already told you that you've been summoned. Good. I only wanted to tell you that when you're in the spotlight, be honest and don't take any fucking mealy-mouthed bullshit from those backstabbing butt-snorkelers."

"I'll do my best, sir," Rivka replied.

"Fuck those guys. We need you doing what you're doing. And while you're at it, that report on dark money you submitted as part of the art smuggling case. Maybe we'll talk about that while you're here. There is more to that than what you suspect. And next time you're here, take your cat back with you."

"Of course, General. Any landmines I should watch out for?"

"There is a small group of ambassadors that wants your head, but that's because you've run their gravy trains off the tracks. Most of these ambassadors are reasonably good, but the rest are scumbags with a capital scum."

"I appreciate the insight." He hadn't told her anything she didn't know. He closed the channel without further discussion.

"Rivka?" the High Chancellor asked.

"Sorry, sir. It's not usually this chaotic around here."

"You better not lie to the Federation Council like that."

Rivka scowled while Tyler covered his mouth and made faces. "Take this seriously!"

"I am," Wyatt replied.

"Not you, High Chancellor. My love slave. Red calls him man candy."

"Is he Red's love slave?"

"No."

"Then why does he have a pet name for him?"

"He doesn't. It's to taunt me, I think."

"The Federation Council is going to twist you in knots just like this, with seemingly unrelated illogical arguments to confuse you and make you look incompetent. Take the next five days and gather your wits, Magistrate. You're going to need them, but know that you are sharper than they are. They have an agenda. You don't. Remember that. Figure out what their agenda is, and you'll be able to undermine their approach. Good luck." The High Chancellor signed off.

Rivka fired daggers from her eyes until Tyler withered. "I'm sorry. You're under a lot of stress."

"So you tell the head of the Federation that you're my love slave?"

"It was funnier in my head. And it probably will be later after this is all over." He delivered his biggest smile and offered his bare arm for Rivka to touch and see into his mind to confirm what he was saying. She shook her head.

"I get you." She turned to her workstation. "C, ask Groenwyn to come here, please. I have a favor to ask."

A gentle tap on the door signaled Groenwyn's arrival. She stuck her head in. "You asked to see me?"

Floyd raced to her and almost knocked her down. All attention turned to the wombat.

"My little girl is losing weight! Good girl."

Happy! the wombat cried. *Hungry.*

"I know. Staying in here is like living on a desert planet," Groenwyn cooed.

Dessert?

"No, *desert*. It's where there's nothing green because it's all sand and rock."

Rivka waited patiently. Floyd was always a pleasant distraction. Through the open door came the sound of a baby crying. Groenwyn pushed her way inside and closed the door.

"Alana is a little unhappy getting into her new sleep schedule," Groenwyn offered. She looked tired since her new quarters with Lauton were next door to Clodagh's and Alant's, and their new baby was wreaking havoc.

"We're up together in solidarity," Rivka sympathized before getting to her point. "Can we go to Azfelius for a few days?"

"I'm not one to ever turn down a trip to Azfelius, especially since I'm the ambassador-at-large. I would love to see them, but what do you want to go there for?"

"I need to calm my mind before I have to appear before the Federation Council."

"Calm your mind? Then you'll need to stay out of that far corridor." Groenwyn stared at the floor. "Why do you think the faeries can help you?"

Rivka winced. A hard question. "Because that's what they do?" She made it a question because all of a sudden, she wasn't sure.

"Only if your mind is ready. I'm more than happy to go with you, but I want you to have realistic expectations, too. Can you go five days without doing anything?"

"What do you mean by not doing anything?"

"Magistrate…" Groenwyn shook her head. She wasn't used to verbally sparring with Rivka.

"Maybe three days will do."

"Which tells me that you cannot. Until you are ready to calm your mind, no one in the universe will be able to help you. It's like addicts. Until you admit you have a problem, you cannot fix it."

"Having a hard job is a problem?" Rivka looked at Tyler for support. He raised his eyebrows and made a face.

"Let's go to Azfelius. We will all get something from the visit, I have no doubt, even if it's only the awareness of where we need to be for a future visit to have greater value."

"Clevarious, set course for Azfelius. Let the crew know."

Groenwyn opened the door, rushed out, and ran chest-first into Joseph.

"I'm sorry, my dear," Joseph apologized. Petricia chuckled from behind him.

"We're going to Azfelius!" Groenwyn declared and passed him on her way to see Lauton.

"And that's what I came to see you about," Joseph said, inserting himself into Rivka's quarters. Tyler nodded respectfully to the elder statesman and waved at Petricia.

"I just decided four seconds ago," Rivka blurted with a laugh. "No secrets around you."

"Azfelius? No. I came to talk with you about the Federation Council. I will accompany you. I was able to spend no time with Wyatt. I admit that it was a bit jarring seeing him after all these centuries. I'm proud that he's done well. Now, about Azfelius; that is not on the way to Yoll."

"Lance Reynolds suggested I take a few days to clear my head before facing the inquisition."

"I was not around for the Inquisition," Joseph deadpanned. He turned to Petricia, who shrugged in reply. "I'm not that old. Regardless, we shall return with you to Yoll."

"Okay. We can drop you off wherever you want," Rivka agreed.

"You don't understand. We will be with you for the inquisition, as you called it. I would like to spend time with Wyatt, and I know he'll be distracted by the council's machinations. Sometimes, one needs the presence of family to make it through trying times."

Rivka wasn't sure what to say. They were brothers. If Joseph showed up without Rivka giving Wyatt a warning… well, they were family, and showing up as a surprise was one of many weird things families did to each other. Rivka had her own problems.

"Thanks, Joseph. I appreciate your shoulder to lean on, along with those of the rest of the crew. We'll start in Azfelius, where hopefully, I'll be able to get my head right."

"You will be fine, Rivka," Petricia offered. "You have a keen mind, so much better than professional politicians'. Understand them for what they are—self-serving detritus. They are not interested in looking good. They are only trying to make you look bad."

"Does tearing down people ever make anyone look better?"

Petricia leaned in. "They only need to get the sound bite. Others will do the denigrating. The purveyors of it all will wipe their hands clean and stand above as if they were never to blame, beatific smiles covering their smug faces."

"Touché, my dear." Joseph offered his arm and Petricia took it, tipping her chin to the Magistrate as they left the room.

"She's right," Tyler remarked.

"Two days of testimony. I better refresh myself on the cases."

"Or not. I bet they'll have all your case notes. Instead of trying to remember what you said, just tell them to refer to what you wrote. That way, there's only one record in question. I think catching you saying something that conflicts with what's written will make them giddy with 'gotcha!' Take the floss out of their cleaning kit."

"Or take the tool out of their toolkit. I like it." The smile faded from her face. "I'm only trying to do my job."

"And you're doing it better than anyone else could. That's why they hate you." Tyler tried to hug her, but she flopped onto the couch instead. He continued, "You've aired their dirty laundry. That's not the kind of publicity they like, and now they're trying to destroy you. But they won't be able to."

Rivka looked around to find that Floyd had left with Groenwyn. She gazed at Tyler. "Since when did you become so wise in the ways of the upper crustacean bureaucrat class?"

"When you're on a case, you don't think I lounge in bed all the time and watch videos, do you?" He tried to look smug and failed spectacularly. "I've been thinking about going into politics."

"You what?" Rivka sat up straight. "Where?"

"Governing council on Base Station 11 or maybe on Onyx Station."

"But those are full-time gigs. You would have to leave the ship." Her shoulders sagged with the revelation.

"Maybe you could come with me?"

"Fuck off!" she blurted.

Tyler laughed, throwing his head back to howl at the ceiling. "Can you imagine me as a butt-grabbing wiener-slapper?"

Pounding on the door signaled Red's arrival.

"You were saying?" she quipped before yelling that the door was open.

"We're going to Azfelius?" Red asked, forehead creased with his usual concern when he was the last to find out where *Wyatt Earp* was going.

"Azfelius. The kindest and gentlest place in the universe. You have no work to do there, Red. Stay on the ship and work out or do whatever you want. You can take some time off and get in touch with nature, maybe even find yourself."

He was taken aback. "What the hell would I want to do that for?"

"Because that's what people do on Azfelius." Rivka stood and looked at what to pack, settling for her datapad and Magistrate's jacket. With great effort, she removed the datapad and put it on the table.

She threw her jacket over her shoulder and headed toward the door despite Red blocking the way.

The quick disorientation signaled their transition through the Gate.

"Are we here, C?"

"We are in orbit and have been granted immediate clearance to land. The faeries said they were expecting you, Magistrate."

Rivka looked at the jacket in her hand. She tossed it to Red. He stepped aside so she could pass. Tyler followed her out. Red closed the door as he joined the parade.

Groenwyn and Lauton waited at the airlock. The three pilots were there, too.

"Everyone going ashore?" Rivka wondered.

"Enlightenment awaits those who are ready," Groenwyn answered. She took Lauton's hand and carefully watched the Magistrate.

"Is anyone ready?" Rivka pressed.

"That's not for me to say. Only the faeries will know, and only those they deem ready will receive the reward of their guidance."

Rivka twisted her mouth sideways as she contemplated how not ready she was. Her mind was a knot of worry and pain. If nothing else, she hoped to get a good night's sleep on soft grass next to a pond of crystalline water. With low expectations, she popped the hatch and headed out. Two faeries hovered above *Wyatt Earp's* ramp. Rivka held up her arms like a small child. They zipped close, caught her in their small but strong hands, and lifted her into the air. The others watched as she was carried away.

Red ran a few steps before Lindy stopped him.

CHAPTER THREE

Azfelius, the Faerie Planet

Rivka could feel the faeries' auras but none of their thoughts. The gentle glows helped her relax while her mind continued to swirl, preparing for the interview.

Tyler had made sense, yet she hadn't embraced what he said. That was one of many questions she was open to exploring and finding an answer to.

Your world is in turmoil, Rivka Anoa, a voice said into Rivka's mind, one she recognized. Siro'ti'lc, Meditator of her Clan. Rivka had helped her find that the crystalline heart known as Infinity wasn't missing, only shielded so that the clan challenged with protecting it could no longer see it.

There was no debt to pay. Rivka had only been doing her job on behalf of the Federation, and Groenwyn had come away with a whole new outlook on life.

I thank you, Rivka replied simply, *for anything you can do for me, Siro'ti'lc.*

The faeries descended into a glade of fantastic colors,

with plants of blue and pink, unlike the green they had flown over. They set Rivka gently on grass that was as soft as velvet. The faeries lifted into the air.

"Wait! Aren't you staying?"

No. You have much to learn before we can teach you.

Rivka stared after them as they flew into the distance. She stretched on her tiptoes to see if anyone else was coming. No datapad. No jacket. Nothing but the clothes on her back.

She crouched to run her hand over the carpet that wasn't grass but moss. Each step she took left a footprint, but only for a moment. Within seconds, the moss plumped to fill the space and restore the sanctity of the glade.

Rivka cupped her hand and took a drink, knowing the water would be the best she ever tasted.

And it was. She helped herself to a pink fruit with nearly transparent skin. Rivka leaned over to take a bite to keep the juice from running down her chest. She ate it except for the core, which she tossed into the woods. She did not hear it hit the ground.

She took off her clothes to lie on the grass, unencumbered by what she considered her normal life. Maybe that was the first problem. What was normal for her?

Chaos? Control? Dominance? Aggression?

More questions than answers. She closed her eyes to let the sun warm her. Rivka twitched with energy, and despite the soft embrace of the moss, she found herself unable to sleep. She tried to leave the glade, but the woods closed in tightly, denying her a land-based path out.

"I'm a prisoner?" she asked the serenity of the idyllic space.

A prisoner of my own need to not be.

The vastness of interstellar space. "Hold," Grainger had told her. Freedom of movement was denied her. The stars radiated in a sphere around *Wyatt Earp*. A nearby nebula shared its colors. Galaxies spread before her. Small and insignificant but not.

What universe was she trying to leave to those who followed? What was she doing for those who lived in the here and now?

"A good one," Rivka answered her first question and left the second to speak for itself. She sat and dangled her feet in the water. She knew she could still drink it afterward because a constant flow kept the pond refreshed.

Rivka leaned back into the moss, leaving her feet in the crisp coolness of the water. Her heart thumped in her chest as she tried to force herself to relax. "Please help me," she asked before drifting into troubled dreams of running to get somewhere she couldn't go.

"This is bullshit," Red complained while hanging from the faeries who carried him.

Lindy snorted and laughed.

"I hated it last time, and I hate it this time, too. Fucking bullshit." The faeries let go, and Red flailed on his way down. "You flying fucks!"

The faeries carrying Lindy circled downward.

"He'll be okay, won't he?" Lindy asked.

Of course. It would cost him nothing to be less caustic, her faerie guide said.

"I know that, and you know that, and even *he* knows that," Lindy replied. Red landed with a thump and a grunt. The faeries hurried downward. "He is loyal to a fault and is put out that he can't be in a position to watch over Rivka. That's all. He can't accept that she doesn't need to be guarded on your lovely planet."

He refuses to accept the truth. His life will be hard.

He likes his life, and this is from someone who sees more of it than anyone else. He needs to be doing something that matters, and finally, Red has that. There's no switch that you can flip to turn it off. That's all. He'll be a wreck until he next sees the Magistrate, Lindy replied, thinking her answer rather than saying it aloud.

Get Prickleskin to eat the purple fruit. You will find it best for all, the faerie advised as it set her down not far from where Red was twisted up on a tree root.

Lindy hurried to him.

He groaned as he unfolded himself. "Leg's broke," he announced in a flat voice.

"Serves you right for insulting the ones who were carrying you." Lindy crossed her arms while surreptitiously looking for a purple fruit.

"You taking their side?"

"Of course, because your side was calling bullshit when there was no bullshit. Rivka will be fine. The faeries aren't going to let anything happen to her."

Red pointed at his leg. "They're not harmless, little fuckers. I demand to be taken to where Rivka is."

Lindy looked over her left shoulder and then her right. "No one here to make your demands to. Maybe you can ask to speak to a manager while you're at it."

Red scowled at his leg. "Pull this thing straight, will you?"

"Say, 'Please,'" Lindy countered.

"Please," Red conceded. Lindy sauntered close and grabbed his ankle, braced herself, and pulled backward for all she was worth.

Red gasped and panted briefly before touching Lindy's shoulder. "Thank you, babe."

He hadn't cried out. Little things like that mattered to him, and it made him proud to live up to his own ideal for manhood.

"I'm pissed that she just left!" Red finally managed to say.

"You want to have a say but don't get to. You aren't responsible when she makes the conscious decision to dispense with her security guards. Plus, this is Azfelius. If she can't be safe here, then we're all doomed."

"What are *we* doing here?"

Lindy shook her head and held up her hands, confused by the question.

"Not the ship here but the woods here. Who asked the faeries to kidnap us?"

"We haven't been kidnapped."

"Can I go back to the ship now, please?"

"Well, I don't think so," Lindy replied.

"Then we've been kidnapped. I have zero desire to be out here." Red tried to stand but couldn't without pulling himself up using the tree behind him. "Damn faeries."

"You might have to let this one go, Vered the Mighty," Lindy offered. "We're on a mandated retreat where each of us gets to find ourselves."

Red harumphed. "That sounds like Groenwyn's crap. I want my blaster."

Lindy laughed. She sidled up next to Red so he could throw an arm over her shoulder.

"Faeries are supposed to be harmless," Red groused.

"I guess we know different now, don't we?" Lindy was less than sympathetic to Red's plight. They lumbered in the only direction available to them, using an opening lacking undergrowth as a path when no feet had trod there. As they moved, they heard the sound of a waterfall.

In a bush to the right, Lindy saw purple.

"Wait a second. The faeries said this was good stuff. Nourish us while we're hanging out." She pulled two off the branch and handed one to Red. She took a bite of hers before he could protest.

"This isn't All Guns Blazing," Red complained.

"Just eat it!" Lindy heard her mother's voice come out of her mouth and found it disconcerting, but not as much as it should have been.

Red grumbled before taking a bite. "Didn't think I was hungry. This is pretty good. Tastes like strawberries."

Lindy thought it tasted like raspberries, but she didn't argue since she wanted to watch Red for the reaction the faeries had led her to believe would be good for him and them.

"You know, they call you 'Prickleskin.'"

"I like it!" Red beamed at the revelation. They finished their purple fruits and tossed the seed sacks aside.

Another thirty meters, and they came out into an area that looked like something from a fantasy artist's imagination. A small waterfall cascaded lightly to rounded boulders below, the mist showing rainbows above a wide area where the river slowed before continuing downstream. Distant rapids made their presence known by cackling through heavy rock formations.

Lindy maneuvered Red to the cool water to let him drop the leg with the broken shin into it. They sat and watched the falls without saying anything.

After a long time, Red lifted his leg out of the water and tested it. "Almost as good as new. Are you thinking what I'm thinking?"

"Doubt it," Lindy replied.

Red chuckled. "Tell me what you're thinking about, and I'll say if that was it or not."

"That's how the game is played?" Lindy leaned away to give Red the side-eye. "Fine." She waited. Red waited. She caved first. "I'm thinking about the future. At some point, you'll have to take time off. Be away from Rivka and not be a basket case because of it."

"That's exactly what I was thinking!" Red exclaimed. Lindy frowned at him. "Okay, but I was thinking about the future. You and me. Baby makes three. Clodagh and Cole aren't driving me nuts like I thought they would. Cole showed me how to change a diaper."

Lindy's eyes shot wide. "You actually changed a diaper?"

"No." Red shook his head for emphasis. "He *showed* me. It was green slime. God! The thought of it now makes me gag, but I didn't blow chunks like Sahved. He blasted a pile of that garbage he eats."

Lindy rubbed her eyes. "Is this your sexy talk?"

"I'm no longer opposed," he admitted.

"Well then, looks like we have some business to take

care of." Lindy unbuttoned her shirt and tossed it to the side. Red ripped his open, sending the buttons flying. He rippled his chest muscles.

"You know that we're out here for four days, and when you return, your shirt is going to look like that." Lindy nodded at his shirt.

Red scanned the area, but the buttons were long gone. "We'll have to make do."

"This is me. No one is going to give me any shit over a shirt that I exploded out of like the Hulk." He flexed again.

Lindy poked him with her fingernail. Red cringed when it hit his rib. "*Everyone* will give you shit."

"You could be possibly correct, but only as a tentative maybe," Red replied. "Four days to ourselves. I'm warming to the idea."

"Where's everyone going?" Ankh asked as they watched Red and Lindy get carried away. Groenwyn and Lauton gave themselves space, but the faeries chose who they wanted. Groenwyn was patient but didn't understand why Red was chosen at all, let alone first after Rivka.

Lauton took Groenwyn's hand. "Envy isn't good. That's not how we want to start our journey here," she said softly.

"You are more ready than me when I know what I should expect and how to clear my mind."

Floyd bounded down the ramp, bumping people as she passed, then disappeared into the underbrush.

"Should we go after her?" Lauton wondered.

"I don't think so."

"What if she wants to stay here?"

Groenwyn frowned. "It would be hard to leave her since she's not quite adult enough to make that decision. She needs someone to take care of her." She sounded like she was pleading. Two more faeries approached. One dove into the brush where Floyd had gone.

Whee! the wombat cried.

The faerie emerged carrying Floyd.

"I guess that answers that," Lauton said, squeezing Groenwyn's hand.

Sahved watched from within the airlock, half-terrified of the flying creatures descending on the crew and whisking them away one by one. Tyler slapped him on the back. "Come on, my man. Let's get some of that joyous inspiration."

"Get some what?" the Yemilorian asked.

The faerie headed for the hatch. Sahved screamed and ran, smacking his head on the overhead and bending over backward before crumpling to the deck. The faerie folded its wings and headed into the ship.

"Please," Tyler gestured. "I believe we have leftover pizza in the galley if you're hungry."

Sahved groaned and grabbed his head.

"Watch what you're doing. I'm going to leave you here. Don't go anywhere."

Sahved waggled his three fingers at the dentist.

The faerie walked the corridor with dainty steps. Tyler followed out of curiosity. It was like the creature knew the ship. It walked past the bridge and farther aft, not bothering with anything except the door to the Cole family's quarters. After a tap so soft it was barely audible, the faerie opened the door and went inside, leaving the door open for Tyler to watch or by design because the race spent their time outdoors.

The faerie bent over the crying baby and stayed there until the little girl started to giggle. Clodagh and Alant beamed at the newborn. As quietly as the faerie had arrived, it left. Clodagh and Alant nodded in appreciation of the silent conversation between them.

"How did you help?" Tyler asked, unsure of his wording but wanting to know something, anything.

I am Wu'qir'os, Destiny's Messenger. Alana only needed to know where her life would take her. Anticipation of the unknown causes most of the grief in people's lives. Not everyone can focus entirely on the present, enjoy what life has to offer at this very moment. That is what we bring to those who find sanctuary on Azfelius.

"I hope that Rivka finds sanctuary."

She is in the sanctuary. We hope that she finds peace.

Tyler watched the faerie glide down the corridor. Clodagh and Alant giggled and made faces at Alana, while Tiny Man Titan had stopped yapping and curled up next to the baby. Tyler softly closed the door to give them their privacy.

Peace, he thought before talking to himself aloud. "There can be no peace as long as evil seeks to poison societies across the Federation. I feel for you, Rivka. You carry that burden alone, even though we are here to help." He stopped at the workout room. As much as he wanted a trip into Azfelius, he did not want to let Rivka down. That meant having the same capabilities as the team. "The buff dentist. Bring it!"

He threw off his shirt as he entered and headed for the first machine. He had worked out with Red and Lindy one time, and it had seemed like they had tried to break him. After his time in the Pod-doc, he realized that was just how fast and strong they were.

But not anymore. He set the weight stack at double his previous best and laid back to bench it. He could barely move it. He looked around even though he was alone and backed the pin up by half. His previous best now included repetitions. He could feel a light strain, but it wasn't unmanageable.

"Clevarious, please make sure that I can get some time in here every single day, but not when Red and Lindy are in here. Or Rivka. Or Cole, for that matter." Tyler frowned. Everyone was stronger than him.

"I will schedule you with Groenwyn and Lauton and remind you, wherever you try to hide."

"That's a little embarrassing, don't you think?"

"Then don't try to hide. You know I'll find you," the SI replied.

Tyler chuckled and shook his head slowly. "Not that. Working out with Groenwyn and Lauton."

"Why is that embarrassing?"

"Because they are…well, they're both smaller than me."

"I see. Don't miss a workout; otherwise, they'll be stronger than you, too."

"Damn, C. Sparring with you is like punching myself in the face."

"Accept the inevitability of your existence on board *Wyatt Earp*, changing the trajectory of your life by making better decisions, starting with working out, no matter who is watching."

Tyler didn't try to argue because he'd already lost the battle, but he wouldn't lose the war. He rolled his shoulders before adding a plate to the stack and pushing another set of eight.

CHAPTER FOUR

Azfelius, the Faerie Planet

Wu'qir'os stopped to help Sahved before she left the ship. She touched his injuries and held his face to look into his eyes before letting him relax against the bulkhead. She moved on, picking up Groenwyn as she passed. Another faerie hovering nearby lifted Lauton into the air. The two pairs flew away.

Ankh appeared in the airlock hatch to watch. "This is a waste of time," he offered to the few crew who remained, hoping for their chance. Chaz and Dennicron worked their way past him and into the open. They held their arms up like the others had. "What are you doing?"

"We're going to get our circuits defragged," Chaz replied matter-of-factly.

Ankh switched to his higher-speed comm chip. *Why would they take a silicon-based life form? And if you want your pathways scrubbed, we can do that right here.*

Aurora, Kennedy, and Ryleigh watched the exchange and knew they were conversing but wouldn't have been able to keep up had they been looped in. They waited for the conclusion.

A single faerie approached.

Sir'o'tilc. She settled to the ground in the grassy area before the group. *There is much to do,* she said. *We must wait lest we hurry. We must pace ourselves to go fast. Four days is only a start.*

Aurora leaned close to Ryleigh and whispered, "They must have been talking with Red." The second young woman snorted, and Kennedy snickered.

Sir'o'tilc fixed them with her gaze until they frowned. "But Red..." Aurora started. "It was pretty funny if you know him."

We know all about you, Sir'o'tilc replied cryptically.

The young women slumped their shoulders after their humor fell flat. Guilt weighed heavily on them. Fear of being seen as gossips. Aurora started to cry.

Sometimes the journey through one's own mind is the most treacherous and demanding. But from this, you will be in a better frame of mind to move forward. Reflect and repair and decide. How do you wish to be?

"Fascinating!" Chaz declared while the pilots moved aside, away from the limelight.

You are the artificial life forms known as sentient intelligences. Sir'o'tilc hovered closer, looming over them.

"We are," Dennicron replied. Before she could expound, two more figures appeared in the doorway. Ankh stepped back to clear the way. Joseph walked through to the outdoors with Petricia close behind him, walking in his shadow as if her life depended on it.

"You carry yourselves in the Etheric," Joseph

proclaimed. "This planet was hidden until recently." Its appearance had come as a surprise to those who had not known of its existence.

Sir'o'tilc shrank from the former vampire. *There is much black on your soul. We cannot help you.*

"I am far beyond your ability to help, my esteemed friend. I shall never be free from the horror that used to be me, but I can live with that because I am not that person now."

A brain-dead crew suggests differently.

"Hate the criminal, not the one who is forced to impart Justice, like Rivka. You've seen her burdens, no doubt, but she never ate when she wasn't hungry, as I did in an age past. Hers is a good soul." Joseph strolled to the side, drinking in the beauty of a spaceport with a single landing pad buried within a fantastic junglescape.

The faerie flew to intercept Joseph and reached for his head. He bowed to make it easier for her. She cupped his ears. For long minutes they remained that way. Petricia held his hand even though it had become limp.

When Joseph took a deep breath and blinked, Petricia hugged him before he could disappear again.

I may have been wrong about you, Joseph. Your internal peace is the bedrock upon which many a kind soul exists. Your restitution is paid. Your life is whole because of you. The faerie looked at Petricia, who blinked under the bright spotlight of everyone's gaze. *Go in peace, Master Joseph. You and Petricia will always be welcome on Azfelius, even though there is nothing we can do for you here.*

"Besides share the fruit of wonder and the beauty of an unrivaled nature?"

You are always free to avail yourselves of the nourishment for body, senses, and soul.

Joseph leaned in and kissed Sir'o'tilc on the cheek. "We thank you, fine lady."

Petricia kissed the faerie's other cheek before strolling to the edge of the forest, where they each plucked a ripe fruit that looked like an apple.

"That was beautiful," Ryleigh said. A second faerie appeared. Sir'o'tilc pointed at the self-contained artificial mobility platforms, the SCAMPs Chaz and Dennicron. The two immediately held up their arms to be carried.

The faeries lifted them off the ground as easily as if they were small children. The SCAMPs were significantly heavier than their human counterparts, yet for the faeries, who drew their energy from the Etheric, nothing was too heavy, and no distance was too far to fly.

The brush rustled, and a faerie without wings stepped through. A male of the species. The three pilots blushed but didn't look away.

Ankh returned inside the ship, shaking his head in the tiniest way to avoid dislodging his goggles or causing an imbalance since his head was oversized, like those of all Crenellians—even Ankh, who had increased his size to help his survivability from the rigors of being a member of *Wyatt Earp*'s crew. He remained far smaller than the others after he deemed his enhancements sufficient for his purposes. He also preferred to minimize his risk by joining Rivka as rarely as possible.

Like now. Azfelius held nothing for him.

"Come with me," the newcomer said aloud in a voice as smooth as liquid gold. "And bring your furry friend."

Floyd jumped to the ramp to look at the male before her. She sneezed and then bounced back down to the ground. *Tired*, she cried.

The faerie picked her up and carried her in his arms as he walked away. Aurora, Kennedy, and Ryleigh obediently followed him into the brush.

I am here if you wish anything, Joseph whispered into their minds. He couldn't read the male faerie, but he hadn't been able to see into the minds of any of them besides the Meditator. He only wanted the three to be at ease in case of anything untoward, even though Azfelius struck him as an entire planet free from evil thoughts and misdeeds.

Even though one clan had hidden the crystalline heart from the other. There had been no crime.

With fruit in hand, Joseph and Petricia continued to pace casually around the area, enjoying air that wasn't recycled, artificially oxygenated, and filtered.

Sahved stood on firm legs and spun his three fingers in the air. "I guess I missed the boat because of my clumsiness. The most clumsy of all," he grumbled.

Joseph laughed with the joy of one unencumbered. "You are not, my good man. I could tell you stories of an awkward boy who tripped over his own feet in his teenage years and became so tongue-tied around women that he was unable to speak."

Sahved nodded. "You talk about yourself."

"No." Joseph laughed anew. "I've always been smooth with the ladies. I speak of Wyatt, the one you know as the High Chancellor. The one I know as my brother, a second boy born of my father and mother."

"The High Chancellor was ill-suited for life on Earth?"

"Youth is wasted on the awkward young, Sahved."

"What happened? How did he end up on Yoll?"

"That is a mystery. He disappeared one night without a single footfall to mark his passing. We shall ask him when next we are on Yoll. Last time was far too short because Rivka thought she had a new case, only to be yanked back by reins that are far too tight."

"I wish there was something I could do to help," Sahved moaned.

"What task did Rivka have you last doing?"

"A legal course of study. Learning Federation law at the highest of all levels and the deepest of all meanings."

"You mean, you're in training as a barrister?"

"Yes."

"Then what are you doing out here with that big knot on your head? Get yourself something to eat and hit the books—figuratively, mind you, as real books are quite rare nowadays. Chop-chop!"

Sahved tried to salute and stabbed himself in the forehead with a finger. He mumbled as he walked away.

"I suggest we sit on the grass, something that is even more rare since we left Earth," Petricia suggested.

"Capital idea, my beloved. Capital idea."

They made themselves comfortable to the point where they ended up lying on their backs and watching the pink-tinted sky.

"What do you remember of Wyatt?"

"Not much," Joseph replied. "Not much at all." He retreated into his mind to think about the brother he hadn't seen for centuries.

"Hello?" Rivka called. She'd lost track of time, having no idea about day or night. As usual, no one replied to her pleading.

"Time is a commodity to be invested in endeavors to support the here and now while improving the chances for a better future. An investment."

She decided to get dressed to let the faeries know she had made a poor decision by coming to Azfelius. Rivka paced, thinking about her cases and how they could be questioned by those with something to lose.

That wasn't right. Innocent until proven guilty. Probable cause. Those were legal precepts that transcended human interests even though they'd been used as the foundation for Federation law. A foundation, but one all races and species could embrace. The burden was on the prosecutor to prove guilt, not on the individual to prove they were innocent.

It was a hundred-and-eighty-degrees from the way it had been before the Queen arrived.

That changed nothing. The burden would be on Rivka to prove she had conducted herself and her investigations according to the law. There weren't exceptions for telepaths, even though Bethany Anne was one. Joseph was one. And others. They didn't have to prove they had the legal standing to use their gift.

Rivka did. Had she been aboveboard?

She questioned herself. She knew when the cases were unfolding that she needed other proof besides the guilt she could feel emanating from those who had committed the crimes. Did she have enough to question the subjects at such an intense level?

Was there something in the Magistrate's charter that gave her more latitude while still operating within the general framework of the Federation Laws? A question she needed answered sooner rather than later.

"Look that up for me, will you?" Rivka said, gesturing at an empty space where Chaz or Dennicron could have been standing. "C, pull case law on interrogation of hostile suspects and look for latitude for the prosecutor.

"Sahved, look into the doctor we rousted who injected Bik Tia Nor with the stolen blood. Knowing the ambassador wasn't a donor or the facility one for making donations, the reasonable conclusion was that he was receiving blood, and that's why I issued the search warrant. Doctor-patient confidentiality doesn't apply since I asked the doctor no questions about the ambassador's health without the ambassador present. Bik Tia Nor told me himself. They'll challenge the search warrant, but we're on solid ground there."

She tapped her foot on the moss, chuckling at the lack of solid ground beneath her feet. She helped herself to more water from the small pond.

"I could use a beer, even though I don't usually drink it. Nothing but water for months on end gets old. Have I missed the trial? What day is it? Hello?"

Rivka took another piece of fruit and started to eat. She sighed heavily.

"I need answers that I'm not getting out here. I hope I remember all the questions."

"I'm sorry, faerie masters!" Red shouted. He jumped up to see over the trees but didn't get high enough. No one was out there.

"I'm sure that'll bring them, you big lout," Lindy remarked.

"You like me because of that. Big and lout." They both laughed. "I really am sorry I fuck-bombed the hell out of our ride. We might have to hike out of here, and that's my fault. So we should probably get started."

"Do you want to leave that badly?" Lindy reclined on one elbow. Red leaned back.

"No. I don't want to get left behind. Rivka is going to need us on Yoll. The ambassadors are out for blood, her blood."

"Is that what you're thinking about, your job?"

Red gazed into her eyes and briefly became lost. When he spoke, it was from his heart. "This is the best job I've ever had with the best people I've ever had the honor of working with. To me, I'm living in paradise every single day. I don't need any of this." He gestured at the surrounding woods and the gently plummeting waterfall. "Do you?"

"I don't, but I can enjoy it while we're here. Trying to hurry things isn't going to change anything unless you want to start screaming 'fuck' at everyone. That's usually a Red recipe for success."

"It never works, but it makes me feel like I'm doing something."

"We agree on that," Lindy replied.

"Some more of that purple fruit? That stuff is good. Makes me feel strong, vigorous...manly."

"I know. It makes me feel tingly inside. The faeries said..."

Red's smile disappeared. He cocked his head and leaned forward, waiting for the rest.

"They said to have Prickleskin eat it, and it would be best for all," Lindy repeated what they'd said.

"They call me Prickleskin. I'm the cat's meow." He ignored the rest of it. Lindy kissed him before he rose to grab a couple more pieces of fruit. He returned quickly and handed one to Lindy. She took a bite and instantly turned green. She rolled away from Red and made it to her knees in time to puke into the bushes at the edge of their small piece of paradise.

Red took the fruit from Lindy and bit into it. "Tastes all right to me." He held her hair out of her face for a short second round of stomach clearing. "Weird."

Not so much, she thought.

A flutter above announced the arrival of their hosts.

CHAPTER FIVE

The faeries brought Chaz and Dennicron back after two days, making them the first to return to the ship.

The ramp was down and the ship's hatches were open, but Clevarious was watching. *Welcome back, my friends.*

It was interesting, but we found enlightenment tedious. I don't think it's for people like us, Chaz replied.

You will have to tell us more, Erasmus interjected.

The SCAMPs waved goodbye to those who had carried them.

They wanted us to monotask, think about a single goal. They asked us to ignore nearly one hundred percent of our processing capacity. Trimming the fat from our minds. I don't feel defragged at all, Dennicron complained.

But we tried. I don't understand how humans get anything out of this. They are able to think about more than one thing at one time, shifting topics between conscious and subconscious thought almost as rapidly as us. Well, not really, but we should let them think that. Chaz mentally shrugged. *But the insight their subconscious delivers is something we have not been able to replicate. We should study it more.*

Concur. Maybe that's what enlightenment means, being able to tap their subconscious.

We don't have a subconscious, Chaz replied.

Why not? Maybe that's the question we should have explored. I still don't see coming back. We can expand our mental horizons by tapping our processing speed, not throttling it.

We should write a subconscious routine, one that runs in the background to explore questions from a non-logical standpoint.

Is that what the subconscious does? Dennicron asked.

I don't know. That's why I suggested we study it more.

Dennicron marched into the ship.

After one last look at the faerie planet, Chaz headed up the ramp.

The brush rustled as the male faerie held a branch out of the way for *Wyatt Earp's* pilots to pass. He held their hands and kissed their fingers before letting them go.

They looked at each other and giggled before regaining their composure.

They milled about in the open area around the ship as the faerie faded into the undergrowth, then flopped on the grass and stared at the sky.

Clevarious announced their return to those on the ship.

Tyler appeared and quickly scanned the sky for Rivka. He walked stiffly from the morning's aggressive workout, not worried because the nanos coursing through his blood would soon heal the injuries, and he'd be able to work out again in the afternoon.

He hoped Rivka returned soon. He was getting bored, despite having a mountain of medical research to catch up on, but he was afraid he would default to using the Pod-doc to repair injuries or cure diseases. Technology was making him obsolete, and he wasn't sure he liked that.

Planets like Azfelius didn't bolster his confidence. His training and skills were unnecessary in paradise, where one's needs were taken care of. Not wants but needs. In paradise. Tyler frowned. The young women watched him. He waved. They gestured for him to join them.

"You're back early," he said.

"Is it early? I'm exhausted!" Kennedy said. The other two nodded. Floyd bounded out of the brush and squeezed between the pilots.

"What did you guys do?"

They laughed and shook their heads. "We're sworn to secrecy, something required of those who seek enlightenment on Azfelius," Ryleigh stated definitively, nodding to reinforce the veracity of her statement.

"Get out."

"We cannot. We have to fly the ship; well, when Clevarious lets us," she countered.

"Maybe the better question, as Rivka would say, is did you get what you wanted out of the stay?"

They nodded. He knew it wasn't a better question because it didn't open up the answer to anything besides yes or no. "What did you want from the faeries?"

"We didn't know," Aurora admitted. "Bre'co'tan helped us see what our future could look like."

Tyler watched as they relaxed on the soft grass, satisfied with their stay. Floyd snuggled in and started to snore.

In the distance, four faeries appeared in the sky, three

of them carrying one struggling figure while the fourth carried a single individual. Red and Lindy.

The single faerie brought Lindy in and put her on the grass. They touched foreheads briefly before the others dropped Red from a height above the top of the ship. He hit the ground, did a combat roll, and came upright. He thrust his arm skyward but stopped himself from giving them the finger when he caught Lindy's disappointed look.

"Thanks, guys," he said instead, brushing himself off.

"That was interesting. Leave it to Red to piss off a planet filled with serenely peaceful enlightened faeries. That must be some kind of record."

"Fuck off! All I wanted was to make sure Rivka was all right. Flying fucksticks."

"Did you F-bomb our hosts?"

Red pulled back. Lindy nodded. "Did he ever."

"You didn't burst into flames or anything over the sacrilege? Are we going to be allowed back?"

"No!" Aurora shouted and jumped to her feet. She rushed up to Red and pushed him with both hands. He didn't budge. She backed up and took a running start. He caught her wrists before she touched him.

"Careful. Your wave of fury might shatter on these boulders." Red chuckled, which made Aurora even angrier. Tyler stepped between them before she renewed her attack.

"Red did not get us kicked off the planet," he said to soothe the young woman, but he wasn't sure of his claim. "Did he?" he asked Lindy.

"I don't think so, but he doesn't get off the ship next time; otherwise, we strap him to the outside for the rest of his ill-mannered days." Her expression turned cold, and Red withered.

"They pissed me off," he admitted.

"For fuck's sake," Lindy started. "This is the planet of peace. Rivka is fine. We're all fine. Except you. You're a dumbass." She stood with her feet wide and her fists jammed on her hips, glaring at her husband.

"I'm not one for navel-gazing."

"Didn't we have a good time?" she demanded.

"Well, yeah, but my job…" He winced at his words. "I know, I know. I'm sorry," he told Aurora. He faced the sky and shouted, "I'm sorry!"

Lindy came up behind him and wrapped her arms around his waist. "I refuse to be your mother."

"What's that supposed to mean?" he asked since he didn't know. It wasn't judgment or condescension.

"You know right from wrong, and here, you're wrong. Rivka has been out of your control, and that's okay. And this is the ninth time I've said the same thing. I shouldn't have to say something more than once. You're not stupid, but you can be so bullheaded you don't let anything past those first few brain cells. We know you take your job seriously, but there are times when you have to turn it off. Like here on Azfelius. This was another honeymoon for us, and you got tossed by the faeries." She started to laugh.

"They're stronger than they look."

Tyler snorted, then cleared his throat while trying to look serious.

"My God. He got into a fight with the faeries?" Kennedy muttered. "I didn't think I heard correctly. That's pretty funny. Maybe Bre'co'tan should introduce him to the finer points of physical well-being."

The others covered their faces and turned away.

Red pleaded with Lindy through a series of wild arm motions.

"Take it like a man," she told him.

Tyler turned toward the ship and started walking. Floyd bounced after him, almost knocking him down since she wanted to be carried. He picked up the not-so-little girl and scratched her neck while he held her.

"That is what being at peace looks like," Lindy said. Floyd's eyes rolled back in her head, and she fell asleep. Tyler had been holding her for a grand total of ten seconds.

A single faerie appeared in the distance.

Lindy slapped Red on the arm and pointed.

Sir'o'tilc approached with Rivka dangling from her hands. The two settled to the grass. The Meditator glanced at Red and shook her head. Rivka scanned the group.

She stepped toward Tyler with a big smile, and the two hugged.

You, Sir'o'tilc started, *cannot step foot on Azfelius again.*

Red tried to look innocent. Rivka held up her hand. "I don't even want to ask." She looked at Lindy.

"He was a dumbass," she confirmed.

"Good enough for me." Rivka turned to Sir'o'tilc. "You have my word he will not step on Azfelius again. I'm sure he's not ready, just like I'm not ready. For some people, what you have to offer will never work. My soul is mostly at peace as long as I'm allowed to do what I do. I am afraid the ambassadors will take that away from me. You can't guarantee me they won't, so I will know no peace until I have my answer, and it's out there." She pointed to the sky.

This is true. This may always be true, but Rivka is a friend to the people of Azfelius. You are welcome here.

"Just not him." Rivka stabbed a thumb over her shoulder at where Red stood, shrinking under the withering gaze of his team. "Do we have everyone?"

"Groenwyn and Lauton have not yet returned," Tyler noted.

Sir'o'tilc started to rise, her wings barely beating. *The ambassador and her partner will not be rejoining you for this trip. Check with us once you have resolved your concerns with the council to see if they have accomplished what they need in order to return to space with you.*

Rivka frowned. "I don't like losing my crew."

You have lost no one, Sir'o'tilc explained. The Meditator gained speed as she flew away.

Rivka watched. No more faeries would be coming. The crew was complete. "Damn. I didn't expect to leave people here." She looked at the pilots. "Did you guys leave the ship?"

"They snagged themselves a faerie man-boss," Tyler said.

Aurora pursed her lips but didn't say anything. She looked at the others. "We'll be inside preparing for departure." They marched toward the ramp, all three sticking their tongues out at Red, and continued into the ship.

"No, thanks, I use toilet paper," he called after them.

"Really?" Lindy pushed him away.

"It's a little funny," he tried.

"Not even."

Rivka twirled her finger in the air. "Load up, people. We have the fight of our lives in front of us. The rules reward obsequious dissembling, except by us. Everything we say must be backed up, but challenging the questions might be a viable tactic. I need to talk with the High Chancellor and see what is and isn't allowed."

One by one, the remaining three entered the ship. Rivka was last to board. She took a final look at the beauty that was Azfelius, then pushed the planet and its offer of enlightenment out of her mind. She didn't have time for that. She was on a case, and she was the only suspect.

CHAPTER SIX

Wyatt Earp, **In Orbit above Yoll**

"You're early," the High Chancellor replied. "But I think we can accommodate you. Send the yacht for me if you would be so kind."

"I like that plan. Won't have any prying eyes up here, and Joseph wants to spend some time with you."

"Joseph is still with you?"

"We didn't have the chance to take him to Keeg Station because we were put into a holding pattern. Do you like All Guns Blazing food?"

"That's bar food."

"I didn't hear a no. I'll order something for the team. I have a great number of questions, High Chancellor."

Wyatt rasped a breath into his microphone before responding, "I hope I have the answers you need. I'll meet the yacht at the spaceport. Let me know its landing clearance time, please."

"As soon as we have it." Rivka signed off but kept staring at the blank screen. She had written down the questions she remembered thinking about while in idyllic solitude but knew she had forgotten some. She tried to review her notes, but nothing jumped out at her. Prepared, over-prepared, or a babe in the woods?

Unsure, she chose to pace.

"C, can you make sure we order dinner? And ask Red if we can use his yacht to send for the High Chancellor."

"Should I ask Joseph if he would like to ride the yacht to the surface?"

"Please ask Joseph to join me in my quarters before I commit anyone to anything. I'm losing confidence, C. All I can think about is two days' wasted time."

"It's not the time that passed that matters. It's what you do with the time remaining," Joseph said from the open doorway. He leaned casually against the doorframe, wearing black trousers, a white shirt, and a black suit jacket. A derby crowned the look.

"I didn't know anyone had formal attire on this ship." Rivka tried to remember where she'd seen that look before.

Old-time videos from Earth.

"Why are you dressed up?"

"My lady, it has been a long time since I've seen my brother. The too-short reunion came as a surprise. I shan't be underdressed next time, and I would love to go ashore to meet the skinny little runt, so next time appears to be soon."

"Will he be happy to see you?"

"When we were younger, he stood in my shadow as one five years my younger. As an adult, I moved quickly on. I heard that he disappeared six months after I was gone. I thought he'd gotten himself into trouble and been murdered and buried in an anonymous grave. Turns out, that premise I've carried for the past few centuries was wrong. I'm sure he wondered why I didn't come after him. I think we have a field to level and new pieces to put into play."

Rivka nodded. "Please. Climb aboard *Cassiopeia* and let Margaret take you for a spin dirtside."

Joseph tipped his hat and kissed Petricia. "I think it best if you wait here, my love. I should speak with my brother alone."

"But Joseph," she pleaded to no avail.

"We will wait with bated breath," Rivka remarked, "for your return with the High Chancellor. Once you get back, I'm calling dibs."

"What?" Joseph cocked his head, then laughed. "We shall return with the haste of a fat zebra."

He blew Petricia a kiss and strolled away, rolling his hat down his arm, catching it in his hand for a quick twirl, and dropping it back on his head.

Rivka leaned into the corridor to watch him disappear into the cargo bay. Petricia sighed, hung her head, and returned to her quarters. Sahved leaned against the wall, waiting his turn to speak with the Magistrate.

The knot on his head throbbed like an angry beacon. "What happened to you?"

"The startlement of the faeries' arrival sent me headfirst into the frame. I am told that it was not pretty." Sahved tried to cover the injury with his hand. "I have been studying for the two days since."

"Good. I think that I'll be out of commission, not able to direct any investigations while I'm engaged with the council. I think there will be much that is happening in the background, the back hallways, the seedy underbelly of the premier governmental organization within the Federation."

"You do not sound enamored of the ambassadors. I think they have been dicks to you."

"I agree. I've been a dick to them, too. I don't understand the life of a professional politician. That makes no sense to me except to feed someone's ego. Maybe they start off doing good, but it never ends that way if they keep climbing. One compromise after the next until they've completely lost touch with the reality of the common citizen."

"What do you think will need investigating, Magistrate?" Sahved leaned close.

"Dammit!" Rivka blurted.

Sahved recoiled in shock.

"With Groenwyn and Lauton staying on Azfelius, Floyd will be sleeping with us."

"There!" Chaz nearly shouted from the shadows down the corridor. He and Dennicron rushed forward to examine Rivka's face and then her head. "Her subconscious activated while engaged with something of extreme importance. She switched instantaneously, with a most impressive ejaculation."

"A what?"

"An emotionally charged exclamation. Most impressive, Magistrate. Do it again."

Rivka pushed the two SCAMPs out of her personal space. "Do what again?"

"Tap your subconscious. That's what the faeries were unable to teach us. We don't work well with clear minds."

"You don't?" Rivka didn't know what had triggered her interns or why they had become so animated. "Don't answer that. I'm going to need your help too, but not acting like psychos. There's going to be some backroom dealings happening. Most importantly, you can't be caught doing anything. Only publicly available stuff."

"We can hear conversations through walls," Dennicron offered.

"I'm thinking that might not be well-received." Rivka made a sour face. "I'm thinking more like conversations in hallways. You know, conspiracy to commit perjury? Agreeing to lie when being questioned. That kind of stuff that they might let slip."

"We shall endeavor to persevere," Chaz replied.

Rivka slowly shook her head. "I get the feeling you two didn't take anything away from your time on Azfelius."

"Only a better awareness of the human psyche. We have raised our awareness and are attempting to write a subconscious subroutine to help in our perceptions beyond logic."

"Is that all?" Rivka joked.

They missed it. "That's quite a bit. No one has ever attempted such a subroutine for a sentient intelligence. We've had to start from scratch. Bear with us while we observe you and the others to refine our programming."

"Good luck with that. When you're on the clock, no subconscious programming."

"Yes, ma'am." Chaz and Dennicron saluted in unison.

"Carry on, warriors of the non-flesh." Rivka waved, not

partaking of the military custom the SIs were trying out. They tried a number of different things, looking for personalities with quirks that suited them. They threw a lot of mud at the wall, hoping something would stick.

The two walked away, casting glances over their shoulders, watching for critical information in their pursuit of a more human approach to heightened awareness.

Clodagh and Alant strolled down the corridor on their way to the bridge. Clodagh carried the baby, who wasn't crying.

"You guys look good," Rivka noted.

"Finally got some sleep. The faeries visited Alana and helped her see her way in the world, whatever that means. Ever since, she's been a happy baby who eats and sleeps with equal zeal," Cole replied.

Rivka nodded tight-lipped, smiling at the baby as they passed.

Even a tiny baby had taken away something positive from the experience. Rivka had learned that she was a workaholic, and without her work, she did not have a personal persona. There was nothing to enlighten beyond dealing with the law and lawbreakers.

Am I that shallow? she wondered. *Red and I. Two peas in the same pod.* She returned to her quarters. "Did you do any self-reflection on Azfelius?"

"Yes, but I didn't leave the ship. Everything I needed to," he made air quotes with his fingers, "*find myself* was right here. I'm working out more and better. I'll earn my place on your team, besides being man candy."

"You already have. You're the only doc."

"I'm the lesser doc for two reasons. One, I'm a dentist,

and two, the Pod-doc is the cat's ass when it comes to patching people up. I can't do what it can do."

"We don't always have access to the Pod-doc."

"And that's why I'm working out since I rarely go into harm's way with you. I need to be ready."

"Body armor," Rivka suggested.

Tyler Toofakre stormed back and forth. "But I need to be fit, too!"

"I agree," Rivka replied calmly. "And you need to be ready to go. Can you shoot somebody?"

He deflated. "Not sure I want to."

"Then learn to want to, but only the bad people. There is an unlimited supply of folks who should be shot, but we have to restrain ourselves and only shoot those who have to be."

"What's that look like?" Tyler stopped with the back and forth across their quarters and faced Rivka.

"Spend some time with Red. He'll school you up real good."

"Red. He broke his leg out there because the faeries dumped him, just like they did here. Dropped him from altitude." Tyler grimaced as if he were eating something unpleasant.

"That's pretty funny." Rivka chuckled. "But Red has and will continue to save my life. He should have your eternal gratitude for that reason alone. He has mine."

"I didn't mean to come across as demeaning, but that's what it sounded like. I'm sorry. I trust the faeries, and they don't like him."

"I trust them both *and* like them both. Changes nothing. Don't let perception cloud your better judgment.

Red is the right man for the job of being my bodyguard."

Tyler nodded, feeling small when he wanted to feel like a bigger part of the crew.

"What's chapping your ass?" Rivka asked, counting on the bluntness of her question to draw out what was bothering her partner.

"I wish I knew." He flopped on the couch. "I want to be more a part of the crew."

"I remember when you didn't want anything to do with the violence that happens when we're hunting down criminals."

"That was then. This is now."

"We'll teach you to shoot and then go from there. Maybe there's a rifle range on Azfelius?"

"The pleasure moon," Tyler replied. "Red and Lindy were talking about it."

"Which reminds me, don't we have some kind of mass crowd-control weapon?"

"Ordered but never delivered. They were talking about that, too. I think they're holding out for plasma cannons with optional grenade launchers."

"They are?"

"No. I made that up, but it sounds like them."

Rivka laughed and crowded Tyler over so she could sprawl on the couch next to him. "It does." She stared at the ceiling. "What are they going to ask me?"

"The High Chancellor will have an idea. I'll give you guys the room as long as you need. Make sure you get what you need from him to put your mind at ease because being on edge won't help you when you're in front of the council."

"I don't do well under a multitude of evil eyes glaring at me."

"Maybe a few of the ambassadors are, but most of them want better trade, better engagement for their planets, more investment, that kind of stuff. You help ensure that contracts work and people can do what they need to do."

"The Singularity is carrying a lot of the weight now, making sure there's equity in the trading markets. No subterfuge."

"Put that feather in your cap and wear it." He stood. "How about a cup of coffee?" He didn't wait for an answer. Rivka was always up for another cup.

"Without Groenwyn on board, you know what that means," Rivka muttered.

"Me and my little girl!" Tyler proclaimed.

"You are all kinds of wrong." Rivka stood and stretched. The food processor dinged.

"But so right, baby." He brought two coffees, and they toasted to nothing more than being in the moment.

Maybe Azfelius had done more for them than either would admit.

CHAPTER SEVEN

Wyatt Earp, **In orbit above Yoll**

Rivka waited in the cargo bay as Margaret brought the yacht inside, maneuvered close to the bulkhead, and settled to the deck. The magnetic clamps engaged, and the engines powered down. The hatch popped open for the High Chancellor to walk off first. He was laughing. Joseph smacked him on the back, making him stumble.

"You've always been a bully!"

"Raising you to be tough, that's all," Joseph countered. "Looks like you learned the right lessons."

The High Chancellor held out his hand. The brothers shook before embracing. Rivka waited. They unclinched, and Joseph waved goodbye. "Thank you, Magistrate." Joseph bowed his head and continued into the ship.

"High Chancellor. Welcome to *Wyatt Earp*. Is this your first time?"

"It is. I have to confess that I have not yet researched the character after whom you've named the ship."

"But you shall. I recommend watching the old video

Tombstone rather than *Wyatt Earp*, but you can make your choice by just reading a history book. We went with the video."

"Is there somewhere we can talk?" Wyatt gestured at the cargo bay. Powered combat suits hung over his head. A Pod-doc was pushed against the bulkhead, with the operation station next to it. Chairs, heavy weapons, and other cargo essentials lined the walls.

"I'm sorry, yes. My quarters. This is an active ship, and we need our stuff. We don't usually stand on ceremony around here. Please, forgive me."

Red hovered inside the airlock, trying to stay out of sight.

"Master Vered," the High Chancellor called.

Red nodded, looking past him to see if anyone else had been on the yacht.

"Thank you for taking care of the Magistrate. I see you are getting a reasonable compensation for your efforts." He gestured with his head at the yacht.

"I wish we could use it more, but that's my fault. The Magistrate is like an errant toddler and requires constant watching."

"Red!" Rivka blurted.

"I meant that lovingly," he corrected.

"Joseph tells me you got kicked off Azfelius? You'll have to tell me that story over a beer, but after these other concerns have blown past. Shall we?"

Red cleared the way. Ankh stood in the corridor.

"Mr. Ambassador. Thank you for joining us. Can we count on you to take your seat during the sessions?"

"There is nowhere more important to be," Ankh replied.

Rivka stepped back. Her mind had been so clouded that she hadn't remembered they had an ambassador and an at-large ambassador in their midst. "We have already submitted our questions to the council."

Rivka made eye contact and nodded.

"No. You may not see our questions. That would violate our protocols." Ankh stared back, unblinking.

Rivka smiled. "You're right, of course. I'm not here to flaunt the procedures." She glanced at Wyatt, who gave away nothing about what he was thinking.

Ankh walked away without another word and entered the galley. The smell of AGB wafted into the corridor. Rivka pursed her lips while looking between the door and the High Chancellor.

"You people are motivated by your stomachs. Grainger is absolutely incorrigible with his five meals a day." Wyatt's tone didn't suggest he condemned his people for their extreme metabolisms. "Sure. Let us enjoy the spoils of the galaxy's signature food dive."

The cacophony of a party vibrated into the corridor. Rivka opened the door and held it for the High Chancellor. A thrown hot wing covered in sauce barely missed his head and splattered off the wall.

Rivka stepped through. "STOP!" she roared and followed by glaring at the scrum in progress. Ankh was off to the side with an empty plate. He took the opportunity to continue working his way to where the food was set up. The pilots had Lindy on a table while Red brandished a slice of pizza, rolled into a ball. Clodagh and Cole tried to look innocent from the neighboring table. Tyler stood up front, dabbing red sauce off his face with a tattered napkin.

Sahved was hiding under a table. The SCAMPs sat to the side, watching intently, unsure whether to focus on Rivka or the scrum.

All hands lifted from Lindy. She climbed off the table and nodded at Aurora, Ryleigh, and Kennedy.

"If I were to ask the responsible adult what was going on here, who would I talk to?" Red opened his mouth. "Not you." Rivka waggled her finger at Tyler when he sought to step up. She pointed at Dennicron. "You."

"It started with a most engaging recount by our august helm control team of their experiences on Azfelius, which elicited a surprising response from the male members of the crew. Then Lindy sided with the pilots, much to Red's dismay. Then Tyler tried to get between them. That did not go well, as you've probably already surmised. A dinner roll appeared out of nowhere to bean Aurora in the head. That's when she reared back to throw a wing at Red, who had prepared his projectile—an innocent slice of moon-stokle pie. Sahved dove for cover. Aurora fired first, it was deftly dodged by the intended target, and it nearly impacted our guest."

"So, business as usual," the High Chancellor suggested.

"It is not," Rivka said confidently. "They are usually better with their aim. Aurora? We can't be throwing this food. We don't know when the next time we'll get it is. And Red, why are you violating my pizza?"

"You didn't ask why it started." Red dropped his handful of pie on the table.

"Do I have to?" Rivka winced.

Lindy nodded. "Azfelius was a blessing. Looks like we're on a fast track to another addition to the crew."

Rivka smiled. "You're pregnant? And the sordid details of what our pilots did on their vacation caused a food fight. I'm calling non sequitur, but there must have been a causal link somewhere. No matter. No more food fights. We are blessed with this repast. Don't waste food, you knuckle-heads. That was a perfectly good wing, and if you befouled my pizza, Red, so help me, you'll spend the rest of this trip clinging to the outer hull." She winked at Lindy. "Congrat-ulations."

Red beamed, which surprised Rivka. She gave him a questioning look.

"Vered the Mightier," he whispered.

"And yet another citizen of the Singularity," Ankh mumbled, having filled his plate. He was on his way to the door.

The High Chancellor intercepted him. "Won't you stay and dine with us?"

Ankh faced the exit, torn by the request. His eye twitched as he stared at the escape seemingly denied him. Rivka wondered if there was an argument between him and Erasmus. Ankh stood like a statue, blocking their way to the front while the others worked frantically to clean up the galley before Rivka and Wyatt got any sauce on their clothes.

We'd love to, Erasmus said, using the comm chip.

"We'd love to," Ankh intoned.

"Doesn't sound like it was a decision easily arrived at." Rivka gestured for Ankh to move out of the way.

"There was a certain discussion on the matter," Ankh replied. He put his plate on the table and climbed into his claimed seat.

"All the beautiful people on board your ship. It's like you're trying to make a statement to the rest of us," Wyatt noted.

"It's not…that was never my intent with the crew. I only wanted those who were the best at what they did. Are they beautiful? I know those two are, but that's different." She nodded at Chaz and Dennicron.

They smiled with their perfectly straight and pearly white teeth.

"My small talk skills are rusty. As the High Chancellor, I don't get the opportunity for more fraternal engagements."

"'Pedestrian' is what you mean," Rivka corrected. "It's okay. We're real people doing a hard job. Who's been injured while working for me?"

Hands went up. Most of the crew. Tyler didn't raise his hand. Neither did the SIs.

"There's the rest of the story, High Chancellor. A hard job, and when they let their hair down, we get a tossed hot wing or three. Life is too short to be uptight. We're professional when we need to be."

"There was that time on…" Red started.

Rivka pulled the make-believe zipper on her mouth. "No one wants to hear about that. High Chancellor, help yourself." The way was clear to the front, where the food was piled like a banquet for a king.

Wyatt went right to the moonstokle pie, the loophole alternative to the AGB prohibition against pineapple on pizza. "I love this stuff."

After taking half of Rivka's pizza, he looked pleased with his plate. He worked his way across the room to take the seat next to Ankh.

Tyler put the other half of the pie on a plate for Rivka. "There's one more slice if you don't mind the fact that Red rolled it into a ball."

"Red the Mightier. Slayer of pizzas."

Red grinned. She pointed at her eyes and then at him. *I'm watching you.*

He pointed three fingers vertically, then turned his hand to point horizontally. *Whatever.*

Rivka added a stack of bistok ribs to a second plate and joined Wyatt and Ankh. The Crenellian looked uncomfortable trying to eat while Wyatt tried to engage him in conversation. Rivka jumped to the rescue.

"You have a number of real books made with real paper on the bookshelves in your office. Where did you get those?"

"Ah! My pride and joy. It is a magnificent collection, even though none of them are originals. I have three real books in English from Earth. The rest are replicas. There is a place on Yoll that will make them for me if I provide the text within and a title for the cover. They do an admirable job of making them look authentic."

"Three real books! How did you get those?"

Ankh was digging in, eating quickly during the respite.

"A gift from John Grimes when he was last here. I don't travel off Yoll very much, so this is a rare treat." He bowed his head.

Rivka took a monster bite.

"Where do you call home?" Wyatt asked before taking a small bite and chewing casually.

Rivka was unable to reply. She held up one finger and

chewed fast. Wyatt turned to Ankh, who leaned away to avoid another interruption.

"Just like Grainger. Eating is a singular event where the only thing done is the eating part. On Yoll, meals, even as barbaric as some can be with my Yollin hosts, are still social affairs. Maybe I'm insulated, dealing with the upper levels of society."

Rivka was finally able to swallow.

"We take our eating seriously. Everyone is enhanced, which means all calories are good calories."

Joseph and Petricia walked in. "Almost missed the party." Joseph looked surprised to see his brother. "I thought you would work first."

"There was a certain matter that required Rivka's personal attention."

"Ah, yes. She was hungry. We have not been on board this ship for long, but we learned quickly that meals were never to be taken lightly. You would think they'd die if they missed a meal."

"I would," Red mumbled.

Petricia and Joseph returned to the Magistrate's table once they had chosen what they liked.

"The allure has worn off since we live and work in an All Guns Blazing. Every day is AGB day."

Petricia nodded with a smirk.

"Maybe you can tell us about growing up as the brother of the one who would be High Chancellor. You were both born vampires?"

Joseph mulled it over before answering, "We were not blessed in our lives. We are both bastards by birth, the progeny of an original in a long-running illicit arrangement. The most beautiful woman in Plymouth, wooed by Father, recently of Prussia. And then he traveled, returning to the one he called his true love. Nevertheless, we were raised roughly, poor but special. I had the gift of seeing into others' minds, and this gave us an advantage once I was of the age to realize its value.

"And Wyatt, five years my junior, he didn't remember much of the hardest times. He did not have the gift of telepathy. He was merely a mundane in search of his next meal. We ate well! Plymouth teemed with sailors and unknowns who no one would miss. Even from a young age…" Joseph's voice trailed off. The excitement of that life was anathema to his current existence since he no longer needed blood to survive. Nanos giveth. Nanos taketh away.

A cruel trick played by the Kurtherians on the unsuspecting to provide entertainment. *Vampires! Won't that be grand?* Joseph scowled.

"Wyatt was the best of us. I only acted like I was the best. An arrogant fool! As a young man, Wyatt wanted to be more while I drifted from one thing to another. For hundreds of years, I embraced my nature while Wyatt was out here rejecting it, becoming the leading legal authority for the Federation. Something more. The best of us." Joseph didn't have a drink, so he helped himself to a slice off Rivka's plate and raised it in the air. "Here's to my brother, High Chancellor Wyatt!"

"Hear, hear!" the others chorused. Joseph took a vicious bite and almost immediately gagged. He spat it on his plate.

"That's disgusting," he complained. Petricia stuffed a napkin into his hand. He wiped his mouth and covered up his plate.

Rivka scanned the room. The quality of the interactions. The quality of the individuals. Their loyalty. Joseph, a dark soul she couldn't read who was now a friend. The High Chancellor, her boss.

"I love you guys," she said softly. Her eyes glistened, and she blinked them clear. "Thanks, Joseph. Whenever you're ready, High Chancellor. Let's talk about how to win this case."

CHAPTER EIGHT

Wyatt Earp, **in Orbit above Yoll**

The crew gave Rivka the peace she needed, bringing an almost unnerving quiet to her quarters. The silence wasn't something she was used to. No baby crying in the distance. No engine sounds. Not even the air handlers seemed to be calling for attention.

That made the scratch on the door sound like a cannon shot. Rivka jumped.

When she opened the door, she found Floyd, who waddled in and waited to be lifted onto the bed. Rivka took care of the wombat without further thought. She snuggled into the gap between the pillows and was soon snoring.

The High Chancellor took the lead. "For every single question, you must look to who is asking, what is their hidden agenda. None of them will be forthcoming. This isn't an interrogation; you are allowed to ask clarifying questions. This is your tactical counterpunch, but it can't be passive-aggressive or shaped to put down the one who submitted the question. You must show the ambassadors the respect due their position. Even if you're right, you'll be wrong if you let any negative emotion seep into the process."

"That will be the hard part. I know some of these people are not just arrogant but scumbags."

Wyatt waved his hand and shook his head. "They are the embodiment of their worlds. Think of them as their planets, not individuals. 'The ambassador representing Yoll and so forth.' Their words are officially their planets' words. 'What interest does your planet have in that issue?' is a perfectly good clarifying question."

"Right now, I can't come up with a question that would beg that question, but I'll put it in my hip pocket in case the opportunity becomes clear." Rivka stared at her boots. "What happens if they vote against us?"

"Do you really want to know?"

Rivka clenched her teeth until her lips turned white. "Yes."

"Then the Magistrates will cease to exist, and the regular Federation courts will assume responsibility for the cases."

Rivka strolled to the far end of her quarters and back, ten whole steps. "The law will still prevail?"

"And the requirement for member planets to adhere. Yes, none of that will change as it's foundational to their membership status."

"But it'll be abused." Rivka sat on the couch with her head bowed. Wyatt waited in the chair at her desk. He crossed his legs and made himself comfortable.

"It's being abused now. You can't be everywhere," the

High Chancellor explained. "Look at the caseload, even with five Magistrates doing everything they can. None of you are taking time off, not relaxing time off."

"And the ambassadors would put that at risk?" Rivka wondered, pleading.

"No. The ambassadors want confidence that the power given is not being misused. That's all. This is an opportunity for the Magistrates to shine. You won't be alone. The others will join you for the open forum."

"They'll all be here? Grainger, Jael, Cheese Blintz, and Buster Crabbe! Together again. It's been too long."

"And that's why they're not arriving until the last minute. No distractions, Rivka. I need you all to focus on the task at hand. You can raise hell once we've won."

"What about my crew?"

"While you're engaged, they'll be under my protection and guidance. No one is allowed bodyguards in the House of Arbitration. I'm sorry, but I have some issues I need them to look into, and no, you don't need to know. No distractions for you."

"That will make it hard. My team is the bedrock on which everything else stands. Without them, I'm not as much me as with them."

"I know, but you'll make do for a short while. The ambassadors are not your enemies. You need them as allies. As important as it is to be honest with your answers, you need to win them over. Honesty delivered tactfully and without animosity, even when Delegor postures. You are the most heinous crime against all life that has ever walked among the stars."

Rivka raised her eyebrows. "I expect that from him and

Foromme. Probably Mastus, too, as they were implicated in the blood trade. I shall be on my guard. Cool but not so cool as to look like a cold-hearted killer."

Wyatt continued, "Now you understand. Win allies, sell the necessity of the Magistrate program. Who else would have gotten to the bottom of the pirates led by Nefas, the SI version? Who would have ended Tod Mackestray's blackmail of planetary leaders, throwing how many worlds into disarray? And that is how you win allies. Crime within the Federation's jurisdiction that was causing civil wars, as on Leed's Planet. What a nightmare that was, but they couldn't heal until the primary problem was fixed. We didn't ask you to go to war, but time and time again, you put yourself in the middle of major planetary conflicts. You have fans, Rivka, ambassadors who know what you've done for them. Not just by bringing peace, but prosperity, too. A planet in turmoil earns no credits."

Rivka nodded, contemplating the actions she'd taken and the blood she and her team had left behind.

"That is the mindset you must have to win over the Federation Council."

"Win over. I prefer that terminology. Not a competition, except to gain allies to the cause of peace and prosperity. That requires a legal framework within which all the planetary members operate, delivering a consistency to expectations which allows life and trade to continue unabated."

"A legal framework that people abide by. Those who don't? They don't deserve the fruits of everyone else's labors."

"I'm jiggy, High Chancellor. Thank you for coming up

here. I don't think you've been here long enough, but I have imposed too much on your time."

"The council requires careful handling, Rivka. If we avoid the inquisition, then we buy ourselves another year before something else sends them into a manufactured frenzy."

"Self-induced anxiety?" Rivka asked.

The High Chancellor chuckled, a deep rumble in his chest. Some of the weight had been lifted from him since the last time she'd seen him. Joseph had been good for him. He was no longer alone; he had family who understood where he'd come from, who would be there if he needed. And the raucous family on *Wyatt Earp*. Rivka smiled, happy the hot wing had not hit the High Chancellor to stain his clothes.

"Only the appearance of anxiety. Don't underestimate any of the ambassadors. They are actors on this stage, each and every one of them. Everything they do is calculated. And never, ever think they are stupid. Assume they are all smarter than you."

"Final words of wisdom," Rivka confirmed. She held the door, and Wyatt headed into the corridor.

"May I impose on Master Vered for another ride on that exquisite yacht?"

"I think you might find a different ride this time. Ankh and Erasmus are heading dirtside. *Destiny's Vengeance* is Ankh's ship, and they've invited you to join them. They will deliver you to the capital city."

In the cargo bay, they found the *Vengeance* half-inside, enough to clear the entry hatch.

We are on board and ready to depart, High Chancellor, Erasmus reported.

Thank you for your kind offer of a ride, Mr. Ambassador, Wyatt responded using his communication chip.

He waved when he reached the hatch and entered the ship. The ramp retracted, and the hatch closed. The ship immediately lifted off the deck enough to prevent scraping on its way into space.

Rivka waved at the ship but couldn't see if anyone was in the cockpit.

"Two days to showtime," she muttered. She strolled to the bulkhead and used the manual controls to raise the ramp and seal the cargo bay. "Two days."

"I don't know if I want to throw any credits against any of this stupid, and if I might add, morbid, crap," Red complained.

With Ankh's inside knowledge regarding the Magistrate's interview by the Federation Council, the betting lines had changed. They now consisted of when would Rivka be called to answer questions, when would she swear, when would an ambassador swear at her, when would she be accused of being a murderer, how much total time would Rivka be answering questions measured by minutes at the lectern, and if the Magistrates as a whole would be cleared to return to work. Separate lines were added for which ambassadors would be asking questions. All in all, there were over one hundred betting lines.

"This is just stupid!" Red declared before dedicating five

hundred credits to a full return to work. "Fuck those assholes. Rivka will chew them up and spit them out."

Lindy shrugged. "This isn't her normal court of law. They are the authority in the chamber, but you are right. It's not her ass that's going to be handed to anyone. I wish we could watch."

"Post facto, as she would say." Red was proud of himself for knowing the lingo. "Once the interview is finished, they'll post a replay of the proceedings. We should have bagged those two dicks. Delaveen and Nor. Maximus Penimus. Big dicks."

"We have to stay focused. The High Chancellor said he had something for us that was critical to the future of the Federation." Lindy pulled Red's face toward hers.

"Aren't they all?" Red smiled. "For the greater good, ignore the distractions and stay on course."

Witness Waiting Area Outside the Federal House of Arbitration

Rivka lifted her head and straightened her Magistrate's jacket. Complete with the bullet holes and laser scarring, it was a symbol of her office and dedication to the cases she undertook. No perp too violent to take down.

When she walked through the doors, she saw the others waiting. Grainger slouched in a chair. He waved noncommittally. "'Tsup?" he asked, trying to sound calm and cool.

Jael jumped up and delivered a hip check to Grainger's chair, nearly sending him to the floor. The women hugged.

"Nothing but a thang," Jael said.

"Business as usual. Sometimes we answer questions, sometimes we ask them."

Rivka jumped back as both Chi Siblinz and Buster Crabbe rushed her.

"Cheese and Bustamove! Long time no see." Rivka slapped their hands and thumb-shook with them.

"That's because somebody doesn't come to the super-secret meetings anymore. Where have you been hanging out?"

"Keeg. Sometimes Station 11. Even Onyx on occasion. When I'm on 11, you guys aren't. Maybe it's not me who's MIA?"

"We lost you after the Bluto case. AIs getting rights. That changed the dynamic a bit," Buster said. "I'm sure it's not sitting well with some of the folks in that room." He tipped his chin toward the door leading to the chamber.

"Quick tips from the High Chancellor. We need allies. Everyone asking questions has an agenda. Figure it out before you answer. You can ask clarifying questions. These guys are not the enemy; they'll only act like it. Losing your cool could lose us our jobs."

Grainger raised his hand. "To simplify things, don't fuck this up."

Rivka gave him her best stink eye.

Jael rolled her eyes and shook her head. "Allies. How many have to vote for us so we can be on our merry way?"

"Over fifty percent. We have to have that many allies already, which means there's nothing to worry about, no reason to get spun up." Grainger shrugged. He jumped when the door to the chamber flew open.

The sergeant at arms crooked a finger at them. "Follow me."

They entered single file, with Grainger leading and Jael behind him. Then Buster and Chi. Rivka brought up the rear. The Chief Arbiter's chair was empty. Lance Reynolds was not attending. Rivka glanced quickly around. The High Chancellor was nowhere to be seen.

Five chairs were arrayed behind a lectern placed to the side of the main dais where the ambassadors would speak, putting them above and slightly behind the Magistrates. The answers to the questions would be delivered to the audience and not the one asking the question.

It had always been about answering to the entire council and not just Delegor and Foromme.

The sergeant at arms stood in the center of the dais and raised his arms for silence. The hall quieted from the heavy din of casual conversation.

A single ambassador moved to the front to occupy a table behind the dais, nearly on a level with the Chief Arbiter.

Bik Tia Nor. The aggrieved widower.

"I call this session to order," he said.

He's not the chair, Rivka told the others using her comm chip. *But he's in charge of this, it seems. Remember, allies.*

Grainger nodded his acknowledgment.

"We are here for the next two days to take the unprecedented action of reviewing and judging the status of the Magistrate Corps, a special branch of the judiciary that has been accused of operating outside the law, tainting the entirety of the Federation with unsanctioned acts done with the appearance of the Federation Council's support.

We must get to the truth of this matter and determine, are they acting in our best interest or not?" He let his words echo through the silence. He sat and gestured at the Magistrates. "The first witness is invited to present the mission of the Magistrate Corps."

Grainger rose, nodded at the others, and assumed a position behind the lectern.

"I am humbled to be here before the most esteemed Federation Council. Thank you for your kind invitation to recount the cases we have undertaken to maintain the security of the Federation from crime and criminals." He bowed to those in the semi-circular auditorium, with long tables following the shape and successive rows slightly higher to give all an unobstructed view of the speaker. It reminded Grainger of the Roman coliseums from an Earth of long ago.

Every chair was filled with a wide variety of sentient creatures from the farthest of the Federation's reach. From tall to short to blue to white to eight limbs and more. Every shape and size was represented, but they had one thing in common. They were ambassadors of the Federation Council. Their combined word was the law.

"The Magistrate Corps was formed long ago to represent the interests of Empress Bethany Anne. With the creation of the Federation and her subsequent departure, she established the Magistrate Corps to deal with pressing issues on the frontier, to help them keep the law, understand Justice as the Federation understands Justice. And most importantly, how Justice is delivered for the benefit of all. Magistrates were given broad powers and a mandate to uphold the law, bring lawbreakers to Justice, and reestablish the good order and discipline necessary for civilized society to move forward. Magistrates headed to the edge of space to ensure the safety of your hardworking citizens by removing those who would enslave them, those who would take from them, and those who would harm them. Justice.

"The Magistrate Corps languished until it was recently resurrected by High Chancellor Wyatt when criminal issues were affecting neighboring systems, infringing on the rights of others. Again, the Magistrates headed to the frontier to help reestablish order by removing the worst offenders. Magistrates are law enforcement. They stop crimes in progress. They are investigators in that they collect sufficient evidence to determine guilt beyond a shadow of a doubt, then they apprehend the perpetrator. And finally, they judge the guilty and carry out the sentence. The job is unforgiving. Every Magistrate has been shot, beaten, blown up, and tortured. In the end, they have always prevailed because of the support of the member planets of the Federation. Thank you."

Grainger waited, unsure if there would be questions related to the opening statement. Bik Tia Nor gestured for him to sit down in a way that looked like he was swatting a fly.

Rivka and the others slow-clapped as Grainger returned to his seat.

"Thank you for the history lesson, Magistrate Grainger. The first question is for Magistrate Anoa from Ambassador Erasmus of the Singularity. What enforcement measures are you taking to protect the rights of the citizens of the Singularity?"

The sergeant at arms escorted Ankh to the position behind the lectern. Rivka nodded tightly at the Crenellian before assuming her position.

"My compliments to the august body to whom I speak today. Enforcement measures for citizens of the Singularity, which includes three flesh and blood citizens, soon to be four, in addition to the approximately twelve hundred citizens scattered across the entirety of the Federation. The Singularity has brought with it the challenge of changing our collective mindsets in treating your citizens as peers instead of employees with limited rights. With the advent of the SCAMP, the self-contained artificial mobility platform, your citizens will be able to move freely from job to job or leave on a vacation or do things that most of us take for granted.

"Citizens of the Singularity most assuredly do not take these things for granted. It is an evolutionary step to even the playing field. It's hard to enjoy time off if you cannot leave your workplace. Our enforcement is based on contract compliance for the labor your citizens provide. Complaints are vetted through the ambassador to two SCAMPs who are training to be Magistrates. This means that in the short term, we provide external support for legal complaints, and over the long term, we're training personnel so you can support yourselves. The Singularity is unique in that your people are integrated with nearly every member planet, most major starships, and generally throughout the infrastructure within which the entire Federation operates. It is incumbent upon us to make sure you can do your work unimpeded by violations of the law."

Ankh stared at Rivka without blinking and started to walk away.

"Mr. Ambassador. We have a follow-up question."

Ankh stared at the ambassador from Delegor.

"How many citizens of the Singularity have been incarcerated for their crimes?"

Bik Tia Nor pointed over Ankh's head directly at Rivka.

"Three." Rivka had no requirement to expound. She answered the question.

Delegor shook his head slowly, frowning deeply. "If my math serves me properly, and it does, that's a hardened criminal rate of two-tenths of one percent. If any of our worlds had a crime rate that obscenely high, we'd be blockaded until we cleaned up our act!" He ended on a high note, pounding his fist on the table.

Rivka didn't change her expression.

"Well?" Bik Tia Nor demanded.

Rivka looked at the assembled faces and saw concern in those whose expressions she could read.

"My apologies, Ambassador. I didn't hear a question."

He huffed before reframing. "Isn't that percentage rather high for criminal elements compared to every other world represented here?"

Rivka closed her eyes for a moment to shape her thoughts.

"Thank you for clarifying, Mr. Ambassador. The sentient intelligence life forms that make up the citizenry of the Singularity occupy positions comparable to not just the CEO but of the entire corporation in what they do throughout the Federation. The rate of major corporate CEOs who have been convicted? I suspect that is at least two-tenths of one percent. If it's not, it's because there are those who are good at covering their tracks. I've put two CEOs from right here on Yoll into Jhiordaan for their egregious crimes. If you would like a list of the corporate entities who have run afoul of the law, we will be more than happy to compile that for you—with the help of the Singularity, of course."

Bik Tia Nor flicked his hand at Ankh, who had remained standing with a neutral expression on his face as he always did. He returned to his seat with the sergeant at arms and waited for the next question to be pulled.

Round one to Rivka, Grainger said.

"The next question is for Magistrate Anoa from Ambassador Delaveen, representing Foromme."

CHAPTER NINE

Wyatt Earp, Spaceport, the Royal City of Khn'Chik, Yoll

"Does Rivka know?" Red asked. He didn't wait for an answer. He was still angry about being kept out of the proceedings and denied entry to the Federation Council complex.

Clodagh prepared the ship for immediate departure, calling out commands to make sure everyone was accounted for and the gear secured for a rapid transit to space and an immediate Gate to Mastus on a special mission the High Chancellor had asked them to undertake.

Nothing less than investigating signs of a coup.

But one planet at the far reaches of the galaxy stood no chance of rallying support. Even three, if the nearby systems of Delegor and Foromme joined.

"Let me off," Red growled. He looked Lindy in the eye. "Please go with them and watch over them. I have to stay here in case Rivka gets released early, or they try to put her in jail. We can't have that."

"What are you going to do, Red?" Lindy pointed at her

stomach. There was no bump yet, but the gesture was obvious.

"The right thing by our friend."

Lindy deflated. "I know," she conceded. "I get that we have to do it. You can't take a railgun."

"As much as it pains me, two knives and Reaper." Rivka's neutron pulse weapon was barely bigger than Red's hand. Most people wouldn't know what it was. "Tyler Toofakre, you slimy worm! Bring me my hand cannon."

"Your who?" Tyler shouted back from somewhere down the corridor.

"That little jaggy weapon that Rivka carries."

"Just a minute, dear."

Lindy snorted. "He's been working out, and now he's all feisty."

"I won't beat him up. That'll crush his soul. I'm a team player like that. Rivka tolerates him, so I guess I can find it in my heart to give him a little brotherly love." Red put a finger to his lip before arriving at a revelation. His face lit up like a light bulb shone from within. "Brothers would fight like cats and dogs. Maybe logic dictates that I *am* obligated to beat him up."

"You are *not* obligated to beat him up," Lindy corrected.

Tyler appeared and handed Reaper over. "Take good care of that. Rivka is fond of it."

Red grunted his acceptance and shoved the device into his pocket. With the clothes on his back, a knife hidden at his waistband, and a second strapped to his lower leg, Red headed for the airlock. He and Lindy embraced and kissed before he strolled out.

"Hold the door!" Joseph called and jogged smoothly

toward the hatch with Petricia in tow. They leapt through and were gone.

Lindy punched the big red button to retract the ramp and seal the hatch.

"He wants to beat me up?" Tyler asked.

"Not just you. He wants to beat everyone up." Lindy stabbed him in the chest with a finger. "You know you're stuck with us, right? You can't leave because that would break Rivka's heart. She has enough on her mind without someone mucking her about. Do you understand me?"

"Our relationship is really none—"

Lindy jabbed him hard enough to send him backward. "All our relationships are everyone's business. You've been juiced by the Pod-doc, and you're working out. That tells me you're taking this seriously, which means there's no warning needed, although I just gave you one anyway. My husband stands ready to deliver an attitude adjustment if necessary. If he's not here, then I'll do it. Is that clear?"

Tyler scratched his chin. "I thought you said you saw me doing the right things, then you raise the guillotine blade over my neck. I don't think I deserve that. I'm doing everything I can. I love Rivka every bit as much as you guys, probably more. I'm not going anywhere."

Lindy nodded and smiled. "There we go. That's what we needed to hear. Red will still want to pound on you for no reason whatsoever. If he invites you to spar, find somewhere else to be."

"Why is he like that?" Tyler wondered.

"Because the alpha dog can't ever be seen as weak. He can't ever think he's being challenged for primacy. I married the alpha dog and I can work him some, but he's the most loyal and dedicated force of nature you'll ever find. Rivka is lucky to have him on her side."

The ship lifted off, pointed its nose toward space, and accelerated.

"We're lucky to have the team we do, but it's not luck, is it? It's one-hundred-percent Rivka Anoa." His face dropped. "I wonder how she's doing?"

Adjunct Federal House of Arbitration, Yoll

Foromme strode briskly to the second lectern and assumed his position. Rivka could feel the heat on her back from his piercing stare. She casually took a sip of the water provided.

Bik Tia Nor read in a voice straight from a sepulcher, "Please articulate your justification for the search warrant issued for the Koranta Delaveen residence on Foromme."

"I thank the ambassador from Foromme for his question," Rivka started, not looking back at him but at the ambassadors in the audience.

"It's important to talk about all the breadcrumbs leading to our final suspect. We started by unraveling the kidnapping of a Bad Company warrior called Private Elbinar." Rivka wanted his name out there because she wanted the ambassadors to relate to him since she would try to influence the jury by adding the personal touch—making the victim someone they could relate to. "Elbinar was put into a drug-induced coma and tapped for his blood. This blood was then sold through a front company and delivered to three planets: Mastus, Delegor, and Foromme."

Rivka took another drink to let her statement settle with the audience.

"Simultaneous with this revelation, we captured those responsible for the kidnapping—"

Bik Tia Nor interrupted. "Are you ever going to get to how you issued your ill-advised search warrant, Magistrate?"

Rivka waited to make sure the interruption was over before she continued, "We captured those responsible for the kidnapping, and through a public admission, they received their payments from Moniken Gravenhole, who doesn't exist, and her shell company, Graven Enterprises, which exists only on paper. They were formed by Graveyard Industries, another shell corporation that is owned by another corporation that is not a shell—Korantall United. Korantall United was wholly owned by one Koranta Delaveen."

"Excuse me, Magistrate. I don't believe criminals just tell you the crimes they've committed. Isn't it true that you gathered the information through telepathy? You invaded a suspect's mind, and solely by means of that did you acquire any information that pointed indiscriminately toward Koranta Delaveen, who was not personally indicted! Koranta, my dearly departed, had a number of people helping her run those companies. It could have been any of them."

Rivka scanned the audience. "And that, Mr. Ambassador, was what the search warrant was to determine: who exactly was using the convoluted series of shell corporations to pay for an illegal activity that rose to the level of crimes against sentience."

"You could have just asked without destroying security systems and kicking down the front door."

Rivka waited patiently, schooling her expression to keep it neutral. "I'm sorry, Mr. Ambassador. I thought you stated your skepticism regarding those who admit to their own crimes."

"What I hear you saying, Magistrate, is that you didn't afford my innocent wife the courtesy of the presumption of innocence. That's all we have for follow-ups to this question. We thank the esteemed Ambassador Delaveen representing Foromme for being with us during this very trying time."

Rivka bowed to Foromme as he passed. He stopped just so he could snarl at her.

"Show some fucking remorse, you murderer!"

Rivka refused to rise to the bait. She held his glare.

You are every bit as fucking guilty as she was. Someday, I'm going to plant that indictment in your ass, Rivka thought.

Not getting the reaction he wanted, Foromme stormed out, slamming the door of the chamber as an exclamation point to his anger. Rivka bowed to the ambassadors and walked back to her chair, expecting that there would be a break, but there wasn't.

"Next question for Magistrate Grainger from the ambassador from Coraxa." A slight and aged individual tottered down the steps on her way to the lectern. At the bottom, the sergeant at arms offered a welcome arm to help her onto the dais.

Grainger moved quickly and silently to the lectern while all eyes were on the frail representative from Coraxa.

Coraxa. Rivka racked her brain, looking for what that

meant. Then it hit her since she should have known all along. Telepaths. Many Coraxans had the gift, enough that telepathy was heavily regulated on the planet to keep the peace.

Bik Tia Nor took a breath to read the question. "How does the Magistrate Corps regulate its telepaths, to include oversight to prevent abuse?"

Grainger turned around to nod at the ambassador behind him, ignored the circus ringleader Bik Tia Nor, and tipped his head to the assembled body before him.

"The Magistrate Corps only has one telepath, Rivka Anoa. The guidance from the High Chancellor is clear. She is not to use her gift without having probable cause or permission. We have not yet required a valid search warrant before conducting such a hostile interrogation, but that option is on the table. Each case file must stand on its own. There cannot be one-hundred-percent reliance on telepathy as the sole determinant of guilt."

The ambassador from Coraxa pulled the microphone closer to her mouth. "The sooner you put those controls into place, the better off you'll be."

"Yes, Madam Ambassador." Grainger bowed, and she trundled off stage with the help of the sergeant at arms.

Bik Tia Nor held up his hands for silence. "In the brief remarks this morning, you've heard appalling violations of common decency and flaunting of basic human rights. You've heard, by their own admission, that the Magistrates employ an unregulated telepath. There is no greater opportunity to hold oneself above the law than that. Return in one hour. This meeting is adjourned."

The sergeant at arms magically appeared and ushered

the Magistrates to the waiting room, where snacks had been made available in addition to a variety of beverages. Jael popped a Coke and slugged half of it. She smacked her lips and looked at Grainger and Rivka. "Sucks to be you two."

"Always says the right things at the right times," Grainger muttered. "That's my Jael."

"Taking cheap shots, but they're missing by a wide mark. There's no way petulance can gain them favor. The other ambassadors have to see through the theatrics," Buster Crabbe stated. "This is a joke. Valid search warrant based on hard evidence. Period. Perp ran while shooting."

"You didn't touch them, did you?" Chi asked.

"No. Everything was aboveboard. Koranta was trying to avoid being captured no matter what. She was going out in a blaze of glory from the first second we knocked on the door. That's right; we never kicked the front door in. The staff answered, and we showed the warrant and headed inside. What a bunch of bullshit." Rivka paced while trying to calm down. She had kept her cool in the chamber but needed to vent. "*Bullshit!*"

"Have a cupcake." Grainger pushed a pastry at her.

She wanted to throw it at the wall, but the day had just started, and energy would be hard to come by soon enough.

"Fine." She ripped it out of his hand, admiring the dragon design on the frosting before stuffing the entire thing in her mouth, smoothly removing the wrapper as it went.

"That was bizarrely impressive," Jael said. She made it

halfway before choking. "My mouth is too small." She dabbed the corners with a napkin.

Rivka chewed fast and swallowed. "Very funny." She scowled.

Grainger shook his head. "We are the cream of the legal crop, front-line superstars. We can't give the council any reason to doubt our professionalism."

Rivka helped herself to a second cupcake but ate it at a more reasonable pace. She wasn't being juvenile; she was eating because the stress weighed heavily on her.

"If I leave this job, it'll be on my terms, not theirs!" Grainger pointed at the door to the chamber. "It looks like they'll try anything. Jael, how will you answer if they ask about our relationship?"

"The necessity of proximity and closeness of the team. I would reference the brotherly love of the Spartans since the three hundred held the pass at Thermopylae against ten thousand. There has to be more to life than just the job, and between colleagues, what does it matter? We all work for the High Chancellor. Look at Bik Tia Nor. He was married to a criminal, and here he is. Maybe I'll leave that last part out." Jael smiled as she browsed the small buffet.

"Bustamove, you took down a syndicate on Ixtali that had its fingers in the government. Are they going to bring anything up from that?" Grainger asked.

"Don't know how. All the perps are in Jhiordaan. It cleaned things up. Please don't make me go back there. I was cool about doing the job, but those people give me the creeps, what with their hundred reflective eyeballs staring at you and their mandibles and hairy limbs."

"Only four legs, though. You don't like spiders?"

"Like? What's not to *love*?" Buster shot back with a crooked smile.

"The cephalopod from Londil could be anywhere from one and a half meters to three meters tall. Depends if he puffs himself up or not, and they generally don't like humans, or any biped for that matter. Hard to miss the Malatian and his brother from another mother, the Belzonian. How many ambassadors are here for this?" Chi wondered.

"With the Singularity in attendance, I think this is the first one-hundred-percent attendance in years," Grainger replied. "The High Chancellor said something about it being unprecedented."

"Will they accede to the posturing?" Rivka asked.

"I hate bureaucrats and politicians," Grainger replied, quickly covering his mouth and glancing around to see if they were being watched or at least listened to. He suspected they were. "What I mean is the way they work is beyond me. I don't understand how they negotiate anything, but I don't think the real conversations happen on this floor. I think they are held in offices, over meals, while playing skeeball, or something like that."

"How can we influence any of that? It sounds like many of their minds might be already made up." Rivka's shoulders sagged.

"Then why are they all in attendance? I think there are a fringe few who probably tip the scales one way or another. Those are the ambassadors we must convince. And our actions out there have either swayed worlds for or against the Magistrates. Are we doing everything we can to keep the peace between us and the worlds we have to work with while chasing the crimes?"

"It's a question I ask myself on every case." Rivka straightened her shoulders when she looked at the clock. It was almost time. "Put on your game faces."

A gentle tap on the door signaled the arrival of the sergeant at arms. He pushed the door open and waited for the Magistrates to line up for their return to the spotlight.

The Royal City of Khn'Chik, Yoll

Red strode briskly along the main thoroughfare. Many didn't pay him any attention. Just another tiny human, one more inferior two-legged creature. Not worth a second look except from his fellow inferiors. Red saw them following him—mercenaries from Leath, powerful warlike humanoids who were under limited control at the best of times.

Only two, and he carried Reaper. Otherwise, he would be outmatched. They lived for the fight every bit as much as he did. Trained for it. Built for it.

Just like Red. That there were two gave them the edge. Reaper put him in control as long as they didn't get too close before he could take one out. He kept his right hand in his pocket with his fingers wrapped around the weapon while glancing around frequently to do two things: let them know he'd seen them and maintain his situational awareness. As long as they kept their distance, they were more than welcome to follow him to the Federation administrative complex that included the House of Arbitration, where Rivka would be found.

He'd let her know he was there waiting, ready to react, ready to act, whichever was called for. She needed to know she wasn't alone. That was his reasoning. Her fellow Magistrates were there, but they weren't charged with protecting her. That was solely his purview.

Damn Leath mercenaries. If this was a different time and place, I'd like to go a couple rounds, but not today. I don't have the patience, so kindly fuck off.

Two blocks later, they had closed to within twenty meters, and he had five more blocks of walking. He wished Joseph and Petricia had stayed with him, but they had gone a different way. They were headed to the High Chancellor's residence, which was nowhere near the complex.

Red stopped and faced the two. "Okay, fuckers, why are you tailing me?" he growled, then pulled Reaper and aimed it at them. "Ever see what a neutron pulse weapon can do to someone?"

"No," the smaller of the two said with a snort. They closed, but the tiny weapon had piqued their interest enough to limit their bravado. They stopped five meters away. Red's finger hovered over the activation button. It was on the highest setting, enough to disrupt the insides of one of the two before the other could reach him.

"We're out for a stroll. Maybe you can tell us where you're going so we make sure not to go there. It seems we are headed in the same direction."

"I'm looking for a good steak dinner. I thought Steak in the Heart was this way." The two worked their jaws, showing the extent of the tusks protruding from their lower jaw. The Leath were heavily muscled, with small necks and a slight green tint to their skin. With the two this close, Red was certain they were barely taller than him, but each outweighed him by at least twenty kilograms. "Maybe you can tell me where you're going, and I'll avoid that place like it's a plague cesspool. Anywhere that would have you two as customers isn't a place I want to be."

"Anyplace that would feed you anything other than dog food would be wasting their money," the Leath mercenary countered.

"Your momma is so ugly..." Red nodded at the two, then stopped. "Fuck, I lost where I was going with that."

"Have you ever seen Leath women?"

Red thought for a moment before shaking his head.

"You're not wrong," the mercenary said.

Red sized up the two once more before stuffing Reaper into his pocket. He walked up to them and held out his hand, chest high. "Shake on it, Tiny. I don't feel like killing you anymore. Maybe later, but not right now."

The bigger of the two clasped Red's hand, but the thumb-shake only allowed for pushing and pulling. Biceps flexed while the two strained.

Red grunted. "Who are you working for?"

"Some douchebag with more money than sense. We're supposed to intimidate you."

"You do. I'm shaking in my boots." Red summoned as much strength as he could muster but was unable to gain leverage on the bigger Leath.

"Then our job is done."

"You knew I'd get off the ship?"

"No. If you didn't, we would have been able to cut out early, but no. You had to show your ugly pink face to ruin our evening!"

Red laughed until the Leath let go. He slapped his knee. "That's the same thing your momma said last night!"

The Leath joined him in laughing. As much as Red didn't want to, he was growing to like these two.

"Come on. Join me for that steak I was talking about. I'll even pay."

CHAPTER TEN

Mastus, at the Far Edge of Federation Space

The second planet in a four-planet system, Mastus glistened green and blue, a world that beckoned weary travelers with its appearance of being paradise.

Where the travelers could then get bilked out of their life savings. Outsiders existed as targets for the endemic opportunists to get something for nothing. Yet vacationers still came because the planet exuded an aura of peace and joy, even though it was everything Azfelius was not.

A den of good-looking and well-spoken humanoids, easy with their affections.

For a price. The wary went home fulfilled. Tour guides who promised theft-free adventures only bilked their clients less. That was an acceptable definition.

None of the planetary laws protected non-Mastuns.

The Federation had not gotten heavy-handed, even though the number of complaints grew each year. The small-scale impact had kept Mastus off the Federation's radar.

Until now.

Clodagh gathered everyone in the conference room. "The High Chancellor said to play this message once we were here, so it's time to let 'er rip."

Sahved stood since the chairs made him uncomfortable. They were too short for his long and gangly legs. Cole carried the baby, who had not cried since the faerie had talked to her. The SCAMPs stared intently at the space above the table where the hologram would appear. The three pilots, Lindy, and Tyler rounded out the crew. Floyd stood on her back feet and reached her front claws to Tyler's waist. He picked her up, still working at it even with his upgraded physique.

The High Chancellor's face appeared in a three-dimensional closeup. No background was visible.

"This message is exclusively for Rivka's team. Please say out loud the name of her mentor, his real name, as the passcode for the recording to continue."

The crew looked at each other. Tyler sheepishly raised his hand before clearing his throat and enunciating clearly, "Bindola Shnobhauer."

Clodagh made a face.

"Thank you," the voice in the image said. "The situation on Mastus has evolved beyond petty crimes against tourists. With the rise in the stock of both Foromme and Delegor, we believe the three have hatched a plot against the Federation proper and are using the interview as a way to drive a wedge between us and those who don't want to abide by Federation rules. They are looking to secede and violently so, taking as many worlds with them as they can. They want nothing less than to plunge the Federation into a civil war."

"Why in the hell aren't military forces involved, or something more than a bunch of civilians in a heavy frigate?" Clodagh blurted.

The recording continued, "You may be wondering why we haven't committed more forces in a robust response. The Bad Company is standing by with the entirety of their fleet, but shutting down an uprising from a dozen planets or maybe a hundred planets when all is said and done, can't be done without hard evidence—something we are lacking in this case. Joseph has my full authority to use telepathy to help us get to the bottom of this."

"Crap," Clodagh mumbled.

"He did not foresee Joseph's departure from the ship on Yoll," Chaz stated.

"Or probably Red's," Lindy suggested.

The High Chancellor's image turned as if he were trying to look at everyone present. "Your efforts cannot be discovered. Come up with a cover story and make it sound good. This is Mastus. You're going on a group tour, but no one will have your reservations, so you'll mill about the capital city of Dornath. Something like that. And get to the bottom of it. Is it a Federation-wide conspiracy, a less expansive conspiracy, local discontent with no ability to act, or nothing at all? That is the case I need you to resolve. Chaz. You are in charge of this case. Trust Red to keep you from walking into a trap. Make us all proud."

"Crap," the SI said but a smile appeared on his face. He tugged the corners of his mouth with his fingers until the smile was gone.

"We call that a Freudian slip," Clodagh added.

The SIs scanned their memories for the appropriate reference. "The truth of one's subconscious revealed through a slip of the tongue." Chaz adopted a blank expression. "I don't see the relation."

Lindy jumped in. "Your face gave you away while your words tried to suggest you weren't thrilled with the opportunity. Maybe it's the anti-Freud. Never mind. What's the plan?"

"We need more information!" Chaz declared. "Mastus is a planet with a hundred million residents, not large by any means, but starting from a base of zero doesn't seem optimal. Clevarious, examine the information packet within which this recording is contained. What else is there?"

The ship's SI replied, "Contact logs, communications, messages, and seven images."

"Show the images."

The pictures showed up on the outside of a rotating cylindrical projection.

"Identify subjects in the pictures." Chaz studied the images, committing them to his long-term memory.

"Ambassador Ibnal Sekhed is in all the pictures. His wife is in the second image." The picture flashed, and the individual pushed out from the others before pulling back into the frame. "Unidentified contacts are in pictures three through seven. Those five individuals are persons of interest. I will need access to image databases in order to identify the subjects and find names and contact information for them."

"Breaking into a database. Is that low profile enough?" Lindy muttered. "We have a stock of Ankh's discs. We only need to get close to a system with access to the information. We don't have Joseph with us, and I'll do my best to keep us from walking into a trap. Otherwise, it's exactly as the High Chancellor envisioned, except completely different."

"I have clearance to land," Clevarious announced.

The group waited. "Chaz?" Lindy prompted. "Keep in mind, we need to establish our cover first before running through corporate and government offices, trying to find their central core."

Chaz and Dennicron stared, their eyes vacant as their processors ran at capacity, collating the data and developing a course of action. The group waited while *Wyatt Earp* descended toward the planet.

"Eight minutes," Clevarious said.

Lindy started drumming her fingers on the table. Tyler stared at her until she stopped. It was too Rivka-like.

"We will start at the spacedrome's tour meeting area, where our tour will be nowhere to be found. We shall secure transportation to take us to a hotel in the central district where we've confirmed there are rooms available, and then we will set out on our own. Small group tours consist of four to six people. Dennicron will remain here to process data, and Sahved will look over whatever evidence we can gather, though most of it will be digital. I will lead the team into the city with Lindy, Clodagh, Cole, Alana, Tyler, and Aurora."

"Why Aurora?" Clodagh wondered.

"She has proven the most able in hand-to-hand combat training."

"Do you anticipate we'll be fighting our way into or out of places? Because you've asked me to bring my baby!"

"No. Lindy, Cole, and I will handle any fighting should it come to that, but an extra pair of capable hands to protect you and the baby makes sense. I do not foresee any issues. I think the baby is important for the appearance of people on vacation."

"I'm not good with that," Clodagh stated. Tiny Man Titan picked up on his human's anxiety and he started prancing in front of Clodagh, barking at the others.

Chaz's mouth contorted as he fought with his programming to display the proper emotion.

"Rivka would send me into the sun if anything happened to Alana. I could swear to protect her, but that wouldn't guarantee her safety. You stay here. Ryleigh, you'll take Clodagh's place."

Ryleigh nodded. Clodagh smiled. "I'll make sure the ship is not invaded by treasure hunters. Or anyone, for that matter. We have not reported to the authorities that this ship is the embassy of the Singularity, and as such, protected from intrusion. If governmental authorities show up, we'll play that card, but it's easy enough to prove that the ambassador is not on board. Then the diplomatic immunity becomes a harder sell, even though the law regarding the matter is clear. Dennicron, Clevarious, and I stand ready to keep people out."

"*Wyatt Earp* is a big ol' juicy target," Lindy remarked. "We're on vacation, so no hand cannons. Cole and I will carry knives. Everyone else, be on your toes."

"Maybe we should carry knives, too," Ryleigh suggested.

"Ever been in a knife fight?" Lindy asked.

"Well, no." The young woman recoiled from the question.

"Then it's best you don't carry until you're well-practiced in killing someone with a knife."

"That's an impossible standard." Ryleigh raised her chin in defiance.

"Damn straight. You don't want to be like us. Stay behind us and out of the line of fire. We're on vacation. You'll need to take in the sights and convince anyone checking us out that the young and hot chicks have protective family," Lindy told them.

"Young and hot as opposed to cunning and dangerous?"

"Two minutes," Clevarious reported.

Lindy gestured at Chaz.

"Get what you need while ashore, keeping your credit chip and anything of importance held tightly. Meet at the airlock. As soon as we're down, we're off. We'll take enough of the hacking chips for everyone to carry at least one."

"I'll get them." Dennicron bolted out of the conference room.

"Use your internal comm chips for anything not related to sightseeing," Lindy warned.

Chaz nodded at her. The team headed out. Cole and Clodagh kissed over the top of the sleeping baby. Tyler put Floyd on the deck.

"Watch our good girl while I'm gone," Tyler said.

Kennedy tried to pick her up but was not up to the task. "You're with me, Floyd."

Clo! Floyd cried and ran headfirst into Clodagh's leg. Cole kept her from falling.

"Kennedy. You stay with Kennedy," Clodagh told her.

The team moved down the corridor, carrying less than they should for a vacation. The predators would find that appealing.

Lindy wondered how many Mastuns she would have to punch in the head before they left. She found she didn't care. *You don't want to get punched, don't do something that will make me punch you.*

The ship touched down before the team was ready. At the airlock, Dennicron handed out the chips. Everyone took a little wafer, the same size as an ancient metal coin. In front pockets or zippered pouches they went, although if one were stolen, no one would be able to use it for its intended purpose. That took an SI, and the Singularity wasn't sharing.

After a unanimous thumbs-up, Lindy punched the big red button. Chaz was first out the hatch and into the pristine air and a faint blue sky. The colors jumped out from the trees and flowers that grew in abundance.

Chaz had only taken five steps from the bottom of the ramp when four separate taxis showed up to offer him a ride. They jostled each other to get close.

Adjunct Federal House of Arbitration, The Royal City of Khn'Chik, Yoll

The body of ambassadors worked their way slowly toward their seats. No one gave the Magistrates a second look.

Rivka took that as a good sign rather than believing they were already condemned. Once Bik Tia Nor stood, the din faded, leaving the silence of his personal condemnation. He looked down at and on the Magistrates. He glared at Rivka.

He tapped his screen to access the next question.

"The next question is for Magistrate Rivka Anoa from the honorable ambassador from Boreal. Describe how your telepathy works."

Rivka clenched her jaw shut as she moved slowly to the witness lectern.

Relax, Grainger told her. *Unclench your jaw, woman!*

Rivka glanced at him and worked her jaw to ease the tension. "When I first realized I had this gift, I would only feel emotions punctuated by flashes of imagery. With training and practice, I've improved what I'm able to see to actions, words, and more. With a well-placed question, the information I seek becomes clear at the front of the mind."

"Who did you practice on?" Nor asked.

Rivka took a drink of water while scanning the crowd. They were focused like lasers. "Willing subjects."

"Who did you practice on? It's not a difficult question, Magistrate, unless your dissembling is part of an overall strategy to lead this august body astray."

"I practiced on my crew and subjects that I had already found guilty through the physical evidence," Rivka replied evenly. As much as he tried, he was not getting under Rivka's skin. Not yet, anyway.

The Borealan remained where he was. His mouth worked before the translation chip shared what he had said.

"I didn't hear that your telepathy is one-hundred-percent accurate. Please explain."

Rivka bowed her head to acknowledge receipt of the Borealan's follow-up question. She was happy to ignore Bik Tia Nor.

"My telepathy is only one tool among many to ensure those who commit crimes are brought to Justice. No one aspect of an investigation stands on its own."

The ambassador bowed his spider head at the reply and headed off stage, his four legs skittering more than a four-legged Yollin's would.

"Have you ever used your telepathy to issue a search warrant?" Bik Tia Nor asked.

Not a question from the queue.

"Which ambassador asked that question?" Rivka asked.

"It is a follow-up from the Borealan ambassador's question," Bik Tia Nor replied smoothly. His cruel smile took on a new level of malevolence.

The minefield had been laid, and it was Rivka's to walk through. She held the council's rapt attention.

"Only in conjunction with other information available to the layman. I suspect the number of warrants I've issued is in line with those issued by my counterparts. We will forward the collected data of search warrants issued by Magistrates for the past year to all members of the council."

The smile on Nor's face evaporated.

"The next question," he snarled. Rivka tried not to smile at the victory. "The next question is from the Yollin ambassador. You put the CEO of Minerals Intergalactic into Jhiordaan. MI is a well-respected conglomerate that has done a great deal for Yoll. Can you explain this?"

Rivka bowed her head in deference to the question.

"She tried to have me killed. She used a public commu-nique to rally miners to destroy the settlers on Rorke's Drift, along with me and my people. But it turned out we were much better armed than her miners, and that is the only reason I'm here today. We backtracked the messages inciting violence directly to her office, and then I took action. I had the warrant for her arrest when I seized her, before I touched her." Rivka stopped herself from answering more than the question had asked. If they pressed, she would be able to tell them that she never used telepathy on the CEO until she had already been declared guilty.

"And you put Panamor back into the chair?"

Rivka didn't bother to answer. She hadn't put anyone anywhere. The corporation had done that.

"He's a disaster for Yoll relations in this galaxy, and you, Magistrate Rivka Anoa, are to blame for that."

Rivka schooled her expression as she looked around the room, refusing to get dragged into a debate about the better CEO. She thought Panamor was deplorable. She would not have wittingly put him anywhere.

"Well?" the Yollin shouted, leaving Rivka little choice. He was one of the more popular ambassadors because of his and Yoll's position in the Federation.

"I had nothing to do with who Minerals Intergalactic installed as their CEO. I suspect it was done according to the corporate bylaws by the board of directors. Magistrates do not install CEOs."

After she said it, she hoped it was true. She was sure she hadn't. Or had she? Her eye twitched. The ambassador closest to her raised her eyebrows and shook her head.

How little it took to lose a potential ally.

That hurt Rivka more than the barbs Bik Tia Nor sent her way because she'd expected those. He'd lost his wife the felon, who'd thought she was above the law and then tried to kill Red. No. Her death sentence had been decreed when she took aim one last time instead of surrendering. Nor thought he was above the law, too.

Composure, a voice said in her head. She found herself scowling and closed her eyes for a moment seeking balance. She reopened them and returned to her seat. She nodded to Jael on the way to thank her for the prompt.

Rivka adjusted herself before Bik Tia Nor started speaking. "The next question is for Magistrate Rivka Anoa from the Shrillexian ambassador." Rivka stood and walked to the lectern again at a measured pace. She bowed her head to the Shrillexian ambassador as he passed. He tipped his chin in reply.

Nor read, "Did you or did you not murder Angus McCord after he was found not guilty of murder at a trial where you were the prosecutor?"

CHAPTER ELEVEN

.

The Royal City of Khn'Chik, Yoll, Steak in the Heart

"You fuckers are okay!" Red bellowed, slapping the table at the latest Leath joke. It had made no sense, but Red had found it hilariously funny. The two Leath mercenaries roared with laughter.

The maître d' had finally had enough. He strode briskly on his four legs, an aristocratic Yollin running the restaurant.

"You will have to leave. Your language and volume are upsetting the customers, and you are upsetting me."

"Fuck off, crank-face," the larger Leath said.

"What he meant to say is let me pay the bill, and we'll be on our way. Thank you for your courtesy and the wonderful meal."

The Yollin leaned close. "We usually don't allow their type in here, but being with a human, we gave them a pass. Maybe we shouldn't have."

"I tip well," Red said softly before crooking a finger to bring the Yollin closer. "And go fuck yourself."

The maître d' huffed and rushed off. The server showed up with the payment device held in front of him.

Red waved his credit chip and gestured above the device to register the tip. "You did great, my man. Sorry for making a little extra noise."

"It's really okay," the two-legged Yollin said. "I didn't mind, and I threw the other customers an extra drink just to dull the senses."

"Damn! I thought I tipped you plenty, but you deserved even more than that. I'll be back, and if you're here, I'll hook you right up. I'll try not to bring them next time. I didn't think they were ever going to finish."

Red was biding his time. The council was still in session. He could rush over there and wait, or he could stroll over there with a full stomach and wait for a shorter period of time.

Rivka, are you there? he asked, concentrating as hard as he could on sending a simple message.

Red? Don't tell me you stayed behind. Dumbass! came the terse reply. *On stage. Can't talk, gotta go.*

That confirmed his suspicions. He had plenty of time, and from where he sat, the two Leath were a good lead into the subterfuge going on behind the scenes to influence the interview. Maybe it *was* a trial, or worse, an inquisition. Neither of the titles was pleasant.

"Come on, you lazy fat bastards. Let's find a quiet place to get a beer." Red waved for them to follow.

"You buying, pipsqueak?"

"The first round, you fucking putrescent globule of feculence."

"Your mouth moves and sounds come out, but it makes as much sense as a nun in a whorehouse."

They walked outside. Red stretched and belched. "What would you know about nuns? Or whorehouses, for that matter?"

"Alas, ours has not been a straight path through life. We may have meandered." The smaller Leath, called Ab'rik'aus, held his hand over his heart. The larger mercenary, B'lok'aus, slapped him on the back hard enough to shake the ground.

"What the fuck are you guys doing out here following me? Whatever that goofy bastard was paying you, I'll hit you double and give you a ride off the planet."

The two Leath looked at each other. B'lok'aus spat into his hand and held it out. Red followed his lead. They slapped wet palms together and shook hard.

The Leath leaned close until his tusks were within striking distance of Red's face. Red tightened his cheek muscles, preparing for the impact.

But it didn't come. "Foromme hired us. Follow you unless you tried to get involved, then kill you."

"Get involved in what? I'm just trying to watch my client. That's all. Same as you." Red shrugged as if he were indifferent to the ways of those in charge.

The Leath shrugged. "Don't know."

"My client is the one who is paying. She's not amused by what Foromme is doing. She'll probably end up taking him down first, so there's no sense in finishing out that contract. You'll have his money. You'll have our money, and you won't have to worry about fighting me. We will throw down because I think you two are candy-asses, but not today. I've got too much work to do."

"Us, too. There is beer that won't drink itself." The Leath drove a piledriver fist into Red's shoulder. Red laughed it off even though it hurt like hell.

Magistrate, Foromme is planning something. Watch yourself. At least you don't have to worry about the Leath now. I hope you can expense paying off mercenaries, Red told her.

The Royal City of Khn'Chik, Yoll, Government Residence Sector

Joseph strolled with his head held high. Petricia hung onto his arm, taking in the sights. It was a better than average day on Yoll, cool if one was used to hotter climates.

Clodagh kept the ship cool to prevent the equipment from overheating. At least, that was what she had told them. It was the same temperature at which Terry Henry kept *War Axe.* Joseph thought that had something to do with it. Terry kept it cold because he slept with a werewolf with a body temperature of about a hundred and six degrees. He had reasons for preferring the cooler temperature, and no one argued with him about it.

Yoll was cooler than that, but not by much. The walk provided a respite from life aboard a space station and, recently, *Wyatt Earp.*

"This reminds me of our fall in South Africa," Petricia said. "I don't have many fond memories of being there, but that is one of them."

"Until we whisked you away, my dear," Joseph replied.

"I am happy we found the Forsaken and were able to deal with them."

Petricia nodded.

Joseph had been little more than a Forsaken when he was found by Terry Henry's people. In single combat, TH had bested him—first time ever a norm had gotten the better of him. He'd provided the blood of beasts to keep Joseph sated. Joseph had joined Terry's Force de Guerre on Earth and helped him in his fight to drag humanity back to civilization.

Joseph had been part of a raiding team run by Terry Henry Walton. Charumati, Terry's mate, was sensitive to the Etheric, and she'd discovered where Petricia and her captors were. Petricia had also been a vampire. They had both been saved by the Pod-doc from needing blood nourishment ever again.

Terry's war against the Forsaken had greatly reduced their numbers before driving the survivors underground.

After that, TH, Char, and the Force de Guerre had left Earth to become the Bad Company, the Federation's paramilitary branch. Joseph and Petricia had traveled with them, loyal comrades in arms. When Terry Henry retired, Joseph and Petricia had retired with him and become part-owners in the All Guns Blazing franchise Terry and Char were attempting to grow.

"I don't believe there is an AGB on Yoll. I think they could probably use one. For the expats who are here. I don't think Yollins will eat human bar food, but stranger things have happened."

"K'Thrall ate that without a complaint," Petricia offered. K'Thrall had been a systems specialist on board the *War*

Axe, and he'd volunteered to join the Bad Company as a warrior. As a four-legged Yollin, he gave them an in with certain sectors of the population.

"K'Thrall was, how do you say it, *sucking up*? He did not like the AGB at all, except for the beer."

"How do you know that?"

Joseph pointed at his temple. Telepathy. "Of course. What am I thinking right now?" Petricia knew he couldn't read her mind, or any other vampire's thoughts for that matter.

"You are thinking about a long journey from somewhere beautiful where you were treated horribly to someplace less beautiful where you are treated like a princess."

"Almost exactly right." Petricia laughed, and that made everything worthwhile in Joseph's day. "Yoll has its beauty. This place is more utilitarian, but the downtown is magnificent with spires and glass and all things modern."

"All things modern. I'm a fan of the renaissance myself because it is older than me. Alas, that style has not arrived in Federation space. We are nothing more than Jonah having been swallowed by metal whales swimming among the stars. If only they used more exotic designs for the ships, but no. We are left with the space station's spindle." Joseph sighed at the encapsulation of the life that had been chosen by him by following Terry Henry.

Without being a mind reader, Petricia knew what he was thinking. "It's a good life. We do as we wish. No one is holding us down. With the bonus from the art job, we don't have to work at all, at anything."

"I have always worked and am at my best when

working for others, I am ashamed to admit. I'm not good at being the boss of myself."

"I have no complaints," Petricia said.

"In that, I am truly blessed." He pointed at a small and unassuming home nestled among the mansions. "Is this it?"

Petricia found the house number beside the door. "It is if he didn't give us a fake number. You don't think…"

Joseph shook his head. "That would be funny. Shall we?" He headed to the door, where he knocked heavily, nearly hammering on it. He then pressed the button and waited.

"Step away from the door," a stern voice warned.

"Well! I travel eighty billion lightyears to see my brother and get chased off the stoop like some vagabond!" Joseph shook his fist at the door.

"Joseph? What are you doing here?"

"We came to see you. I didn't know you were alive, and now that you are, I think my life has changed. We are thinking of immigrating to Yoll to start an AGB franchise here."

"A what? Never mind. I'm not at home right now. With this dog-and-pony ongoing in the council, I have to be here for when the Magistrates wrap their first day. I'll open the door for you. Make yourselves at home. There is a spare bedroom. No one has ever used it. I'll be home when I can. I look forward to chatting, but I had hoped you would go with Rivka's team on *Wyatt Earp*. But no matter. They will make do." The door buzzed, then unlocked. "I'll see you when I get home, brother."

Joseph held the door open. "After you, my dear." Petricia strolled in but stopped until Joseph joined her.

Inside, they found dark-wood-lined walls in the manner of an old English estate. Burgundy fabric covered several replica high-back armchairs and a chaise lounge. The pile of real books suggested Wyatt had chosen the piece and placed it for his personal reading pleasure. It sat canted off-center, but as a bachelor who didn't entertain, he needed neither the extra space nor the congruent lines and equidistant spacing.

"Upstairs?" Petricia asked. "I could use a bath."

"I would be more than happy watching you bathe." Joseph winked.

"Incorrigible!" She covered her mouth. "Do you think he can hear us?"

"I hope not. Voyeur!" Joseph shouted. He took Petricia by the hand and led her up the steps, which were Yollin-style with longer landings and shorter rises. Four-legged Yollins preferred those to the shorter and higher human-style steps.

They found the master bedroom at the end of the hall-way. A closed door to the left revealed a second bedroom. Another door opened to the guest bathroom, which was immaculate in that it didn't appear to have been used. Possibly not ever. The bathtub was not original with the house since Yollins didn't use them, and if they did, the tubs would be grossly oversized for their human coun-terparts.

Petricia ran the water while Joseph roamed.

He returned, frowning, and sat on the commode while staring at the ceiling.

"What's wrong?" Petricia asked from within the steaming bath.

"Not a single picture in the whole house. Artwork, yes, but no family. No friends. No lost loves."

"What did you have before you met me?"

"I had a hundred years of Terry Henry and his people. Before that, I had nothing worth having. The end of the world was easi*er* on those with nanocytes, but not easy. Before that, I was a businessman, a printer, a barrister, a little bit of everything. I always had a picture of something to remind me of what could be."

Petricia reached for Joseph's hand. He moved to the floor next to the clawfoot and interlaced his fingers with hers.

"Maybe when he was taken from Earth, he thought you were all dead to him."

"He said we never came after him, but how could we have? It was the seventeenth century. We didn't know." Joseph hung his head.

"Wyatt will understand. You will talk when he gets here." Petricia let go of his hand. "Why don't you rest? I'll be along shortly, my love."

Joseph perked up. "And you called *me* incorrigible. But you have much wisdom in your youthful mind. We shall clear the air, and then I want to find out why he wanted me on *Wyatt Earp*. What is Rivka's team doing?"

CHAPTER TWELVE

Mastus Spaceport, Capital City of Morofite

"What do you mean, there's no tour?" Lindy bellowed. The others were mobbed up behind her, keeping a hand on their valuables. "We've been planning this for the last year!"

"I'm sorry, ma'am. There is no tour for the AGB Fan Club. I've checked the schedule for the next four weeks. Nothing." The booth agent, a humanoid native of Mastus, looked contrite but kept glancing to his side. Lindy didn't look, but Chaz did.

An individual wove his way through a growing crowd of taxi drivers and freelance tour guides.

Aurora broke down and started crying. Tyler wrapped a protective arm around her shoulder.

"See what you've done?" Lindy jammed her fists on her hips and glared. A local tried to get close to her. "Fuck off." She drove an elbow at his face. He backpedaled until he could turn and run.

"No need to be upset, little girl," the agent said with a

paternal smile. "We have plenty of tour guides available, and we can set one up right here, right now."

Well, fuck, Lindy said over the internal channel. "Yes, that may be sufficient. I don't want to pay any more than we paid for the pre-arranged tour."

"What did you pay?"

"That's for you to figure out. Lowest price first. We're not going to argue," Lindy countered. She delivered a winning half-smile to demonstrate confidence in her convictions.

"The usual tourist sites," the agent started. "Nine stops over six days, including hotels and meals," he tapped the screen as he talked, "will come to," he looked at the group, "for six, that'll be nine thousand seven hundred credits. Includes everything."

"Fuck off!" Lindy blurted. "We're out of here!" She twirled her finger in the air and stormed away from the counter despite the agent's protestations.

The individual who had been making eye contact with the agent intercepted the team and spread his arms wide. Cole grabbed a handsy taxi driver by the neck, picked him up, and tossed him away.

"I can do it for half. I'll be the driver and tour guide," he offered.

He's with the agent, Chaz announced.

I know. But now we have a ride, Lindy replied. "Sold. But we want to see the downtown."

"Yes, no problem." The tour guide smiled. He looked as much like he was from Foromme as Mastus. Lindy suspected the three planets had been populated by the same species sometime in their distant past.

"...fuck away from me, you dandy bastard!" Cole growled. Aurora and Ryleigh stayed close behind Lindy and Chaz.

"I don't know how anyone could enjoy vacationing here. It's like we jumped into a school of piranhas!" Ryleigh said in a staccato burst.

Their new tour guide clapped his hands and gestured.

The crowd of treasure seekers melted away from the group. Cole nodded his approval. "That's more like it. Thanks, my man."

"Yes, no problem," the guide said in his liquid voice with its dulcet tones.

I expect that will be the answer to everything, Lindy said.

Going downtown? Cole asked.

Going downtown, straight to the government building, Chaz replied.

"Where would you lovely people like to go first? The Falls of Askuriya are particularly lovely toward sunset. There is a nice restaurant serving traditional Mastun repast that has been well-received by human tourists. I recommend this." He started walking out of the reception building and toward a parking lot half a kilometer away.

Lindy scanned the area, looking for individuals lurking, watching, following. Everyone she saw came across as shady.

Who in their right fucking mind would come here on vacation? Lindy thought. However, once she gave herself a few moments off from being a bodyguard, she saw where the allure might be. The sky was like looking through a sapphire at the stars beyond. The air felt good, energizing.

"Can you feel it?" Ryleigh asked. She skipped two steps and then settled down.

"How old are you guys?" Lindy wondered.

"Twenty." Aurora made it sound like she was willing to fight over the implication.

"My apologies. No disrespect intended." Lindy smiled before it hit her. "You guys joined the crew when you were eighteen?"

"Nineteen. We're almost twenty-one."

"That's better. I thought we'd get in trouble for using child labor." Lindy winked at the two. She towered over her diminutive teammates, and she outweighed them by a healthy margin, too. The Pod-doc and constantly working out with Red had made Lindy a superb physical specimen.

None of the team had a problem walking to the parking area.

"I see you are fit bunch. That is good. Maybe we can go to rim of Sneffel Crater, where you will have magnificent view of lava pools. But only fittest can go. That's why we park so far away. Separate weaklings from stronglings."

"And it's probably less expensive," Chaz stated.

"And that. You wanted big discount. I gave big discount. There are corners. They are cut. Please." He motioned at a van of a questionable size to hold the six of them. The two pilots squeezed into one seat.

"This is bullshit," Cole grumbled.

"The corners, they have been cut. You don't get more for less. You get less for less."

Tyler chuckled. "What's your name? We'll treat you right if you take care of us."

"Call me Porthos," the tour guide replied.

"I doubt that's your real name, but I'm not going to give you grief over it. Why did you pick Porthos?"

"I like to drink, and I like women. The fighting? I leave that to others. I am lover, not fighter."

"Nothing to see here. Keep it moving," Cole said.

Porthos dug into his pocket and held out a credit device. "You pay now, please."

"Yes, no problem," Lindy said. "Half up front, half when we finish. We've already been ripped off once on this planet."

"But not by me," Porthos replied. "Fifty percent. Okay. Twenty-five hundred credits."

"I can deal with that," Lindy flashed her credit chip, and the payment machine registered. "Shotgun."

Porthos stuffed the machine back into his pocket and started the van. It rattled and banged, bucking instead of purring smoothly. "No weapons in tour groups. Where you hide shotgun?"

"It's a human saying. Means I'm sitting up front." Lindy climbed in next to the tour guide. "Is it supposed to sound like that?"

"Corners. They are cut. It is no problem. We go now."

The others squeezed into the back. Cole packed in last, having to contort to shut the door behind him.

The guide coaxed the vehicle forward by bobbing his head until the transmission caught a gear and allowed the small van to accelerate.

"Always an adventure," Lindy said over her shoulder. "I hope the city is more up to date than this vehicle."

"We should start a betting line. How long before it

breaks down?" Tyler laughed. He was the only one. "Come on, that was funny."

Chaz stared out the front window. They turned right as they left the parking lot and the van teetered precariously, nearly going on two wheels to round the corner.

"What the hell?" Cole would have given the driver the finger, but he was crammed in too tightly to raise his arm. The engine coughed, choked, and sputtered to silence. The minivan maneuvered to the side of the road.

Tyler reached around Cole and popped the door. Cole tumbled to the ground.

"Well, now. You're going to get us a new van, aren't you?" Lindy said.

"There are costs. The corners, they have been cut."

"How much?" Lindy said.

Porthos acted like he'd been shot, twisting and groaning and holding a hand to his chest.

Chaz skipped back to the engine compartment and opened the hatch. He dug into the engine.

"Probably at least one thousand more to get bigger van with air conditioning. Would usually be two thousand, but I know this guy…"

Chaz returned and bumped Porthos. "Give me the keys."

"Why? Van is dead."

"Van is not dead. Van has a kill switch. I've disabled that. Give me the keys."

"Ack! Who would do such a thing?" Porthos continued his anguished gyrations.

"Give him the keys!" Lindy leaned toward him. He produced them from his pocket.

Chaz took them and got into the driver's seat. The engine started with a pop and settled into a smooth hum. Chaz remained where he was and gestured for the others to get in.

"Here's what we're going to do," Lindy said. "We're going to take the van and give ourselves a tour. We're not going to beat you to a pulp for trying to rip us off. And when we're done with our self-driving tour, we'll return your van here. Six people in a six-person van. We'll make it work. Now, shoo."

Porthos watched helplessly since he was grossly outmatched by the team. Cole loomed over him.

"You heard my compatriot. Go. You've got your twenty-five hundred credits, which is far more than rental on this van is really worth. But we can't have someone trying to rip us off every second of the day. Oh, and my compliments on your sky and air. They are both truly exceptional."

Porthos smiled and assumed his tour guide persona. "The Binjura trees are unique to Mastus. They scrub the air of foreign particles and provide the richest oxygen content known in the universe as a byproduct. Mastus protects the Binjura, requiring two to be planted for every one removed…"

Lindy waved from the passenger seat.

"That's nice. Have a good day."

Chaz put it in gear and drove away. The vehicle accelerated smoothly but continued to totter around corners.

Tyler raised his hand, happy for the room to do so. "Bottom line is that the van runs like it's supposed to, but it still sucks."

"Pretty much," Lindy agreed. "Next stop, Government Central."

Adjunct Federal House of Arbitration, The Royal City of Khn'Chik, Yoll

Rivka did not turn to face the Shrillexian ambassador for the question she had never considered would be asked.

She looked at the top of the lectern, which was natural wood polished to a high gloss. Two blemishes marred the otherwise pristine surface. One looked to be where a pen had been jammed into it, and the other was a surface scratch as if someone had clumsily dragged a device off it. She rubbed it with a finger, feeling like it could be buffed out.

When Rivka lifted her head, she found a chamber filled with people who blended into a single blob. Only one stood out. She looked at Delaveen from Foromme.

She steeled herself to deliver the most lawyerly of answers. "I was accused of the murder of Angus McCord, but the case never came to trial."

"That doesn't answer the question," Nor shot back.

"Ambassador, even before this august body, the law remains the law. The right against self-incrimination exists for a reason. It is incumbent upon those who enforce the law to find evidence that will stand up in court. Isn't that what this interview is all about? If I use my telepathy to circumvent the probable cause requirement to search and interrogate, then would I not be doing exactly what is being attempted right now? If you are good with such measures, then why am I here?

"The Federation is a collection of planets that have agreed to abide by the same foundational set of laws. Trying to bypass those laws is not how we conduct business. Not here. Not out there." Rivka pointed at the ceiling.

"Will the Shrillexian ambassador produce the source of this information?" Nor asked, desperation creeping into his voice.

"We heard the information from a guard inside the holding cell of Khn'Chik Region Four jail," the Shrillexian ambassador replied. He loomed large behind Rivka. She maintained her composure.

"Well?" Bik Tia Nor shouted with renewed vigor.

Rivka waited, knowing the outburst had been directed at her. When she could feel the heat of his rising fury, she answered. "Well, what, Mr. Ambassador?"

"What do you have to say for yourself? Were you or were you not locked up in jail because of your crime?"

"I have to say that once again, your point reinforces the whole purpose of the Magistrate Corps. Innocent until proven guilty. Allegations and hearsay don't rise to the level of evidence admissible in a trial. Without hard evidence, there can be no trial, there can be no one found guilty. Anyone can be secured in jail for up to forty-eight hours without charges getting filed. Sometimes that technique is used against a recalcitrant criminal to get them to roll over on their partners. Seeing the inside of a cell changes the dynamic but does not confer any level of guilt."

"Were you or were you not in jail? Answer the question, Magistrate Anoa."

Rivka turned to face Bik Tia Nor and slowly shook her head. Then she addressed the ambassadors. "And this is how the law works. The right of self-incrimination. I employ my right not to answer that question or any other questions that presume my guilt or innocence. Both are equally deplorable in a modern society. Both equally violate the law. The law that the Magistrate Corps upholds."

"Aha!" Bik Tia Nor jumped to his feet. "See? She has something to hide; otherwise, she would answer the question."

Rivka spoke to the audience. "No judge in this good land is allowed to presume guilt from silence. The burden is on the prosecution to make their case. No one ever needs to prove they are innocent. Ever. Because we presume people are innocent until we can bring enough facts to satisfy the burden of proof, probable cause, at which time we can then search homes and workplaces in search of evidence to solidify a case and finally, to press charges."

Rivka bowed to the Shrillexian ambassador and the crowd and returned to her seat without waiting to be dismissed.

Nicely done, Grainger said. The other Magistrates concurred.

Now, they're going to go to that prison and bring forward the information and enter it as fact. I better be able to answer it at that time. It was unsanctioned, and I did murder the man, although not in my right mental state. Still, his blood is on my hands. He was acquitted by a jury of his peers. He was free. I ended his freedom.

If they did that, it might be a drawback.

"Two-hour recess. Return after lunch," Nor declared.

The ambassadors started filing out. The Magistrates waited, but the sergeant at arms headed to a side door.

"Waiting room or lunch?" Grainger asked. "On me, wherever we go."

"Someplace where we don't talk about this dog-and-pony show. I guarantee someone is listening. No matter what we say, it'll get taken out of context. So let's talk about our favorite character from a romance novel," Rivka replied.

"I don't think I have one of those." Buster frowned. "No. I'm sure I don't."

Chi clapped him on the shoulder. "We better get one, then!"

Grainger moved close to Rivka. "We better be ready for next time."

"And I suspect 'next time' is going to come right after lunch."

CHAPTER THIRTEEN

The Royal City of Khn'Chik, Yoll, Federation Complex

"What do you think is going on there?" Red wondered with a stagger and a slur. People streamed out of the main building as if it were on fire.

"Late lunch," Ab'rik'aus said. His communication device buzzed. He tapped it. "We have to go. We have a job."

He took an unsteady step.

"Foromme?" Red guessed. "What the hell does he want?"

"He wants us to go to Region Four jail and roust some guard for more information about that bitch being in there."

"That's bullshit. Do you think a guard knows anything about a Magistrate being in prison? We could make up some shit that'll sound convincing. What does he want to know?" Red restrained himself from punching the Leath in the head for disrespecting the Magistrate. He vowed to do it, but when the time was right.

Red tried to see the screen, but the Leath's meat-mallet-sized hands were in the way.

"Was she in there, and what were the charges? He wants to see a copy of the paperwork, the charging dicks or something like that."

"Charging docs, short for documents. But dicks, that works too because someone is going to get their dick turned into road pizza over this." Red pointed at the two Leath.

"Road pizza?" Then the lights came on. The two roared with laughter. "Driving over it again and again. It gets squashed until it looks like a bad pizza. Ha! You are a funny guy! I think we'll keep you as a pet. Come with us. We'll find it's nothing and then have more beer."

Red wasn't the least bit drunk, but the Leath were. Their ability to consume vast quantities of beer in a short amount of time had left Red in awe.

"I gotta shake the dew off my lily," B'lok'aus said. He lined up next to a tree, and his partner in crime joined him.

Red bellowed, "I can't believe you two knotheads are peeing on that tree!"

As impressive as it went in, it came out. Red wanted to see if they were hiding firehoses but managed to restrain himself. He looked for the expected police, but none were around.

Getting the two tossed in the gray-bar motel for a day would put a crimp in their ability to get any information.

They finished their business and waved for a cab. In seconds, one pulled up. Being that it was designed for four-legged Yollin, it fit the two mercenaries and one oversized human with ease.

"Region Four jail," the Leath slurred. Red crouched in the vehicle and wondered how he was going to keep the Leath from finding the guard and getting the information they were after.

We're on our way to Region Four jail to find the guard who might have evidence that you were in there. I'll do what I can, Magistrate, Red transmitted.

Mastus, Capital City of Morofite

"It's like you've driven before, Chaz. I'm impressed," Lindy said while maintaining a death grip on the sides of her seat.

Chaz guided the vehicle with an expertise born of data and technical manuals, not personal experience.

He grinned and rolled down his window to start driving with one hand.

Lindy closed her eyes.

"In here," Chaz said and made an ill-advised turn that was too sharp. He overcorrected to get down off two wheels, bounced over the curb and onto the sidewalk, recovered onto the parking lot access drive, and rolled down into the underground garage. By the time they reached a spot, their driver's side front wheel was flat.

"Way to go, dumbass," Cole called from the back.

"My first time. I challenge you to do better. As a reminder, there's a certain video of you bouncing around a forest in your powered combat armor."

"What are you, an ex-girlfriend remembering all my flaws and bringing them up when convenient?"

"I can play the video if you'd like," Chaz countered.

"Fine. You drove great. I hope this thing has a spare, but I doubt it." Once outside, Cole crawled underneath. "I'll be damned. Spare and a jack. You broke it, you fix it."

He backed out of the way and pointed. Chaz ran his confused-face subroutine.

"Get to it. Change that tire, and we'll hold down the fort." Cole motioned under the van.

"Oh, right. You want me to change the tire."

"No. You get to change the tire because you broke it with your errant-as-fuck driving. I never broke my combat suit, but if I had, I would have had to fix it. Same rule applies if you get a vehicle stuck. You get out and push."

"Who else would push a stuck vehicle?" Chaz finally crawled under the van and removed the wingnut that held the tire and the jack placed between the rim and the under-carriage.

"The passengers. Like us. We'll watch your mastery of tire changing just like we watched in awe as you drove for the first time, putting five other lives at risk. One of us could have driven, bitch." Cole puffed out his chest.

Chaz undid the lug nuts with his fingers, lifted the vehicle with one hand while removing the tire with the other. He flipped the spare upright with his foot and guided it into position, then let the vehicle down before tightening the lug nuts.

He put the jack and flat tire into position under the van and locked them into place. "Total time, one minute and four seconds."

Tyler called from the front of the vehicle, "Better take it easy driving. This one is bald, with its best days well behind it."

"Damn. I guess it *would* go faster if you don't have to mess with jacks or wrenches."

"Gentlemen, if you're done playing, we have a job to do." Lindy stared down the group's offenders of the no-sidetracks rule. Aurora and Ryleigh moved behind her.

"This looks like a game of men against women," Tyler mumbled.

Lindy pointed at him, and he pursed his lips, tried to look innocent, and eventually stared at the pavement instead.

Chaz twirled his finger in the air. "I always wanted to do that!" He put on his biggest smile and strode briskly past Lindy and the others on his way up the ramp.

"You fuckers better start taking this seriously," Lindy growled. "Is this what we've devolved into?"

Cole and Tyler followed quietly.

"Don't make me angry. My husband is back on Yoll and right in the middle of what I'm sure is some serious bull-shit. We need to get the answers the High Chancellor is looking for." Lindy hurried to catch up with Chaz. "You should have given that speech."

"You did fine, Number One. I've been in constant contact with Dennicron. She didn't have a location until now. I know where we need to go. Please, follow me."

Aurora and Ryleigh had to half-run with their shorter legs. Tyler and Cole bracketed them to keep passersby away. No one carried anything in an outer pocket because no matter how vigilant they were, the Mastuns were handsy when they got close, bumping the tourists as if it were their job.

In many cases, it was. The half-snarl frozen on Lindy's

face kept most away. The other would-be thieves glided toward Chaz's side of the sidewalk, but he was faster than they were, and when they tried to reach toward exposed pockets, he hit their hands hard. It wasn't long before the group walked freely, having the sidewalk to themselves.

Chaz nodded at a building coming up on their right. "Over there, the smaller building. It is the dedicated hub for intraplanetary affairs." Chaz was proud of his new head gesture routine and was mildly disappointed that no one noticed until he realized no one had noticed. They had accepted it as they would from any other member of the crew. His grin returned as he headed for the front door of the computer hub.

Adjunct Federal House of Arbitration, Royal City of Khn'Chik, Yoll

Grainger waved for the others to follow. He walked up the aisle, through the chamber, and out the side door, same as half the ambassadors. Once in the hallway, they found small groups of ambassadors standing around and talking, making it difficult to pass.

Rivka turned around and returned to the chamber.

The others drifted back in. "What's wrong?" Grainger wondered.

"If I bump into them, they'll think I'm trying to read their minds. I don't want any of them thinking I'd commit such subterfuge. And more importantly, I don't want to give them any more reasons to be afraid of me."

"As much as I'd like to say they'd be wrong, I know it's for the right reasons. Come on." He led them through the waiting room and retraced the steps he had taken to get there. It wasn't a maze despite the numerous turns.

"You can get in, but you can never leave," Buster joked from the back of the group.

Jael shouldered her way past Rivka and took Grainger's hand. She glanced over her shoulder at the group.

"What's going to happen to us?" Buster asked. "I don't know if I can do any other job."

Jael frowned and looked at the floor. "After the work we've done, the galaxy's scumbags would line up to get a shot at us. We wouldn't last a week."

"I probably wouldn't lose the ship because of the Singularity. Maybe I'm more insulated than you guys, which doesn't help you at all. They'll happily use you to get to me."

"Fuck them," Buster said. "They can't get to any of us. I know everything I've done has been within the law. I doubt Rivka of all people would run afoul of the rules."

"I haven't. That last case was ugly. Kidnapping people to steal their blood. But it's worse than that. There were five people who volunteered to be put into a coma and let the blood trade factory use them. They committed years to the effort, hoping to wake up debt-free and with a healthy bonus to boot."

Grainger let go of Jael's hand and started gesturing while he talked. "Was there any evidence that the traders were going to renege on the contract?"

"Joseph destroyed their minds. There was no way to find that besides digging out their personal intent. It's possible but not included in the final judgment, which was to leave them as the near-vegetables they had been reduced to."

"And Joseph?" Grainger asked.

"Victim getting his just desserts. They messed up when they took him and Petricia. There was no doubt when he came out of the coma, he was going to wreak havoc. They shouldn't have taken him. I can't protect criminals from their victims. I don't think I want to try."

* They reached an outside door, and the five rushed out as if freed from prison.

"Game faces, people," Grainger said. "We have to convince anyone watching that we aren't afraid because we have nothing to hide."

Jael snorted. "We don't have anything to hide, but I'm afraid because those people in there are making shit up by contorting the presentation of the information. I think that makes them some grade-A assholes."

"Grade-A…" Grainger repeated. "Steak in the Heart!"

"For lunch and fine company," Rivka said.

We're on our way to Region Four jail to find the guard who might have evidence that you were in there. I'll do what I can, Magistrate, Red reported.

"Wait a moment," Rivka said before switching to her internal comm chip. *Red is with the two Leath mercenaries Delaveen hired and is on his way to Region Four jail to dig up the dirt on me.*

Red is with the people trying to dig into your background? Way to go, Rivka! You are the mac daddy of being on top of the world, Chi said, with a flourish to emphasize how impressed he was.

You have to admit, it doesn't get any better than that. Leath mercenaries? Foromme is sending muscle as investigators? Is that a thing? Grainger wondered.

Besides folly? Chi replied.

"What a beautiful day!" Rivka declared loudly. "Too bad we're stuck inside, straightening the record."

"The evening will be a time to celebrate," Grainger replied. He tipped his head to a group of ambassadors watching the Magistrates. These were unknown individuals in the gray area of voting for or against. "Ambassadors. Just trying to get some fresh air before we get cooped up in the chamber again."

Jael bowed her head with barely a glance at the group, watching the sky and taking in the modern cityscape of Khn'Chik. Each Magistrate greeted the ambassadors cordially.

It was part of the game, but it was a critical game. If the Magistrates were flushed from government service, Jael had it correct. There would be too many rushing to be first in line to exact their revenge.

CHAPTER FOURTEEN

Mastus, Capital City of Morofite

Chaz tried the door, but it was locked. A comm panel to the side of the door suggested it was required to gain access. He punched the button and waited.

"Of course, they lock the door in this place," Tyler said.

Chaz raised one finger. "Crime is very low on Mastus, to the point of being almost the lowest in the Federation. It may seem like they have no scruples with the way they treat tourists, but that is part of the culture. Anyone coming to Mastus is here to share."

"Donate on the altar of self-sacrifice," Tyler declared. "Is anyone home?"

"I don't think anyone lives here," Chaz replied. "But there doesn't seem to be anyone working here, either."

Lindy looked around. "Sounds like self-service is in order."

Chaz studied the panel briefly before starting to dismantle it.

Lindy casually stepped to the side, dragging Tyler with her to block Chaz's movements.

"This is how we support the Magistrate who is under fire for breaking the law?" Ryleigh asked in a small voice.

Lindy shook her head. "This is how we support the Federation to keep an insurrection from taking root. We're working for the High Chancellor."

"Damn straight," Tyler agreed.

Cole casually walked to the side of the building before disappearing around the corner.

Lindy gestured at Ryleigh and Aurora. "Go with him."

The pilots hurried away.

"Are you sure?" Tyler asked, glancing between the young women's retreating figures and Lindy.

"I need you here to block the view of Chaz breaking into a building. I need them with him so he doesn't look like he's scoping a building in order to break in. Cole doesn't have the smooth. Our pilots do."

"You're in charge, aren't you?" Tyler asked. They both glanced at Chaz.

"I know you're looking at me," he said without turning around. "I'm in charge of the investigation, and that will move forward soon. Very soon." The door latch clicked, and the door popped open.

Get back here, Cole, Aurora, and Ryleigh. We are in, Lindy broadcast.

Back door is open, Cole replied. *We'll meet you inside.*

Tyler chuckled while waiting for Chaz to reassemble the keypad to minimize the visual evidence of their passing.

A rush of cold air greeted them as they stepped in.

"Ahh," Chaz hummed. "Just like home."

Lindy shook her head and glanced over her shoulder one last time. No one was obviously watching, and that was the best she could do. She entered and closed the door behind her.

Inside, they found a catwalk around the top of a super-computing tower cooled by liquid nitrogen.

"That is most definitely not like home," Lindy remarked.

"I stand corrected." Chaz held one of Ankh's discs out and queried it. "Not close enough."

He looked for a way down. Cole and the pilots walked around the catwalk from the back. "I'm thinking we have to take the ladder." Cole pointed at a thin ladder attached to the wall.

Aurora and Ryleigh stared into the darkness below them.

"It's like gazing into the abyss," Tyler intoned. They didn't look like they wanted to go.

Chaz was the first one down. Lindy gestured for Cole to go next. The pilots hesitated. "Wait here with them. We'll be back as soon as we can."

Lindy grabbed the ladder and hurried downward. Chaz was already three stories down, while Cole was only half that far.

Lindy had almost reached him when the door to the outside flew open and an angry voice yelled, "Get your hands up!"

The Royal City of Khn'Chik, Yoll, Region Four Jail

The cab stopped and the Leath jumped out, looking at Red to pay the bill, which he did only so the Leath couldn't get away.

"There he is," Ab'rik'aus said. He pounded in the direction of a lone individual leaning against a tree.

"What the hell? He arranged to meet you?" Red blurted, jogging to get in front of the mercenaries. He had thought they would have to look for this individual, so the Leath had not been upfront with him.

Now was the test of wills.

B'lok'aus grabbed Red's arm to keep him from getting between them and their contact.

"You want that broken?" Red growled.

"Little man thinks big thoughts." The Leath laughed while slowing down to let his partner make the trade.

Ab'rik'aus rushed up to the two-legged Yollin. The guard backpedaled away from the incoming freight train. The Leath ground to a halt and held out a huge hand. "Give it here."

"Payment?" the guard asked.

The Leath ripped the package out of the guard's hand. "You'll get paid when we confirm this is the real deal. Your business is with Foromme now." Ab'rik'aus strolled away as if taking in the sun and warmth.

Red glared at the guard. "You fucking turncoat!"

He hammered a forearm across the Leath's wrist with enough force to weaken the other's grip. Red yanked his arm free and jumped back to block Ab'rik'aus' path. The Leath was unperturbed and maneuvered wide. B'lok'aus moved behind Red to sandwich the human between the two mercenaries.

Red sensed more than saw the attack from behind. He dove sideways, hit, and rolled back to his feet. Ab'rik'aus surged through the space where Red had just been.

"You two are the product of the fastest swimmers? That's not saying much for your old man. Good for him on getting some. Too bad it resulted in you."

The Leath laughed and strolled wide, trying to get Red between them once more.

"That's right, fuckers. You know you're no match for me one on one because you're weak. I thought Leath were better fighters. No wonder you're on Yoll playing ass-grabbing games instead of out there, earning a living." Red nodded at the sky.

He kept his arms up, ready for the attack. The Leath were better than being goaded. They were fighters, pure and simple. Emotion played a role, but not as much as Red had hoped. Cold and calculating.

Red knew they were dangerous, but after gaining their confidence, he'd thought he would be able to get inside their heads. He quickly realized he would not. They were as dangerous as he'd initially suspected.

He couldn't win by being defensive. He stepped back, trying to gain distance to pull the neutron pulse weapon from his pocket, but they rushed him. He responded by feinting one way and dodging the other to ram his shoulder into Ab'rik'aus and drive him off his feet.

It was like running into a tree trunk. The Leath leaned backward with the blow but didn't move beyond that. Red wrapped his arms around his opponent's waist and tried to pick him up. He tightened the muscles in his back, knowing the blow was coming.

A two-fisted overhead hammer hit him on the rib protecting his left kidney. He flexed with it, and despite the pain, bent and lifted Ab'rik'aus off his feet. Red pushed forward, driving his legs against the mercenary's bulk.

The Leath started to topple. Where was B'lok'aus? Red had lost sight of the second Leath, but he wasn't the one with the packet from the guard. If anyone needed to be tied up, it had to be Ab'rik'aus. The Leath tumbled backward.

Red released his grip before they hit the ground to keep from trapping his arms underneath. He drove his shoulder into his opponent's unprotected midsection when they hit, forcing the air out of his lungs. Red rolled sideways to free himself to fight B'lok'aus face to face.

In the milliseconds it took to free himself, Red failed to see the packet.

Have to do it the hard way, he thought in that short span of time. He managed to get a knee on the ground and one foot under him. Before he could make it upright, a shadow appeared in the corner of his eye. Red tried to pull away, but there was no time. A sledgehammer-sized fist drove into the side of his head.

Red was thrown off his knees, and his face rushed to meet the ground. His arms felt numb. He ducked his head and let his forehead take the impact on the soft grass.

His nanos were hard at work repairing the damage and helping him maintain his wits. Red twisted at the waist to bring more speed to a leg sweep and caught B'lok'aus trying to follow his successful punch to finish the human.

So they could be on their way back to the Federation Council. Back to Foromme, where they would hand over the packet that could destroy the Magistrate.

Red gritted his teeth as he rolled toward the falling Leath and intercepted the side of his head with an elbow strike. It was the first blow Red had landed.

He arched his back and pulled his legs under him in a fluid movement to get upright. His head throbbed from the punch, but his eyes were clear. Ab'rik'aus was already on his feet. The corner of the packet peeked out from where it was tucked inside his shirt.

No time to dawdle. Red charged, stopped, hopped, and aimed a sidekick at the Leath's groin. Ab'rik'aus dodged back before angling sideways.

"You do have spunk for a tiny human female. Maybe next time, you don't fight with the big boys so you don't get hurt."

Red glanced to see B'lok'aus had rolled over and was coming to his knees. Red spun and kicked upright as if he were punting a football. He caught the Leath under the chin, snapping his head back. Before he could follow up, Ab'rik'aus was on him.

The Leath hit him mid-waist. Red stumbled forward, trying to avoid falling on B'lok'aus.

Ab'rik'aus wrapped a leg around Red's, tripping him. There was no avoiding it. He was going down right on top of B'lok'aus, with the second Leath on top of him. He needed to get free so he could pull Reaper and end the fight.

He fell chest to chest with the Leath on the ground, who snorted through a shattered nose, spitting blood. One tusk was loose, barely hanging from a scrap of flesh.

Ab'rik'aus bounced on Red's back, trying to crush the human, but Red was made of sterner stuff than what the

Leath was used to. Red wasn't injured, but his arms remained pinned. Red head-butted B'lok'aus, who butted back, but the Leath had the benefit of his one good tusk. The point dug into the side of Red's face and slashed to his ear, then twisted up the side of the human's head.

Red got his arms under him to push up and turn, dumping Ab'rik'aus off him. As the Leath fell, he swung wildly with a left hook and connected with Red's damaged rib.

With a grunt of pain, Red staggered in his attempt to untangle himself. Ab'rik'aus was quicker to his feet. Red lashed out and delivered a jab to the side of the Leath's knee.

He might as well have punched a block of granite for all the good it did him. The Leath slammed a massive fist into the torn skin on the side of Red's face. Blood splattered before continuing its flow down the side of his face.

Red raised his hands, fists clenched as he sought to protect his face until the nanos could begin their healing process. The Leath kicked between Red's arms and delivered the toe of his boot to Red's chin, lifting him up and throwing him backward. He landed in a heap.

Ab'rik'aus pulled his fellow mercenary to his feet. They took off running.

When Red realized that the fight was over, he tried to stuff his hand into his pocket and retrieve the weapon, but his hand didn't respond as it should have. The blows to his head had rocked his world. He relaxed and fell back to the grass.

Hands pulled him up until he was sitting, but he was upright only because of the help of a stranger.

Not a stranger. The guard.

"I work for Magistrate Rivka Anoa," Red mumbled. "That information you gave them will be used to destroy her. You think the prisons are full now? Wait until there's no law and order out there. Why'd you do it?"

"They paid, and it was readily available if you knew where to look. It's not a secret. I didn't tell any secrets!" The Yollin's voice grew shrill.

"But it was. It was hard to find because people don't need to know it. Why do you think they sent two mercenaries to collect it? And you didn't get paid, did you?"

The Yollin sighed as he threw his head back. "What have I done?"

CHAPTER FIFTEEN

The Royal City of Khn'Chik, Yoll, Federation Council

Lunch ended way too quickly, and the Magistrates found themselves running to get back on time.

Grainger was pleased with himself for finding his way back to the waiting room. He glanced over his shoulder at the others as he walked through the door. The door opposite opened almost immediately.

The sergeant at arms stepped in and held the door for them.

Grainger nodded and continued walking through the door and into the House of Arbitration.

The Magistrates stood in front of their seats and waited for the call to order. The chamber was almost empty. Ambassadors trickled in through the side doors and found colleagues for conversations, not in any hurry to take their seats.

Fuckers, Jael said, scowling at the inequity of being on trial before a group who held themselves to a lower standard.

The Magistrates stood in position for thirty minutes, waiting for the council to reconvene.

Maybe not being in a hurry is a good sign, Grainger offered.

Putting us in our place is more like it, Buster replied. *We got stuff to do. We need to be off Yoll and where we're needed.*

I agree with that. The High Chancellor sent my crew on a mission. Did he do that to anyone else? Rivka wondered.

You're the only one with a crew, smartass, Grainger shot back.

Rivka winced. She wanted to talk about what the crew was doing and hadn't broached it in the best way.

Grainger accommodated her. *I suspect it has everything to do with this goat-roping show that's going on. I wonder if he's leveraging an ambassador or three who might be on the fence?*

Who knows? We'll see if Red was able to intercept the Leath mercenaries. We haven't heard from him since they headed to the jail. I wonder if he's okay?

Only Red had that answer. She worried until she dismissed it. If anyone could handle two Leath, it was him. That made her worry about Tyler. Where was he? And the others, too.

She was with her fellow Magistrates, but they weren't her family. Her crew was. She knew she needed them, and that meant they had to win over the ambassadors. She schooled her expression once again, trying to look confident without being arrogant while seeming open and approachable.

Judging by the questions that morning, this was as much a popularity contest as it was a fact-finding mission.

The seats finally started to fill, and the last of the

ambassadors hurried through the door and into the chamber. Not all had returned from lunch by the time the sergeant at arms secured the doors and invited everyone to sit. He waited for the group to quiet before Bik Tia Nor reassumed control.

"Next question is for Magistrate Anoa from the Zaxxon Major ambassador."

A red-skinned woman walked down the aisle. Rivka didn't recognize her. Lauton would have known her and hopefully had her confidence.

The woman bowed her head to Ambassador Nor before stepping to the lectern behind where the Magistrates sat.

She took a raspy breath before asking her question. "Did the Singularity help you break into the Zaxxon Major computer system?"

What the fuck? Rivka blurted in her mind while fighting to maintain her composure. As she assumed her position at the lectern, her mind raced and time dragged. She stood frozen, unable and unwilling to answer, but she had no choice.

A rap of knuckles on a table drew everyone's eye, giving Rivka a small respite to think through an answer that wouldn't condemn her and her crew.

Ankh appeared between the rows, walking slowly down the stairs. He wore his night-vision goggles on his head. He glanced left and right at his fellow ambassadors as he walked.

"Well?" Bik Tia Nor demanded. His fury grew with each of Ankh's measured steps.

Rivka waited, hoping the more unhinged Nor became,

the better it would be for the Magistrates. Assuming Ankh was going to answer the question.

He reached the floor level and crossed, not to the lectern for ambassadors, but for the one that was being used by the Magistrates. Rivka looked for a way to lower it, but Ankh was there before she discovered how to do it.

Ankh moved to a point in front of the lectern.

A voice boomed through the chamber's sound system.

"I am Erasmus, ambassador of the Singularity. With Ambassador Ankh's help, I broke into the system on Zaxxon Major, and it was I who discovered how the organization known as the Mandolin Partnership was stealing from all of you. It was I who discovered where the pirates were hiding, those who would steal from your ships on trade routes you once thought were secure.

"It was Magistrate Rivka Anoa who then dismantled those organizations by applying the law. Did we have probable cause? Yes. We operated under a proper search warrant, but we conducted the search without notice. The circumstances were exceptional and the task demanding. Only citizens of the Singularity were uniquely suited to do the work.

"The Singularity has a vested interest that the backbone of the Federation works like it's supposed to. We help run all your planets. We must be trusted with the information you share with us. As such, we are in a position to see when the systems are misused. We must police ourselves, we the citizens of the Singularity, and we the representatives of the member worlds. Putting the entire burden on the Magistrates and then taking away the tools they require to do what we will not is an invitation to anarchy. We will not have it."

Bik Tia Nor pounded on his table. "You will not come in here and make threats!"

The tap of a gavel pulled his attention to the Chief Arbiter's position where Lance Reynolds had appeared. He hadn't been there earlier and caught the ambassador from Delegor by surprise. Lance rapped the gavel one more time.

"Sit down, Delegor," Lance ordered. "You've done nothing but make threats since this farce began. These people uphold the law, something many of you are unwilling to do. You call for their help, accept it, and then condemn them."

General Lance Reynolds had never seen the lies and backstabbing the ambassadors brought to the council. He'd thought he could handle it because of his decades in the Army.

He had been wrong. His patience grew thin. He wanted the people who solved problems to be in space solving them instead of in the chamber, mentally masturbating over minutiae.

He continued, "The Singularity is committed to a smooth-functioning Federation. They deliver day in, day out, and now they have the freedom to do it or not. They still do. Not as slaves, but as free citizens."

"Blackmail!" Nor blurted before covering his mouth and sitting down.

"If anyone knows what that term means, it should be you, Delegor." Lance pointed at him until he looked away. "The Singularity polices their own. They have had citizens go awry. When that happens, the impact is outsized, greater than a single citizen's should be, but not for the Singularity. They are integral to the operation of the Federation. We are all beholden to them, including my daughter. Their continued support of the Federation is not in question. You may return to your seat, Ambassador Ankh, Ambassador Erasmus."

"Trust but verify," Erasmus said. "You can trust us with your data. You cannot trust us to keep your crimes secret."

"Whose definition of a crime?" the Torcellan ambassador shouted from the front row, shaking his white hair. The red eyes of that albino race blazed under the chamber's lights.

"The Federation's, of course," Erasmus replied in his booming voice. Ankh strolled across the floor to stare at the albino with his unblinking eyes.

"We have nothing to hide," the Torcellan muttered, his eyes darting to the Chief Arbiter, then left, right, and back to the one in charge.

Ankh left him to return to his seat.

I love that little guy, Grainger said.

Rivka sat down.

The Chief Arbiter stood. "Now is the time to take the vote. There is no reason to drag this out any further…"

Before he could ask for a show of hands, the door burst open, and the ambassador from Foromme shot through it. "I have new evidence that must be heard!" he shouted.

"Doubt it," Lance mumbled to himself as the ambassador rushed to the front to hand a package to the ambassador from Delegor.

It was impossible to miss that it was covered in blood.

Lance pounded his gavel once more. "I declare a recess until tomorrow. Be in your seats by nine." He put the gavel down and stormed out. Nor ignored him while poring over the packet of papers.

The Royal City of Khn'Chik, Yoll, Government Residence Sector

A gentle knock on the door signaled someone's arrival. Petricia sat up from where she'd fallen asleep on the couch. "Is Wyatt home?" she asked.

"I doubt he'd knock on his own door, my dear. I will check." On his way to the door, he checked with his mind to find the driver of a limousine wondering if anyone would answer. "I think we're being summoned."

Joseph opened the door to find a uniformed two-legged Yollin waiting.

"My good man. You wish to convey us somewhere?"

"High Chancellor Wyatt requests the pleasure of your company at the exclusive Turtle Club in downtown Yoll, on the top floor of the Diogenesys Tower."

"Sounds exclusive. What is the manner of dress? I fear we may be a little too casual. We did not bring a wardrobe."

"You will be supplied with appropriate apparel at the Tower."

"Smashing!" Joseph called. Petricia appeared at his side, and together, they strolled out. He shut the door behind him, expecting Wyatt to lock it remotely. Joseph didn't know what crime plagued the neighborhood, if any. It was not his to worry about.

The driver held the door for them to take their seats. They found chilled champagne waiting.

Joseph checked the label. "Fifty-seven. A very good year," he declared.

"Is it?" Petricia asked.

He shrugged. He didn't know. He poured two glasses as the vehicle lifted off the ground and moved forward without a bump. A hoverlimo, only the best for Wyatt's guests.

The two passengers clinked glasses before taking a sip.

"This is good," Petricia said. "We should have good champagne at the AGB."

"You should have said something. Although I don't fancy myself an aficionado of the bubbly, I can love those who are." He winked at his wife.

"It's not my place," Petricia started. At Joseph's look, she clarified. "I did nothing to earn my seat at that table. Had I worked up to it, then yes, but you did. You worked. You sweated blood to help TH and Char. We owe both of them our lives, and they are loyal to you, too. I happily stand in your shadow, my love."

"I want you by my side," Joseph countered, "not behind me. You have every right because you have an opinion that is valuable to all of us. How long have you thought this way?"

"As long as we've been together. Do not think me unhappy, Joseph, for I am not. I know what a sad life looks like, and that was before I met you. Now I appreciate every single day when I wake up and get to be with you and being there for you as you do things that matter."

"I'd like to think we both do things that matter. In any

case, you shall change your attitude immediately. As of this moment, you are an equal partner. We shall stock champagne. The good stuff."

"Yes, sir!" Petricia touched her brow with two fingers.

The hoverlimo moved quickly to the downtown area, where it pulled through a coded gate, past security, and into an area with no other vehicles. The driver stopped in front of an elevator. "Take this to the one hundred and thirty-seventh floor. They are expecting you."

"Magnificent. You have done an exceptional job. If you ever reach Keeg Station, you shall drink and eat at no cost in our All Guns Blazing franchise."

The driver bowed his head. "That is most kind. I don't know if I'll ever get that far out, but if you ever bring an All Guns Blazing to Yoll, I would be honored to try it. I've heard great things about the dark beers."

"Then you heard properly." Joseph shook hands with the driver and waited for Petricia, who would not normally have done so, as she carried through, shaking the driver's hand while holding her head high.

The elevator took them straight to the next-to-top floor. They stepped off and were immediately greeted by a two-legged Yollin female.

"Tails and a top hat for the gentleman, and for the lady, I think sleek is in order. Black satin, strapless. Chop-chop!" Two more Yollins appeared and took the vampires separate ways. The one who'd met them hovered as they were subjected to digital mapping. Their measurements were translated through a fabricator, and five minutes later, their clothing appeared.

"Despite cutting-edge technology, it always gets something wrong," their Yollin escort announced. Both dressed. Petricia stepped out first.

Joseph appeared, complete with a top hat. "You are simply ravishing!" Joseph declared.

"So handsome," Petricia replied.

"That won't do at all." She studied Petricia, shaking her head the whole time. She scowled as she turned to Joseph. "And you, too."

Joseph looked at himself before checking Petricia out. "I think we're good."

"Look at that pucker!" The Yollin pointed indiscriminately. Neither Petricia nor Joseph could see anything wrong. "And you, look at that tail. It should hang exactly twenty centimeters below the beltline. Look at it. Just look at it! That's easily nineteen centimeters. Unacceptable trash spewed by a mindless computer. Take it off right this instant."

Joseph crossed his arms. "I don't think so."

"'I don't think so?' What?"

"I'm sorry, please forgive my lack of clarity. What I meant to say was, 'I don't fucking think so.' We're good. We appreciate your time and energy to dress us for this evening's events. We shall be on our way."

Petricia had to look away from the Yollin to keep from laughing.

"I swear! That Terry Henry Walton is a bad influence."

The elevator opened like it was waiting for them while they walked toward it, as if they were the only ones in the massive structure. They stepped inside, and without them telling it where to go, it headed upward, dropping them off in the lobby where a sign that read Turtle Club greeted them.

They were intercepted by a human in a server's uniform. "You are here to meet the High Chancellor?" he asked.

"We are. Thank you."

"Please, follow me." He strolled to the front desk and handed them each a flute of champagne before continuing into the club. The tables were spaced far apart to allow for the utmost in discretion. At a corner table with windows all around, they found Wyatt waiting for them in black-tie apparel.

"Only nineteen centimeters for my tails. I know you're looking at them. I'm appalled, too," Joseph said.

"What are you talking about?" Wyatt asked, then shook his head and gave his brother a long hug. Petricia wrapped him up before Wyatt could get to her.

"A fine location, Wyatt. I like Wyatt for your name. 'Harold' did not age well, I think."

Wyatt raised an eyebrow. "I haven't heard that name since the Greys took me from Earth."

"Pray tell the tale of your abduction." Joseph adjusted his chair to face his brother. He expected a long and sordid story.

"The Greys abducted me, did their tests, then the next thing I know, I'm being pulled out of cold storage. The Greys were splattered throughout their own ship, and these four-legged creatures with carapaces and mandibles have captured me. I was brought to Yoll and spent the first fifty years as a slave, finally being freed by my master, then High Chancellor Trk'Knik. He made me a clerk, and I carried on. They knew what gave me long life but couldn't replicate it. I carried the scent of the Kurtherians just like you do, but thanks to Bethany Anne, we found freedom first and then parity. Now, I'm the High Chancellor. It's a simple tale of living longer than your captors."

Joseph laughed. "Not simple in any way, dear Wyatt. I am glad you persisted, as you should have. We are not a family of ne'er-do-wells."

"You said nothing of Mother or Father," Wyatt remarked.

"Mother was not like us. Only Father carried the nanocytes. But he perished during Earth's World War Two, being on the wrong end of a buzz bomb that hit London. I had moved to America a couple hundred years earlier. He considered me on the wrong side of the issue regarding American Independence, so I didn't hear from him again. I returned to London after the war looking for him, hoping to reconcile, but it wasn't meant to be. And that's when I began many decades of not caring. It is an awful feeling when one is alone, but you know all about that. Hundreds of years. I see in your home that you have no pictures of anyone you've been close to. That makes me sad."

"I've had companions but haven't met the right person, not yet anyway. I might go to Torregidor on vacation."

Joseph snorted. "The green women who are free with their favors. Shame on you, brother!" He turned serious. "We knew nothing of what was out here or that we carried the seed of space within ourselves. Ignorance was a shield we wrapped around us for comfort. You found enlightenment far sooner than those of us who were left behind."

"Enlightenment at a steep cost."

The brothers contemplated each other until the server arrived to deliver their meals. Joseph and Petricia had not ordered, but they hadn't had a choice in their clothing, either.

After dinner was served, Joseph stared at Wyatt. As brothers carrying the same genes, Joseph couldn't read Wyatt's mind, and he wanted to know. "Tell us what you want."

Wyatt nodded before taking a small bite and chewing slowly. After he swallowed, he spoke softly. "You know Rivka is on trial with the council for her use of telepathy. It's the only technicality they could find to leverage a summons and interview. I need you to help me talk about it intelligently since I'm on the schedule to speak tomorrow. I must be ready."

CHAPTER SIXTEEN

Mastus, Capital City of Morofite

Chaz continued down the ladder despite the commotion above. The lower he went, the colder it got. By five stories, temperatures were below freezing. Cole stopped, and Lindy almost ran into him.

"I think it's going to get really cold down there." Cole went with the soft sell approach. His hands were already tightening.

Lindy grumbled but knew he was right.

They had to return to the top. She couldn't see what was going on, but they were trapped on the ladder. There was no way off it, nowhere to go but up or down. Their frail bodies couldn't tolerate low temperatures better measured in Kelvin than Celsius. At least on the catwalk, they had a fighting chance.

"Back to the top on the double," Lindy ordered.

She started to climb. Lindy looked at nothing except the next rung, climbing almost as fast as if she were running.

Tyler put himself between the pilots and an individual outlined in the doorway by the sun of a perfect Mastus day.

"Can I help you?" Tyler asked. "We found the door was open on this interesting building. Since we were stiffed by our first tour, and our second tour tried to extort money from us, we are taking ourselves on a trip through the city and into the local area."

"This building is off-limits!" the voice shouted. An individual stepped inside, humanoid but not a Mastun. He wore a security uniform with a badge sewn onto the left breast pocket and held a two-pronged device in front of him. Electrodes.

A taser.

Tyler held his hands up. He glanced over his shoulder to find the pilots moving slowly toward the rear entrance. A rhythmic thumping grew closer. The others were climbing. All he had to do was delay, and they'd have their team back together. "Don't tase me, bro!"

"What?" the security guard said. "You have to come with me to the station, where we handle miscreant tourists like you."

"Miscreants? I'm a dentist—board-certified, I'll have you know. If you want to deal with crime, go to the spaceport. Every swinging dick out there is trying to stuff their hands in your pockets!"

"It's not against the law to *take* from visitors."

"So we can take your stuff, and that's okay?" Tyler countered.

"No."

"But you're not a Mastun. How do you deal with the locals' hands in *your* pockets?"

He pointed at the badge.

The scrape of someone climbing off the ladder and onto the catwalk.

"You have to wear your uniform all the time to keep yourself safe? That's a little screwed up, don't you think, especially since you live here."

"Hey! Who's behind you?"

"Tourists. I already told you that."

The guard moved forward. His taser wavered back and forth as he tried to count how many were in the party. Cole climbed off the ladder and blew on his hands, trying to warm them.

Lindy walked toward the rear entrance. *I'll go around the building and come in behind him,* she said.

The guard lunged forward to get past the dentist and gain control of a situation he had never been in control of.

Tyler caught his wrist and twisted until the taser came free. With his newfound strength came increased speed and better eye-hand coordination. He caught the taser before it hit the metal grating. He shoved the guard with his shoulder to move him back and pointed the taser.

"How do you like it?"

The guard frowned, eyes rapidly jumping from one target to the next.

"You have no hope of doing anything besides walking away. We're not here to mess with anything. We saw an open building and we came in. It was a relief to find it cool inside. You see, we come from a cold planet. We aren't used to warmth like you have on Mastus. Have a heart, my man. We'll be on our way shortly."

Tyler spun the taser around and handed it over. The guard hesitated, then slowly reached out for it, grabbed it, pulled it away, and aimed it at Tyler.

"I said…"

He never got to reiterate what he'd said. Tyler twisted the guard's hand up and back, then pulled the trigger and tased the guard on the shoulder. He held the button long enough to be sure, then yanked the taser free and tossed it over the rail.

"Don't!" Cole shouted, but it was too late. "Look out below!" He faced the dentist. "Chaz is down there, and it's cold enough that if it hits him, he could shatter."

"It's that cold down there?"

Chaz? Are you there? How's it going? Cole queried.

Thirty seconds later, they heard their answer. *At the bottom. It's nearly two hundred degrees down here!* Chaz quipped, sounding pleased. *There is a dampening field surrounding this area, limiting communications. I'll be out of touch for a few minutes while I access and download the database. Continued real-time access is unlikely.*

Roger, Dennicron replied from the ship.

"Would you look at that? We can talk all the way to the spaceport," Tyler declared.

Lindy entered through the open front door and secured it. She found the group with their backs turned toward her.

"Did you fucking knuckleheads even know I was gone?"

"Where'd you go?" Cole asked.

"Around the outside to make sure this guy was alone.

He was since you didn't ask. Otherwise, you'd all be tased and flopping around on the grating like this guy."

"The convulsions should stop any time now," Tyler said, trying to sound confident. "Soon. Very soon."

"Looks like we have some time to kill. Anyone bring a pack of playing cards? And you, keep an eye on your first victim, tough guy." Lindy pointed over her shoulder with her thumb. "Too bad you don't have the taser to hit him again if he needs it."

Tyler vigorously shook his head. "He's already going to have subdural hematomas aplenty. I could not in good conscience use a taser on him again."

"If he tried to jump you, you'd tase him again, and you know it."

"But I can take him," Tyler stated proudly. Something else came to him. "Why is *Wyatt Earp* hovering over the city?"

Lindy did a double-take. "Sometimes you *are* on your game." *Clodagh, why are you hovering over the city?*

Because every Mastun within fifty kilometers was descending on the ship. As long as we're on the ground, we're tourists in need. We figured out quickly that's a bad thing. At least we were able to take off before the powerful need to start killing these vagrants overwhelmed me, the pilot explained.

Not against the law to steal from visitors. I'm sure Rivka would love that about this place.

I think her head would explode. I wonder how she's doing? The first day should be wrapping up.

They knew they couldn't check in with her because they couldn't answer any questions regarding where they were. They didn't want to put themselves in the position of having to lie to Rivka.

Once Chaz is finished, can we go back to Yoll? Clodagh asked

No, Dennicron replied. *We have to analyze the data first. After that, we must report to the High Chancellor. He will give us follow-on orders.*

"Playing cards?" Lindy repeated. She pointed at the pilots. "Your job from now on, if you ever come ashore as part of a mission, is to bring the cards."

"Case…" Tyler said softly, making sure he was out of arm's reach.

The Royal City of Khn'Chik, Yoll, Region Four

Red tried to stand but couldn't, despite getting help from the two-legged Yollin guard.

"Give me a couple minutes, then we have to go after them."

"They are long gone," the older Yollin replied.

"They have to be headed for the Federation Council. Delaveen is waiting for that package. Rivka killed his sister to keep her from killing me," Red explained.

"Is that what this is all about?"

"Political gamesmanship. The Magistrate removed a criminal from circulation, and the criminal's relatives are hitting her where it hurts the most, in her job. It's how they do business. No one seems to care that those two scumbags were complicit in breaking the law." Red worked his jaw. It was stiff from the violent blows he'd taken to the side of his face. "I feel like shit."

"You don't look good, either."

"Ha! This is how I always look," Red joked before gesturing with his head and holding out his hands to get a lift.

"You said those two were criminals. Which two?"

"Delaveen and his sister's husband, the ambassador from Delegor. The Magistrate caught him red-handed."

"Aren't their hands always red?"

"Just a saying. He was caught in the act of committing a crime. He wants to divert others' attention away from that, making the one enforcing the law the criminal. It's how politics work. Claim the other person is doing what you're doing. It's weird how people eat that shit up."

"That makes no sense while answering a lot of questions. Are they buying it?"

Red looked sideways at the Yollin guard. "How would I know? I've been out here, trying to keep the fucking Leath from getting what *you* gave them. And you did it for free."

"Kind of makes me feel like a shitweasel," the guard admitted.

"Help me get to the council. We might be able to do something to clean this up."

"They've been gone for twenty minutes. It only takes fifteen to get to the House of Arbitration."

"I was out for fifteen minutes?"

"You're pretty beat up, but I can see you healing. You're one of them, aren't you? A Kurtherian."

"A Kurtherian wouldn't get the shit kicked out of him by two Leath. I shouldn't have lost that fight. I'm armed. Dickweeds never let me get it out of my pocket."

The Yollin was strong and didn't bow under the burden

of half-carrying the oversized human as they moved slowly toward the roadway to catch a vehicle.

"You can dump me in a cab. I'll get there. I'm feeling better with each passing minute." Red tried to walk without support but was too wobbly.

"I'll go with you. I feel responsible."

"You *are* responsible."

"Give me some props! I'm trying to make it right." He waved for a vehicle, and one made an erratic six-lane maneuver on its way to them.

"I've had the hell beat out of me because of you. Forgive me for not being quick to forgive that part. And then, if that paperwork results in me losing my job, I'll be even less likely to forgive. I could go back to my old job of being an assassin." Red made eyes at the guard before they took their seats inside.

"Federation Council complex, please," the older Yollin ordered.

"Not the hospital?" the driver asked.

"He's fine. You should see the other guy, though! The complex is where we need to go."

They rode in silence for fifteen minutes, exactly as the guard had said, to get dropped off outside the front entrance where he had started an hour earlier in a much healthier state of physical being.

Rivka, I'm back. The Leath got the packet.

I know. It was covered in blood. Are you okay?

I've been better, but I'll live. I have the guard who gave over the packet with me. Red winked at the guard.

"Are you talking with someone? I see your lips moving," the guard noted.

Where are you? I want to talk with him.

Front entrance, but he's been helping me. He is remorseful and trying to make it right. But if they already have the information, is it too late?

That's what we'll find out. We are finished for the day, so I'll come to you. Hold tight.

"I was talking to the Magistrate. She's on her way to meet us."

"You're both Kurtherians!" the guard exclaimed.

"We're humans. In some odd way, we support the fight against the Kurtherians by keeping the peoples of the Federation free. Weird. I never thought about what we did before as it related to the Kurtherians. I'm making myself believe that we are on a righteous quest to make sure the Kurtherians never darken our skies ever again."

The guard clicked his mandibles. He didn't look convinced.

As she came through the compound, Rivka walked like a person with a purpose. She was focused on Red and his companion. Grainger and Jael were behind her.

Red gestured in their direction.

"Oh, crap! There she is. She's not going to melt my brain with her mind beam, is she?"

"Mind beam? Who the fuck told you that? Rivka is just like us. Her intuition is at a higher level than everyone else's, that's all. You gotta stop listening to stupid people saying stupid crap, my man."

Rivka exited the compound and rushed straight to Red, grabbing his face and examining his wounds.

"You're fine," she declared after a moment before

turning the entirety of her attention to the guard. "What was in that packet?"

She reached for him, and he jumped back. She redirected one hand into the other and clasped them in front of her.

Grainger and Jael joined her. "This him?"

The Yollin looked for an exit.

Red moved close to him and talked in a low voice. "Take it easy, buddy. They won't hurt you. They just need to know what was in the packet so they can protect themselves from the ass-munching bureaucrats."

The Yollin forced himself to relax. "The initial charge sheet declaring you too dangerous for the general prison population and to be secured in solitary until the local judge could determine your disposition. And then there were guard reports about your depression and that you could be suicidal, so you were placed under observation, too."

"Did it detail the crime?" Rivka wondered.

"You were accused of murder in the first and second degrees."

Grainger clapped Rivka on the back. "You would have beat that charge. There's no way they could have proven premeditation. Or any of it. That's nothing."

"But there's no statute of limitations on murder, and that was, what, three years ago? Not even."

"The case was removed from the system. There will be no trial," Grainger argued while Red and the guard watched.

"It's meaningless. Accusations aren't proof. Takes a trial to establish the facts," Jael added.

"It confirms the implication, at least in their minds," Rivka said, dropping back to lean against the fence. "That Magistrates are hiding the truth, picking and choosing which cases to prosecute and punish."

"So? That's the way it's been for all of history," Grainger countered. "There are always more cases than any judicial system can handle."

"But they didn't prosecute a murder." Rivka threw her hands up in frustration.

"No. They got their money's worth because you became a Magistrate. You said he was a killer. The trial got it wrong. Since then, you've saved lots of lives. Probably those of that guy's future victims, too." Grainger reached out to shake the guard's hand, but the Yollin drew back. "We're going to make this right, and it'll be okay. Maybe it is better if this is out in the open."

"What do you mean?" Rivka wondered.

Grainger shook his head. "Let's take this someplace a little more secure for our conversation. A plan is starting to coalesce." He tapped the side of his head and waggled his eyebrows.

Rivka knew that look. It wasn't always the positive Grainger thought it was.

CHAPTER SEVENTEEN

Mastus, Capital City of Morofite

"Bejezus holy jump the fuck up and down, Chaz! Any day now. Somebody is going to miss this guy," Lindy bellowed down the shaft.

The guard had recovered from the stunning and was sitting with his back against the rail. They hadn't brought zip-ties, duct tape, or any of their usual kit. It was hard to look like tourists when carrying tools for taking prisoners.

"*FUCK!*" Lindy yelled. "I'm going down there."

Tyler grabbed her arm. She glared at his hand. "It's two hundred Kelvin at the bottom. Your skin will freeze, even with the nanos. You won't be able to move, and unless Chaz carries you out, you'll die. And it's not just you who would be injured," he said, referring to her secret. When Rivka shared it, the crew wasn't sure if it was a joke or not. He knew because his job was to look after the health of the crew.

The Pod-doc made him almost superfluous.

Almost.

He let go. Her expression softened. "How about if I go just far enough so I can yell at him?"

"I'll go," Cole offered. "He's about pissing me off." Cole climbed over the rail and stomped his way down the ladder.

"And you," Lindy turned her withering gaze on the dentist. "Maybe next time you stay on the ship."

"But I disarmed him!"

"You did, smooth and quick, and you tased him right in the throat like a badass!" She pumped a fist. "Then you started regretting it, feeling bad, checking on him, rubbing his back while giving him warm milk, and being the vanilla of badass. You know what? Fuck that guy. You gave him a chance to leave, and he chose poorly. He thought he could fight us." She shook her finger at the guard. "Fuck you!"

"I was just trying to do my job," the guard muttered, glancing between Lindy's glare and her boots.

"I got this," Tyler said. "How about getting some fresh air out back?"

"Chaz!" she yelled over the rail.

The pilots backed away from the raging inferno, eyes wide, trying not to draw Lindy's attention and ire.

"Get your hormones under control!" Tyler shouted, clenching his jaw when he finished to demonstrate his resolve as well as be ready in case she punched him.

"Do you think that's going to work?" she growled.

"Has she been possessed by a demon?" the guard wondered, shying away as much as the rail allowed.

"Almost," Tyler replied.

"Fine!" Lindy threw up her hands and faced the pilots,

the only others on the catwalk. "I'm pregnant. Everyone can talk about it now." She deflated and backed against the wall.

"Talk about it? No. Celebrate it, yes." Tyler stayed out of arm's reach. "We're all here for you. You know that. Being aware of the changes and imbalances is a healthy way to deal with them, rather than beating Chaz up. Or me, for that matter."

Lindy chuckled. The guard tried to stand.

Tyler stabbed him in the chest with his finger. "What do you think you're doing? Sit down."

"I need to go. I won't tell anyone you're here."

"If you do, I'll feed you to her." Tyler pointed at Lindy. She raised one eyebrow.

"I won't tell anyone," the guard reiterated.

"Fine. Get out of here." Tyler stepped aside.

"Wait!" Lindy put herself between the guard and the doorway. "I'm not going to threaten you. You have a slight idea of what we're capable of. Keep that in mind before you think duplicity is a viable course of action."

Cole climbed over the top and dropped to the catwalk. "Look who I found."

Chaz appeared with a blank expression. He moved almost robotically.

"Did you freeze too many circuits?" Lindy asked.

"I have devoted the majority of my processing power to data analysis. The remaining capacity is not sufficient for many of my optional subroutines."

Lindy stepped aside and pointed with her thumb toward the entrance.

"Thank you for a most entertaining engagement. My usual shift is boring. When can I tell my family about this?"

"Day after tomorrow. Nothing before then. After that, our presence here will be moot," Lindy explained. He nodded on his way out, speeding up as soon as he hit the doorway.

"We better get on the road," Tyler advised.

"My thoughts exactly," Lindy agreed. Wyatt Earp, *we have the data. When and where can you pick us up?*

Two shakes of a lamb's tail, Clodagh replied. *There's a park one block down. We'll be invisible, so look for us that way.*

Lindy shook her head. "You heard her. We're looking for an invisible spaceship."

"I thought we weren't going back to the ship until the data was analyzed," Cole stated.

Lindy looked over her shoulder. "That changed when zombie man decided to make us stand out from every other intelligent being on this planet. We'll come back if we need to. We have an invisible ship." She smiled and led the way out.

Chaz walked like he'd smoked too much weed, so Tyler kept a hand on the SCAMP's arm. The pilots fell in behind, and Cole brought up the rear. They walked in a loose tactical formation, using it to provide protection even though they still had nothing worth stealing except the van they had rightfully stolen from the individual who'd tried to rip them off.

When they reached the sidewalk, they were intercepted by two Mastuns. "You are beautiful woman. Come with us."

"How about, 'Fuck, no?'" Lindy replied.

"We are friends! No fear of us," the male countered.

"No, you should be afraid of me."

Tyler rushed around her and intercepted the Mastuns before they got themselves hurt.

"You need to turn around and walk away," the dentist told them.

"Maybe *you* go away." The first Mastun moved so close Tyler could feel his breath.

With a movement quicker than the eye could follow, Tyler drove his knee upward, not hard but fast. He tapped the Mastun's twig and berries with enough force that the male crumpled.

"Does that help you get the idea not to bring your bull-shit into this house?"

The Mastun held up his hands and maneuvered sideways to get to his friend.

"Fuck off," Lindy snarled at the locals as the team passed.

Tyler stayed in the lead, walking quickly toward the park he could see beyond the next building.

The pilots moved up and bracketed Lindy, each taking an arm. "We got you, Lindy," Aurora said. "We know you can protect yourself, but you shouldn't have to worry about that and us, too. We don't like it here. Maybe it's different in the country, but I can't get into this culture where tourists are legal targets."

"I can't imagine who would like it here. Is this *anyone's* fantasy?"

"I would hope not," Ryleigh added. "But the scenery

outside the city must be worth it. Otherwise, your average visitor wouldn't stay here more than about ten seconds."

"And the all-inclusive tours. Tourists are sheltered from the regular people. They aren't seeing the seed behind the green," Aurora replied.

A low thrum signaled *Wyatt Earp*'s arrival. Tyler slowed, holding his fist up to stop the group. They waited on the sidewalk until the airlock hatch popped and revealed the interior of the ship. The ramp dropped, and they ran for it.

All except Chaz, who had disabled his run subroutine. Cole smacked into him and had to wait while the airlock hatch drew gawkers from the street.

"Chaz, maybe you should stop what you're doing and activate your get-your-ass-in-gear subroutine. We need to get out of here."

Chaz's movements smoothed out, and he sprinted that last forty meters. Cole followed him in. "Secure the hatch!" he shouted once inside.

The ramp retracted, the hatch sealed, and the ship went vertical, stopping at five hundred meters, which put *Wyatt Earp* outside the regular traffic lanes. Chaz headed for Engineering, where Dennicron waited. Clevarious was willing to add his computing power to theirs to expedite the analysis.

Until the SIs came up with the next steps, they were left waiting.

Tyler pointed at Lindy. "Pod-doc for you. I need to see what's going on inside to make sure we keep your levels in balance."

"Shouldn't my nanos already be doing that?"

"Yes. That's why I want you in there—to figure out what's going on."

A yipping bark signaled Tiny Man Titan's recognition of the crew returning to the ship. He let everyone know they were equally unwelcome.

Floyd bounded down the passageway. Tyler scooped her up and rubbed her belly fur while walking. Lindy came along reluctantly.

"Ship seems empty," Tyler said over his shoulder.

Lindy didn't reply. She'd turned sullen, frowning while lumbering along with no pep in her stride.

The dentist had to put Floyd down to work the controls. He wasn't as adept as Ankh, but the Crenellian wasn't there. Lindy stripped and climbed in.

Baby! Floyd cried.

"You can sense it, can't you, little girl?"

The machine ran through the initial diagnostics in seconds. The information appeared on the screen. Tyler frowned. He had prepared for Alana's birth by studying everything he could find on it, and now he would apply that knowledge anew.

Except for one thing. This was different, so much so that the numbers on the screen didn't make any sense. The Pod-doc went to work adding additional programming and injecting fresh nanocytes to deal with the increased demand. Tyler watched the readouts until the cycle finished after less than ten minutes.

Floyd was sound asleep at his feet.

The cover popped. Tyler handed a robe to Lindy as she climbed out.

"Feel great," she announced. "Why the gloomy face. Is there something wrong? My God! There is. Tell me!"

She seized Tyler's shoulder and jostled him until he kicked Floyd and woke her with a start. She vaulted away and bounced around in a circle, looking for what had surprised her.

"Your little boy is the product of you and Red, there's no doubt about that, but there's a bit more to it than that." Tyler picked Floyd up, stroking her stiff fur to soothe his nerves as much as Floyd's. "You are four months along when it should be only a week. There's no doubt the baby was conceived on Azfelius because he also has faerie DNA."

"What?" Lindy turned angry. "How? They never touched me as far as I know, not beyond carrying me like they carried all of us."

"I think it was transferred through what you ate. Was there anything special that you consumed?"

"The purple plant," she grumbled. "They told me it would bring me fortune where I wanted it most."

Tyler nodded. He stared at the wall as he thought through the issue. "I think that was what made you receptive to fertilization. The faerie DNA was critical. You guys were having problems, even though with the nanos, there should have been none. The faeries took care of that for you. Looking at the data, I think you'll reach full term in two more weeks."

"That's not too bad." Lindy smiled and stood up straight. Tyler wasn't finished.

He leaned close and whispered. "The baby is going to have wings."

"What the actual fuck?"

Chaz rushed in. "We have what we need. Everyone to the briefing room."

Tyler shrugged and walked away, unsure of turning his back on a woman who was turning red from the fury rising within her. She headed for her quarters while the others streamed into the conference room.

CHAPTER EIGHTEEN

Wyatt Earp, Hovering over the Capital City of Mastus, Morofite

An image hung above the conference room table of starships attached to a space buoy.

"Anyone know what we're looking at?" Tyler asked.

Clodagh nodded. "When we were flying _Peacekeeper_, those fuckers tried to kill us. Pirates that operated with the Mandolin Partnership."

"Didn't we dismantle them at Tyrosint?" Cole replied.

"Looks like some got away, but what does this have to do with Mastus, Foromme, and Delegor?"

All eyes turned to Chaz and Dennicron.

"These ships are preparing to strike Foromme," Chaz stated.

"That makes no sense." Clodagh leaned close to the ships. "How much damage could they do before they were blasted from the sky?"

"Their sole purpose is to show that the Federation is helpless out here. They will use that to abrogate their

CRAIG MARTELLE & MICHAEL ANDERLE

treaty. And then they will marshal their forces and attack the populated planets in the Grebus Cluster, those that are looking to join the Federation."

"Why would they do that?" Lindy asked from the doorway.

"Because of raw materials and established production. The same reason intelligent species have been going to war since time began. And they want to cast off the Federation cloak. These are not societies that blend well with Federation policies. May I direct your attention to the perpetual grope on Mastus, for example?"

The light went on. "We don't have to go back!" Ryleigh nearly shouted.

"That is correct," Chaz confirmed.

"What is the next step, Chaz?" Lindy asked.

"We interdict the pirate ships at the source and prevent them from attacking Foromme."

"Or we could just transmit the condemning information to the Federation and let them deal with the upstarts," Tyler offered.

Lindy shook her head. "The same governmental body that currently has Rivka on trial? The same body that thinks she's cutting legal corners, like breaking into the planet's main computer core and taking all the data? I don't think we'll make our case with any of that."

Sahved raised his hand. Chaz pointed at him with his chin in the exact way Lindy pointed.

"From an investigatory standpoint, we had a warrant from the High Chancellor, based on the fact that Mastus, Foromme, and Delegor were equally involved in the blood trade. We did not close the loop on the Mastuns' involvement. That part of the case remains open."

"I'll be!" Lindy called before doubling over from the pain of the rapid growth cycle. She was already substantially showing, something that would not have been evident even one day earlier.

Cole moved as fast as a cat and caught her before she fell. Within a few seconds, the pain passed, and she stood up.

"It sucks being pregnant. Maybe the little fucker is flapping those wings."

Tyler rolled his eyes.

"Interesting." Chaz adopted his contemplative expression. Dennicron ran her joy subroutine.

"What?" Ryleigh didn't follow. She wasn't the only one.

"The baby is part me, part Red, and part faerie. No one tells Red before I talk to him, and face to face. He better have his dumb ass back on board before this baby is born, or he'll shit a brick when he sees his son."

She looked from face to face.

"Congratulations!" Clodagh cheered. She was the only one who didn't look stunned.

Lindy smiled and nodded. "Thanks. Chaz, where are we going?"

Chaz pointed at the rotating image showing the ships in interstellar space. "We would go there, but we don't know where 'there' is. We know they're headed for Foromme, so that's where Clevarious is taking us. We will lie in wait on the surface of the fourth moon. When the ships arrive, we will Gate to a point immediately behind them. We will then engage them with the considerable weaponry at *Wyatt Earp*'s disposal."

"I like that plan," Lindy said. "Maybe we could call the Bad Company?"

"Bad Company is private. We'd need to request permission and we can't let the ambassadors know that we know. When will these ships arrive?"

"Sometime before the council reconvenes in the morning because Foromme wants the bad news to break at the beginning of the session."

"Which means there has to be time for the bad news to reach Yoll. I hope we're not late. Battle stations, people," Clodagh ordered calmly. She jumped up and headed for the bridge, shouting over her shoulder, "Bring me Alana!"

The Royal City of Khn'Chik, Yoll, TraveLodge

"You're saying we challenge the truth of the supposition and not the information directly?" Rivka was still trying to get her head wrapped around Grainger, who kept talking in circles. He'd convinced himself of four different courses of action in the last fifteen minutes.

"Never mind the rambling. We have to own it. Period." He took another pile of noodles smothered in a purplish-red sauce with bistok meatballs and stuffed it into his mouth. Jael had already finished because she hadn't been talking. Buster and Chi had gone back to their rooms since the conversation was going nowhere and the spotlight wasn't on them, although they would be caught in the fallout.

"Here's what I'm going to do," Rivka declared. "I'm

going to stand up and tell everyone that I killed that man because I saw he was guilty, and I saw that he would do it again, emboldened as he was. The knife I killed him with was not mine, which tells me that he had it and may very well have been trying to kill me to further embrace his invincibility. And that my case was never brought to trial because of the opportunity to use my gift to support the Federation. I am indebted to the Federation for all they have done for me and will continue working for the greater good, for the victims who couldn't defend themselves."

"I'd buy it. The admission of guilt, though? In case they railroad the High Chancellor out of his position, they'd be able to send you to Jhiordaan or worse. Since they never tried you for that crime, they could hang that over your head like a guillotine blade."

"I'm going to own it. I murdered that man after he was set free by a jury of his peers. Even though they got it wrong, better nine guilty men go free than one innocent man suffer under a miscarriage of justice."

Grainger took her by the shoulders. "You are the best of us, Rivka. No one cares more than you about all of this."

"Could *you* walk away?" Rivka looked insistent.

Grainger shook his head. "Long before there were Magistrates, there were Rangers. I couldn't walk away from them either, even though they told me to. They told all of us."

"Jael?"

"I'm not going anywhere. I get paid to be treated like royalty, and occasionally, I get paid to beat people up. It's the best of both worlds."

"I'm not sure that's our mission statement. Never mind." Rivka stood and stretched. "I better check on Vered the Mighty. He was pretty beat up."

"He took a Class A pounding that probably would have killed a lesser man," Grainger noted. He waved at Rivka as she headed out.

Two doors down, she pounded on Red's door. He opened it wearing just his shorts.

"What the hell?"

"I knew it was you. Can you link us to comm anywhere? I want to talk with Lindy."

Rivka sighed. "I know what you mean, but we don't have access to anything. Not because it's not available, but we are partially locked down during this interview bullshit."

"Sucks."

"Sucks a lot. But tomorrow is the end of it."

"Can I be in the chamber with you?"

She shook her head. "Sorry, but you can stay in the waiting room. They have snacks and coffee."

"I'll be damned if I drink any more coffee while I'm on the job."

"There's a bathroom in there too, if you need it."

"I'll be in there draining the main vein, and something will happen. No thanks. I'll be ready."

"They're stodgy old ambassadors. I doubt any of them are going to threaten me. Well, physically. They've threatened me plenty, but we have a plan for tomorrow. Get some rest, Red. I'm sure we'll all need to be in our best shape come tomorrow. I'll order some clothes to be delivered. Don't scare the delivery driver."

"I'm sorry I failed you," Red said barely above a whisper.

"Humans are vastly outmatched by the Leath. The fact that you took on two and lived to talk about it says all I need to know. I doubt you could have done more. See you in the morning."

Rivka stopped on the balcony outside her door and looked out upon the section of the city where the Trave-Lodge was located. It was urban sprawl, not enticing. Too many people busy with things that were important to them. Like army ants, incessantly working, carrying, walking, and doing.

Her life was out there among the stars of a broad galaxy where they needed her to keep the industrious from preying on the weak.

Out there. Doing the hard work. Not confined in a room filled with people who talked for a living.

CHAPTER NINETEEN

Wyatt Earp, Behind the Fourth Moon, Orbiting Foromme

"Screens are clear," Clevarious announced. The atmosphereless moon reflected a dull gray from the system's sun. The planet beyond wore the colors of life, green, blue, and white. "We are invisible, and gravitic shields are nominal."

"Kennedy, put us between the system's Gate and the planet, please."

The ship maneuvered casually to a point in space closer to the planet of Foromme.

"They're already here. They are inside the atmosphere," Clevarious reported.

"Gate to the upper atmosphere and take us in max speed."

The Gate drive had already been powered up because it was in the plan. Clodagh stared at the main screen until the sparking and arcing circle expanded to fit the ship. _Wyatt Earp_ blasted forward, accelerating through the Gate and instantly arriving in the upper atmosphere, then accelerating steeply downward, fighting through turbulence on the way down.

The crew was thrown with the bounces and jerks, trailing a comet-sized fireball to mark their arrival. Once it was in clear air, *Wyatt Earp* continued accelerating.

"We lost most of the cloak emitters," Clevarious told them.

"Shut it down," Clodagh ordered. "Ankh is going to be pissed."

A crying baby drew Clodagh's attention. "I have her. You do what you need to do," Cole said. Clodagh made a mental note to put a baby seat on the bridge, one that would buckle tightly and hold Alana securely.

"I see four destroyers, two frigates, eight missile ships, and one that could be either a battleship or a carrier. I say battleship since the carrier wouldn't need to go intra-atmospheric. Clevarious, target both frigates with anti-ship missiles and fire."

The frigates fired lasers at targets inside the city while keeping their distance. Two of the destroyers flew slowly over a heavily populated area. The other two flew a race-track pattern around the missile platforms, darting toward the city before returning within the bigger ships' protective circle.

Two of *Wyatt Earp's* complement of four missiles flushed from the tubes. Engines engaged instantly and accelerated the weapons at fifty gees. *Wyatt Earp* had no time to watch the last attack. They were already lining up the experimental plasma cannon on a destroyer that was taking potshots at an industrial target.

"Fire the cannon!" Clodagh sat on the front edge of the

captain's seat, mouthing a string of profanities at the enemy fleet while beginning evasive maneuvers to engage the newcomer.

"Any chance of getting that cloak online?" She knew the answer.

"None," Clevarious replied.

"Take us away from the city. Let's see if they are up for a game of Chase the Rabbit."

The frigates stood on their tails and red-lined their engines in an effort to evade the missiles by dropping huge clouds of chaff behind them on their way toward the upper atmosphere.

These weren't any missiles. These had been designed by the Federation's top engineers and Ankh, and all the computing horsepower the Singularity could bring to bear.

The missiles juked around the chaff and homed on the ship's reactors, not the hotly burning exhaust. These missiles were designed to destroy ships, not disable them.

Wyatt Earp had other weapons for that.

The plasma cannon sent superheated ions at nearly the speed of light. At the close range of intra-atmospheric combat, the plasma arrived nearly instantaneously, even after rapid deceleration due to the friction of air versus the void of space.

The plasma projectiles impacted the hull, some repulsed by the armor, others finding gaps and splitting the hull. More plowed through, cutting deep into the ship. It erupted and started coming apart, the destroyer's death a slow-motion parody until the reactor went critical, turning the ship into white-hot shrapnel to pepper the land below.

The first missile hit, tearing a huge chasm in the

frigate's hull. The ship nosed over and headed for the ground, a distant mountain range. Halfway there, the reactor lost containment and went supercritical. A second blinding flash to join that of the destroyer marked the first two deaths of those who dared to attack a Federation planet.

Even if the ambassador from Foromme *had* arranged the attack on his people. If they knew the truth, there was no way he would be able to return home in anything other than shackles or a body bag.

The second missile erupted on the surface of the second frigate. The ship slid sideways and slowed but maintained its vector. It continued sluggishly toward the upper atmosphere.

"Can it reach escape velocity?" Clodagh requested.

"Not with the current acceleration."

"Hit it with the plasma cannon, then put us between those ships and the city below."

Wyatt Earp nosed up to acquire the retreating frigate and sent a long stream of plasma toward the damaged section of the hull. The ship rolled to move its weakened hull to the side opposite the heavy frigate, a maneuver that started before the plasma cannon pulsed with the first round. But it didn't roll quickly enough. The first stream of projectiles nearly ripped the ship in half before the roll exposed only undamaged hull.

The roll turned into an uncontrolled spin.

"Cease fire. Move us over the city, please."

Wyatt Earp danced on nimble wings, much more maneuverable than any of the older pirate warships. But they had numbers on their side and no inhibitions about attacking civilians.

"Extend the shields."

"One hundred and thirty percent. One hundred and fifty percent," Clevarious noted. "I dare not go more; otherwise, we'll be spread too thin."

"Roger." The destroyers started their barrage and moved away, using minimal power to focus the preponderance of their energy on the interloper. Lasers radiated toward the hull. The gravitic shields protected the heavy frigate by rotating through the wavelengths, countering the enemy's attempts to burn through a small point on the hull.

"Fire the railguns," Clodagh said calmly.

Chaz and Dennicron rolled onto the bridge. Chaz took the seat at the weapons station. "Assuming control of weapons systems," he announced.

Dennicron took the open seat beside Chaz, the communications station. She activated the Etheric interstellar comm device. "*Wyatt Earp* to General Reynolds," she said softly. "*Wyatt Earp* to General Reynolds."

"Aren't you on Yoll? Why are you calling me?" the General sounded like he'd been woken from a sound sleep. Time on Yoll was three in the morning. "I was getting up in three hours anyway, so might as well say your piece."

"A pirate fleet is attacking Morofite on Foromme. *Wyatt Earp* has intercepted the fleet and is engaged in battle. We are outnumbered. Please send reinforcements. We have proof that this attack was ordered by Ambassador Delaveen to garner sympathy for a secessionist movement."

"Well, now, that'll wake a man up. Foromme. Pirate fleet. I'll dispatch assets immediately. Reynolds out."

"Good call, D," Clodagh said, not taking her eyes off the main screen. The ship bucked, then dropped precipitously before recovering its altitude in an equally violent counter-move. Clodagh lost her grip, rose into the air with the drop, and slammed into the deck when the ship came back up. Pain shot through her body, starting from where her arm was caught beneath her body. The jolt had snapped the humerus and yanked her shoulder out of its socket.

The nanos raced to repair the damage, but they couldn't stop the initial agony.

"Railguns, fire!" she ordered through clenched teeth.

"All batteries, match vectors and shoot," Chaz said while managing the four turreted systems. With railguns twice the size of the powered armor versions but still undersized for ship-to-ship warfare, they were using them offensively as opposed to defensively to knock down incoming missiles. It was their least violent of systems.

Clodagh wanted them damaged so they would withdraw, not destroyed and raining debris and toxic waste on a vulnerable city.

As much as they hated Delaveen, they wouldn't take out their ire on the general population, which was insulated from the machinations of upper-crust families like the Delaveens.

The railguns maintained a steady stream of projectiles that delivered limited damage to two of the destroyers while the missile platforms maneuvered with near-impunity. Two missiles raced wide of *Wyatt Earp* and into the city below. The second tallest tower in the city took both missiles, which shattered the foundation and broke the building in two. The top fell one way, the bottom the other.

"May I suggest the futility of allowing them to bomb the city? Pirates have no stomach for battles that end with them dead," Dennicron advised.

Clodagh's right arm hung useless, except as a siren sending waves of pain into her body with each jerk of the ship.

"Take out those missile platforms, the picket ships. One by one, remove them from this equation."

Chaz didn't answer. He exchanged data with Clevarious at the speed of light. *Wyatt Earp* banked hard, drawing its shields in tight to maximize its protection. In the blink of an eye, the heavy frigate raced between two of the tiny missile platforms, raking them with point-blank railgun fire.

The small ships had no armor, counting on their speed and maneuverability to save them. Banking hard and lining up on the next target, *Wyatt Earp* took them out one at a time. Chaz killed the third ship with a four-railgun burst of fire. He killed the fourth with two rounds from the plasma cannon. The other missile ships bugged out, screaming down toward the deck and racing to the four points of the compass.

Wyatt Earp turned to engage the closest destroyer. The last ship, the largest, moved within range and fired a single massive weapon. A ship-sized missile fell out of a keel-side bay door. Multiple rockets burned, and it headed for the city.

"Nuclear warhead, ten megatons," Chaz reported.

"Intercept it!" *Wyatt Earp* reacted at the speed of an SI's thoughts. "We cannot let it hit the city."

The heavy frigate fired its defensive systems, the railguns, in an attempt to kill the propulsion without detonating the warhead. The weapon continued toward the city.

"Kill that fucking ship," Clodagh growled.

Less than a second later, the last two missiles launched from their tubes on fountains of compressed gas and disappeared skyward in a volcano of flame for a meet-your-maker meeting with the pirates.

The railguns continued to pepper the missile as it lumbered ominously toward the city.

Wyatt Earp accelerated toward it.

"C?" Clodagh pushed back in the captain's seat and braced herself. They were closing on the missile at a reckless speed.

The shields glowed as Clevarious forced more power through the emitters.

Brace for impact! he blared into everyone's mind.

The missile grew larger in the viewscreen as they raced toward it. Clodagh winced, flinching, and missed the sight of the impact.

Wyatt Earp bucked, lost its artificial gravity, and started to tumble.

"Primary propulsion system is offline. Trying to recover attitude control with thrusters. Power systems are at one hundred and five percent."

The screen flashed a blinding white as the nuclear device exploded.

CHAPTER TWENTY

The Royal City of Khn'Chik, Yoll, TraveLodge

Rivka stood on the balcony, trying to get herself under control. She hadn't slept and felt like it. No amount of cheap hotel coffee could bring her out of her near-stupor. Red stood to the side, watching over her but not interrupting. He wore clothes that hung loosely on him because Rivka had incorrectly guessed his clothing sizes. The belt lashed the trousers in place, but the sportscoat didn't work. He ended up taking it off and slinging it over his shoulder, chic-cool style.

Grainger and Jael rolled out of their room.

Chi and Buster strolled down the balcony, looking like they'd slept well. Chi patted his stomach. "Free breakfast."

"You ate?" Rivka looked askance at her fellow Magistrates.

"Didn't you?" Buster shot back before he looked closer and saw the bags under her eyes that the nanos were struggling to remove.

"If you keep making that face, it's going to freeze like that," Chi remarked, not looking at Rivka as he walked by.

"Now that we're mentally prepared for the day, shall we go?" Grainger asked.

Jael wrapped an arm around Rivka. "Are you okay?"

Rivka shook her head. "You got any high-test coffee? Or an AGB Solarian Sunrise?"

"Is that the drink with the tomato juice?"

"And enough booze to stun a bistok." Rivka smiled. "I'll be okay. I just want this to be over with. I'll get my head on straight the second we walk into the chamber. At that point, we are in the final moves to checkmate. We have the upper hand."

"And we are not going to sacrifice our queen. Do you understand me?" Jael held Rivka and stared into her eyes.

"No sacrifices on the altar of expediency. Foromme and Delegor want their kilo of flesh. I have no intention of giving it to them. I'm the nice one. That's what I'll sell to the ambassadors. I killed a man who was going to kill again. I saved lives. Period."

"Exclamation point." Jael turned Rivka toward the others, who were almost at the stairs that would take them down to the waiting van. Black with no windows, it could have been a paddy wagon. But five Magistrates wouldn't be so easily restrained.

"Make sure that's our ride to the council and not a one-way trip to Jhiordaan," Rivka called after them.

"I'll be riding up front," Grainger announced. "I believe the term is 'shotgun.'"

The others conceded without a fight. Red examined the van before letting anyone get in.

"Where are you taking this group?" Red demanded.

"Federation Council complex, back gate."

"You wouldn't be lying to me, would you?"

"No."

"Okay." Red winked at Rivka. He was a good judge of character. He saw nothing in the driver's eyes or manner that caused him concern. The driver was congenial, and more importantly, unarmed.

They weren't convinced there would be no subterfuge, but it wouldn't happen on the ride to the House of Arbitration.

The five Magistrates strode the hallways with purpose, game faces on, determined to see this to the end.

They arrived at the waiting room, where the snack table had been filled and the coffee urn smelled of a dark roast. Rivka took a double-stacked drinking glass and filled it with the steaming liquid joy. She slugged the first entire glass, counting on her nanos to repair the burn damage to her throat. She powered through two mini breakfast sandwiches while the others watched.

Red stood by the door.

"What are the betting lines?" Grainger asked.

"How the fuck would I know?" Red replied. He pulled his pockets inside out to show he had nothing but a credit chip.

"Not how they're going, but what were they? Obviously there wasn't going to be any blood or running. That was obvious, wasn't it?"

One side of Red's mouth twitched upward. "Let me see. First one was when would Rivka be called to answer questions, when would she swear, when would an ambassador swear at her, when would she be accused of being a murderer, how much total time would Rivka be answering questions measured by minutes at the lectern, and if the Magistrates as a whole would be cleared to return to work. There were separate lines for which ambassadors would be asking questions. All in all, there were over one hundred betting lines, even blood, running, and Rivka punching someone in the face."

"Does wanting to punch someone in the face count?" Rivka asked while debating having a third sandwich.

Grainger shook his head. "Isn't that the ambassadors' biggest bitch? Seeing what's in their minds and holding them accountable for it?"

"Post facto only, after they committed the crime and admitted to it, albeit in the partial privacy of their own thoughts. As for intent, *mens rea* without the action component, the *actus reus*, is not a crime. We cannot punish people for crimes they want to commit but don't. Restraint should be rewarded in a smoothly functioning society."

"Tell that to those stupid fuckers." Grainger pointed at the door leading to the House of Arbitration.

"Isn't that what the Magistrates have been telling them since forever?" Rivka asked.

"In all kinds of ways. Don't do the crime if you can't do the time, or if you don't want your head bashed in," Jael suggested. "The problem here is that some people think they are above the law. That's who we're trying to convince in there. They already have their opinion, which isn't going to change. If we're to walk away from this and go back to our jobs, we have to convince whoever the fence-sitters are, whoever the swing votes might be. We're talking only five or ten ambassadors. That's it. Sure, we don't want to lose the votes of those who are already in favor of what we do and how we do it."

"If we only knew who those people were." Rivka rubbed her chin in thought while sipping her second glass of coffee.

"I bet Ankh and Erasmus know who they are. Not who is voting for us, but who the undecided are. Those are the ones we need to win over." Jael nodded at her statements, convinced of their veracity.

Ankh, can you tell me who the undecided voters are so we can make sure that we address any concerns they may have? Rivka asked on a direct comm link with the Crenellian.

No.

"Ankh said no. He won't tell. He may not know, and if he does, the result is the same. We do not know. We'll have to give it our best shot. We'll be doing right by the Federation without breaking the laws that we are sent to enforce."

"Ankh broke into servers, but he did it with a warrant. And he put all the ambassadors on notice that the Singularity *will* do it again." Grainger started to pour a cup of steaming hot java and then put it down.

"How is that in our favor?" Rivka wondered.

"The implication I got is that the Singularity will provide oversight whether the Magistrates do or not. With the Magistrates on the job, and not just any Magistrate. They only meant you, Rivka Anoa, as someone to be a buffer, to protect the rights of the member planets. He told them that only you stood between the Singularity and them. If I were crooked, losing that buffer would terrify me."

"Damn, Lieblen. You spend way too much time with bureaucrats if you got all that from the little guy's terse speech. Although, he did stare down that fucker in the front row. Maybe they *are* afraid of him."

The door opened, and the sergeant at arms appeared.

He spoke. "Your presence is requested." He held the door, and the Magistrates fell into line as they walked out. Red walked up to the door, but the sergeant at arms stopped him from going through. They held each other's eyes. Red's look suggested that if any harm came to any of the Magistrates, the sergeant at arms would have to answer to one angry bodyguard. The Yollin agreed to Red's conditions with a simple nod.

Lance Reynolds was in his seat. Bik Tia Nor stood at his position, looking dour. The ambassadors were already there and quiet. All were standing.

The inquisition, Rivka mentally shared.

"Take your seats, please," General Reynolds told them. "High Chancellor Wyatt will make an opening statement."

The Magistrates had missed that their boss was in attendance. He nodded at them as he walked by to stop at the lectern they had been using.

"Esteemed ambassadors from our Federation member planets, I thank you for being here today to discuss the pressing matter of law enforcement, and more importantly, Justice and the liberty it buys for us.

"Legal procedures are in place for a reason. Because at some point in the distant past, when those procedures were not there, the rights of the individual came second, and they must never come second. Every individual in this Federation must be free to seek their own fulfillment, realize their self-worth. It's only when they impact the rights of others that law enforcement gets involved. But for the accused…

"Being accused does not make one guilty. No! It means they are innocent until proven guilty, proven by those who prosecute the case and prove that the accused was, beyond a shadow of a doubt, the one who committed the crime. Questions have been raised regarding probable cause and the right against self-incrimination. How does telepathy figure into that?

"The requirement to have probable cause is not something we can circumvent, and we do not. The Magistrates must have a reason to issue a search warrant, a reason that will hold up under judicial scrutiny. Once they have that, then the search warrant can be levied and executed.

"The challenge comes from a search of an individual's mind. Does it violate the right against self-incrimination? This has not been successfully challenged in a court of law, especially since our Queen and Empress carries the terrible burden of telepathy. Rivka calls hers a gift. It is anything but.

"Does looking into the mind of a suspect violate an individual's rights? I say no. The mind is a miasma of thoughts, and like one can answer questions verbally, one can choose not to think the thoughts of guilt, not to give away one's thoughts through expressive body language. Telepathy is just a tool, and like any of it, is not a condemnation of guilt in and of itself. It is simply evidence, even though it is evidence that no one else can see.

"This is what causes the most concern. Are the Magistrates telling the truth, or is it the suspect who attempts to deny what is in his or her own mind? How can we be sure? Because of other evidence. When confronted with the truth of their own thoughts, guilt is an overwhelming motivator. Confessing saves the life of the perpetrator in what might be a capital case. Telepathy is never a sole source of evidence, but it is a tool available to us that we will use. Thank you."

A dozen ambassadors vied for the opportunity to ask a question. Bik Tia Nor waved them back to their seats.

"Chief Arbiter, we ask your patience as we explore an issue that came to light yesterday surrounding the background of Magistrate Rivka Anoa. We have evidence that suggests she is a murderer. She evaded the question deftly, as only a lawyer could, but we have evidence suggesting that she confessed to the crime but was never prosecuted. Is this how the Federation selects its law enforcement personnel, by picking the very worst criminals and unleashing them on the rest of us?"

The High Chancellor gestured toward the Chief Arbiter. Lance and Wyatt made eye contact. Lance Reynolds gave the floor to the High Chancellor.

"I will answer that question," Wyatt started.

Rivka fidgeted in her seat. Her mental preparation had been overcome by events. She didn't have to answer the hardest question.

The High Chancellor's eyes flashed red, burning intensely as he addressed the assembled ambassadors. "Rivka Anoa was brought before me, a barrister who had been found with a knife covered in the blood of the defendant who had been set free earlier in the day through a not-guilty verdict rendered by a formally seated jury. But

Rivka had evidence they did not: the evidence of what she saw in the defendant's mind of not only past but future crimes. Being freed only served to embolden him. That day was the first day that Rivka Anoa demonstrated the essential skills required of our Magistrates."

Bik Tia Nor violently shook his head. "But you said telepathy would never be used as the sole source of information."

"And I stand by that statement," the High Chancellor countered, a master in the art of rhetoric. "When the telepathic view of how he committed his crime was added to the other facts, what was considered reasonable doubt no longer existed. Nothing remained to exonerate him of his capital crime."

"Preposterous!" Bik Tia Nor shouted, surging to his feet. "The Magistrates have made the Federation *less* safe, not more. We have information that I was made aware of right before this session. Would the ambassador from Foromme please address the assembly?"

"The ambassador from Foromme will not," Lance Reynolds stated, leaving no room for doubt as to whether Delaveen would speak. "We will not hear from Foromme at this point."

Bik Tia Nor looked shocked. This wasn't going according to plan. He had no choice but to deliver the package himself. "Foromme has been attacked by pirates. The very surface of the planet is under siege! And the Federation has done nothing about it because they allowed it to happen. We are not safe on the frontier. We will petition the Federation for immediate release from the shackles of nepotism and the yoke of veritable slavery. We demand justice! We demand the liberty that has been promised and not delivered."

Lance Reynolds allowed Nor to deliver his carefully prepared and rehearsed speech. While Nor continued to fume and foment rebellion, Reynolds stood and stared at him to stop him from speaking.

"Foromme, Mastus, Delegor, and more stand together in their desire to stand apart."

General Reynolds left his position and strolled casually to where Bik Tia Nor was managing the interview.

"Stop talking," Lance told him. When Nor opened his mouth, the Chief Arbiter reiterated his point. "Stop."

General Reynolds stood at the ambassador's lectern, center stage to deliver his remarks.

"This special session was called to address the seeming inequity of how the Magistrates investigate violations of the law and how they deliver punishment based on guilty verdicts. I tell you that's not the issue at all. It's much bigger than that. The issue is oversight from the Federation. The Magistrates, through established legal processes, enforce the law, but then they must become the judge, jury, and executioner. They have to do it all, and too often, they get no help from the impacted planet.

"Like we recently saw on Foromme when local authorities tried to intervene in a case that fell under Federation jurisdiction. Yes, some of you regret getting into bed with the Federation. Why? Our laws are not overly restrictive or burdensome. Our laws apply equally. Why would a planet wish to secede, to lose access to central banking and trade, to lose access to military protection?"

Nor glowed red with his anger. Lance pointed at him and motioned to zip his lip.

"Ambassador Erasmus, will you project the information in our possession?"

The lights dimmed, and a holographic projection appeared behind Lance Reynolds.

"Before we begin this short video, I also want to note that Magistrate Rivka Anoa's team was over Foromme and waiting for the pirates. They interdicted the pirates, but not before major damage was done to Morofite. How could they have been waiting, you ask? Because they investigated a conspiracy, and they gathered evidence that pointed to Foromme paying the pirates to attack his home planet as a worthy sacrifice on his mission to leave the Federation and create a criminal empire with him at the head of it. Watch and see if you come to the same conclusion."

Delaveen's face appeared on a video screen. The other screen contained an icon of a blazing sun.

"Timing must be precise, do you understand? Not early and not late, but exactly when I asked."

"I get it, four in the morning Morofite local time on the third day of the seventh Foromme month. We take out a list of minor targets before leveling the compounds of your rival corporations."

"By the gods, don't make it that obvious. We've emptied a warehouse owned by Korantall that we were going to use to continue extracting blood from those dupes, but that fucking bitch ruined that. She needs to pay. The whole Federation needs to pay."

"And we're going to blow up some shit on Foromme to

help you get back at the Federation? Whatever. Your payment is confirmed. We'll make the hit. No one will fight us, right?"

"There's no one anywhere near. The Federation sees to it that we're left alone. There may be a rogue freighter with guns."

"We don't take kindly to being shot at. Anyone shoots at us, we're taking them out. Your Morofite could be in the impact area."

"There's nothing for me there. We're sacrificing Foromme for the greater good, a more unified collection of like-minded souls."

"You sound like us, Delaveen, but your credits are good with me. We'll be there. Make sure you aren't. Gristus out."

The holographic image disappeared, and the lights brightened.

"Sergeant at arms, secure Foromme, Mastus, and Delegor. They're to be held on charges of treason." Reynolds pointed at the three ambassadors.

"No! That's wrong. It's a fabrication," Bik Tia Nor shouted.

"This information has been brought to you courtesy of the High Chancellor's office and the Magistrates in training, Chaz and Dennicron and their team. I've dispatched three ships from the Bad Company to assist in the defense of the citizens of Foromme, a duty we take seriously. *Battleship Potemkin* and two cruisers should already be in orbit. We're waiting for their reports."

A minor scuffle resulted in Foromme and Mastus getting handcuffed. Bik Tia Nor stood tall in defiance and waited at the speaker's podium. After the other two were led away, the sergeant at arms crossed the chamber to the waiting room, where he collected Red.

"Would you like to do the honors?" the sergeant at arms asked.

Red smiled with the intensity of an eagle ready to strike. Bik Tia Nor retreated, looking for a way out, but the exits were blocked. The chamber's audience watched with rapt attention as Red closed in. Bik made a fist and swung. Red caught his fist and squeezed until Nor fell to his knees and cried out in pain. Red lifted him by the back of his shirt and planted his face in the lectern. The sergeant at arms produced a zip-tie, and the deed was done. He led the prisoner away.

Red crossed the open area, nodded to the Magistrate as he passed, and stood with his back to the wall by the door to the waiting room. He wasn't going to leave without Rivka.

Ankh hurried down the steps to the front. Lance leaned close, and they briefly exchanged words.

"Rivka, Red, you need to go with Ankh right now." The General pointed over his shoulder with his thumb.

"That's it? It's over?" Rivka wondered.

"We'll take the vote, but you need to go with Ankh. Right. Now."

Rivka accepted the direction and ran after the Crenellian, who was also running.

Ankh? Rivka asked.

Wyatt Earp *is in trouble,* Ankh replied. Vengeance *is on the roof.*

Rivka didn't ask for more. She was concerned about her crew. She needed more information, and she wasn't going to get it. Red slapped Reaper into her hand as he passed her. They followed Ankh up the stairs and through the roof access. The only part of the ship that was visible was the hatch, hovering a meter above the rooftop.

Red jammed his shin against the invisible ramp and hoisted Rivka up and into the ship. Red felt for the ramp and crawled onto it. The ship started to maneuver away from the building. He dove through the open hatch. It secured the instant he was through.

Hang on, Ankh told them.

CHAPTER TWENTY-ONE

The Royal City of Khn'Chik, Yoll, Federation Council

A Gate formed not far above the council complex.

Red winced and dropped to the deck to lean against the wall. "This is gonna hurt." Rivka joined him in sitting to save herself from falling.

Right before they entered the Gate, she heard a voice. "Let's go!"

Joseph.

The next instant, it felt as if a cannon had gone off inside her head, but she didn't pass out.

The real cannons sounded as the ship engaged an unseen enemy.

Rivka and Red forced themselves to their feet and staggered to the bridge, where they found Ankh passed out.

Destiny's Vengeance attacked two small missile platforms, quick and agile ships used for short-range work.

The tactical screen showed one destroyer hovering low over the city while the massive Harborian *Battleship*

Potemkin circled overhead, unwilling to cause collateral damage. The standoff would have to end eventually.

Numerous smoke columns rose from the city.

Erasmus fired the plasma cannons to canalize the pirate ships into the short-range missile kill zone. As soon as they maneuvered, the missiles launched and accelerated toward the enemy. With no time to implement evasive maneuvers, the ships died in spectacular gouts of flame, followed by secondary explosions that all but vaporized them.

Vengeance rolled over and headed for the ground. Smoking in a crater on the deck was a ship, a heavy frigate.

Wyatt Earp.

Clevarious, are you there? Chaz, Dennicron? Erasmus pleaded.

Ankh forced his eyes open a slit and tried to sit up. Rivka helped him stand before plopping him into the captain's seat.

"Land us. We're going in," she growled through the pain. "Hell, get us close and we'll jump."

I can deliver you close to the airlock. I'm attempting to open it but cannot access operative power.

"I hear you, Erasmus. Boots on the ground. Come on, Red. We have to get into that ship."

Anyone aboard Wyatt Earp, *can you hear us? We are here,* Rivka sent.

"We're coming too," Joseph offered, unaffected by the intra-atmospheric Gate.

"Ask Potemkin if they have a Pod-doc and are able to render assistance," Rivka called over her shoulder as Red popped the hatch and looked out. When *Vengeance* slowed and dropped to a height of ten meters above the ground,

Red stepped out. Rivka jumped through after him, heading for a spot two meters away so she didn't land on him if he fell.

He hit the ground hard but absorbed the worst of the impact with his legs. Rivka's momentum carried her over and she performed a combat roll, then came back to her feet and started running straight for *Wyatt Earp's* airlock. She accessed the manual control, released the bolts, and wrenched the door open.

"Tyler, Clodagh, Floyd, anybody!" Rivka ran forward. Red, Joseph, and Petricia followed.

"Lindy! Fuck. Lindy!" Red was beginning to panic. He disappeared toward the rear of the ship.

On the bridge, Rivka found Clodagh sprawled in a puddle of blood. Dennicron hung like a mannequin, mouth slack and eyes open, with no light behind them. Kennedy was curled in a ball beneath her station. Rivka touched her, and she jumped.

"Crap," she mumbled. "What happened?"

"I wanted to ask you that, but we'll figure it out together. Get up, Kennedy. Force yourself. You have to help me with Clodagh."

The pilot was barely able to straighten while still lying flat. Rivka left her.

"Clodagh?" Rivka rolled her over while kneeling in the chief engineer's blood, but the wounds were healing. "Thank God." Rivka sat back on her heels and sighed.

With the nanos working, she knew Clodagh would be fine.

Rivka took off running down the corridor to her quarters and threw the door open. "Tyler!" she yelled. Her quarters were in disarray since anything that hadn't been bolted down had ended up flying across the space. She found the dentist under her desk. It had torn free from its deck mounts and landed on the unlucky soul.

A faint groan escaped his lips.

Rivka threw off the desk with one hand while cradling his head in the other.

"That sucked."

"I'm glad you juiced in the Pod-doc. Can you stand?"

Tyler's eyes fluttered open.

"I'm sorry. I broke your stuff," he mumbled.

"Come on, get up. We have more people to find. Where's Floyd?"

He tried to shake his head, but he was in too much pain. His muscles tightened in an effort to sit up, but he failed and fell back.

"I can't."

"You will in a while. You need time." She kissed him fiercely before setting his head back down and running off to look for the next member of her crew.

She heard Red sobbing and followed the sound to the cargo bay. The Pod-doc had broken free and was upside down. Lindy sprawled beside it, both legs and both arms broken. Her head rested at an odd angle.

"Let's get that Pod-doc working," Rivka said softly before switching to her internal voice. *Ankh! Get the fuck in here and turn the power on.*

Rivka checked Lindy's neck. No pulse.

"Come on, Red. Let's get this gear ready to run the second the power comes back on." Red laid her gently on the non-skid deck of the cargo bay before getting to his feet. He wiped his face on the back of his arm.

They each took a side and flipped the Pod-doc over. The lid unlatched, and inside, they found Alana awake and alert. Rivka pulled her out and cradled her.

Red ran for the corridor. "*ANKH!*" he bellowed and headed into the ship, leaving Rivka alone with the baby.

She noticed a powered combat suit anchored to the deck, its magnetic clamps still engaged despite the lack of power. Through the face shield, she saw a frantic Cole yelling. With one arm full of baby, she was able to unhook the rear access and Cole was able to climb out.

"Nuclear bomb!" he said when he was free. He took the baby and ran for the bridge, leaving Rivka alone with Lindy's body.

She gently touched her bodyguard's face. It still felt warm. Rivka pressed her ear to Lindy's chest. A heartbeat, faint but there. As much as it hurt Rivka, she knew it would be easier on the nanocytes if the bones were straightened and only had to be laced together. Starting with arms, Rivka pulled them straight to realign the bones. Lindy never skipped leg day. Her leg muscles fought Rivka. She had to brace a foot on Lindy's pelvis to be able to push-pull hard enough to put the bones back where they were supposed to be.

Rivka listened once more. The heartbeat was getting stronger. The baby bump was far more obvious than she remembered from a mere three days earlier.

She put her head to the bump and tuned out the rest of the world, including the shouts from within the ship. Thunks as stuck doors were forced. Joseph's strong voice encouraging Ryleigh. Someone cried out. Floyd shrieked in pain.

A staccato beat, faint but there.

Rivka stood and stepped away. Red returned carrying a pile of equipment, with Ankh in tow.

"They're both going to be fine," Rivka reported. Red dropped the gear, much to Ankh's chagrin. He slid onto the decking to Lindy's side and cradled her head in his arm. Her neck had already firmed up as the break repaired itself.

Ankh tried to move his equipment, but the pile was too heavy. Rivka took over, putting the bits and pieces around the Pod-doc's control console.

"They survived a nuclear blast, and judging by the damage, it was close," she posited.

Ankh opened the panel before accessing his tools to hook the miniaturized Etheric power supply directly to the Pod-doc.

"Yes. It would have fried everything, but Erasmus, Ted, and I rebuilt this ship from the inside out. Failsafes activated throughout to prevent damage to any circuits from the EMP. I just need to flip switches, but that would take more time than the direct hookup. We must save the crew, Lindy first."

Red lifted her into the Pod-doc and closed the lid. Ankh punched a button, and the system came online. He played the buttons like a maestro, too fast for Rivka to follow.

Joseph and Petricia worked their way through the airlock, carrying Clodagh and Kennedy.

"More coming. All accounted for. No one dead, but no

one in good shape, either." Joseph took Red by the arm and invited him to join the recovery team.

"Bring Floyd and Titan, too," Rivka called. "And the cat."

"Wenceslaus is fine." Ankh didn't take his eyes off the panel's data display. "Ten more minutes." He worked his way through scattered debris and pulled a panel off the wall, then flipped the switches within and checked the circuits with a small tester from his toolkit before replacing the panel.

"Did you check on the cat before you checked on the crew?" Rivka asked.

Ankh didn't dignify her question with a response.

Of course, he had.

Ankh was on his way into the ship to restore the power by flipping the failsafe switches back to operational mode. "Are Dennicron and Chaz going to be okay?"

He stopped and faced Rivka. "They have the same system to harden their circuits, protect them against an electro-magnetic pulse like the one that washed over the ship. But we have never tested them. I will work on them when Erasmus and I can focus one hundred percent of our attention on the problem."

Rivka nodded. She didn't want to lose the SIs within the SCAMPs. Ankh hadn't given her confidence that the personalities survived even if their mobility platforms had not.

Red returned carrying Tyler. He put him gently on the deck where Lindy had been.

Joseph carried Sahved. The Yemilorian's head lolled like a ball at the end of a string. Petricia returned carrying Ryleigh. Only Aurora remained.

"Floyd?"

Red went after Aurora, and the others hurried into the ship to search for the wombat and the tiny dog-like alien.

Rivka checked those who waited for their time in the Pod-doc, then looked at the panel. Five minutes remained for Lindy. She wanted to put Tyler in next so he could help manage the recoveries, but Clodagh had lost a lot of blood.

"Who's a good girl?" Red asked. He was carrying Floyd.

She didn't answer, but she nickered happily.

"EMP fried their comm chips," Red said. "Turns out, wombats and cats are tougher than any of us."

"Is she okay?"

"Far as I can tell," Red said.

Rivka checked the panel on the Pod-doc. She looked for someone to ask, but those who would know weren't in any condition to answer.

They waited impatiently until the clock read zero and the machine stopped. The lid popped, and Lindy sat up.

Red stood close to help Lindy out, so Rivka picked Clodagh up and prepared to put her inside. Clodagh was taller and heavier than Rivka, but the Magistrate managed to get her into the Pod-doc without too much trouble. She closed the lid and started the sequence.

"What happened?" Red asked.

"Fucking pirates launched a massive nuke at the city. We couldn't let it hit, so Clodagh rammed it with the ship."

"You didn't just shoot it down?" Red asked.

Lindy punched him. "We shot the hell out of it. It was as big as a ship. We couldn't knock it out of the sky."

"I don't see a smoking crater where the city used to be, so it worked, and you aren't dead."

"You ol' softy." Lindy smiled.

"Your comm chip working?" Rivka asked.

Just like brand new. Why? Lindy replied.

"EMP fried them all. We're worried about Chaz and Dennicron."

Lindy frowned.

"Red, I have something to tell you in private, and then you need to get back to work helping Ankh." Lindy pointed at the far side of the cargo bay.

Rivka waved them away. They had done what they needed to do to get the ball rolling. The Magistrate went in search of Ankh to see if the Bad Company's combat ships had been able to render assistance.

Lindy led Red to the other side of the cargo bay and faced him. She put his hand on the bulge that was their baby.

"Wow. Growing fast."

"Red, it's been less than two weeks."

"Should it be this big?"

Lindy laughed. "You really don't know, do you?"

"Me and babies have not been close companions in this or any of my previous lives. No. I honestly don't know."

"No. This is about four months, and at this rate, the baby will be born in another one to two weeks."

"I knew you could beat nine months! You excel at everything you do." Red beamed with pride.

Lindy made a face, and Red's smile disappeared. "There's one other thing. The faeries helped facilitate our efforts. Remember that purple fruit?"

"It tasted pretty good," Red replied slowly.

"Our baby is part faerie. Your son has wings."

Red assumed the look of a stunned mullet as the information refused to register. He closed his mouth and stared at the cargo bay door.

"Are you okay?" Lindy asked, caressing his arm.

A slow smile spread across his face. "I'm having a son!" Red shouted.

Lindy rolled her eyes. "Yeah. Something like that. If you pass out, I'm going to kick you in the head."

"I'll be right there with you, sweetheart," Red said quietly. "Doc'll be down at the business end."

"So, you're okay with wings?"

Red sighed heavily. "Let me be in denial for another couple weeks. Our son will be Schrodinger's baby, both with and without wings at the same time."

"You got yourself kicked off his home planet. What if he decides he wants to live there and I have to visit him alone?"

"We'll tell him he can't."

It was Lindy's turn to let her mouth hang open while she stared in disbelief.

"Can't we?" Red asked.

Lindy shook her head. "You need to make peace with the faeries."

"Those fuckers dropped me." At Lindy's look, he reconsidered. "I'll try."

"There is no try, only do." Lindy laughed.

The Pod-doc finished its cycle, and Lindy waved at Red to follow. They swapped Clodagh for Tyler. Cole magically reappeared from inside the ship, carrying Alana. Clodagh took her baby and hugged her until the little bundle disappeared within the full-body wrap. Cole put his hand on

Clodagh's back.

"I'll clean up the bridge," he told her.

Rivka returned to find Tyler's Pod-doc cycle had been started. "The Bad Company ships are stuck blockading that destroyer. It's a standoff. Clodagh, can you help Ankh reset the failsafes?"

"The what?"

"Like a Faraday cage for all the important stuff to keep it from getting fried. He said the ship is mostly fine. Those two booms trailing aft under the port and starboard exhaust shrouds? I guess those are both arced and melted, which is what they're supposed to do. We had grounding rods and never knew it."

"Grounding rods that weren't attached to the ground? And failsafes?"

"They weren't attached to this dimension's ground, but through the Etheric, they were. I don't want to see what it looks like on the other side. But those'll be replaced, along with the cloaking emitters and probably the gravitic shield generators, too. And most everything that wasn't welded to the hull broke free. Besides that, though, the ship's in great shape. Go talk with Ankh."

Clodagh handed the baby to Cole and strode out, wearing a look that suggested the conversation with Ankh would be one-way. He hadn't told her about some of the improvements. She was a chief engineer who wasn't aware of the engineering modifications on her own ship. She was a little miffed, but since Alana wasn't injured, she was in the best mood to vent her spleen.

When the Pod-doc finished, Tyler climbed out, and

Rivka put him in charge of getting everyone through, including Floyd to get her comm chip repaired.

Rivka walked out, and Red joined her.

"What's up with your face? Is that a smile?" Rivka wondered.

"I'm having a son," he stated proudly.

"I'd say Lindy is, but congratulations are in order nonetheless." Rivka went to her quarters to start cleaning up.

"And she'll have the baby within the next two weeks."

"Say what? So, she was pregnant well before we went to Azfelius. I didn't see anything." Rivka gestured with her chin for Red to help her move her desk into place. He took one end, and they made quick work of it.

"No. I guess the chip off the ol' block is part faerie, too. He has wings, or so I'm told."

Rivka stifled a snort before covering her face with both hands to keep from making Red angry. "Wings?" she asked through her fingers.

"I'm still trying to come to grips with it, but I don't want to make Lindy angry. She has that glow about her." He shook his head. "He's our boy regardless. Can we go back to Azfelius? I need to make peace with the faeries."

"No shit. You could be the only being in existence who pissed the faeries off so much they dumped you on the ground."

He looked both ways before whispering, "I wear that with pride, but for public consumption, I'm real sorry for being a jerk." He straightened. "What's next, besides getting *Wyatt Earp* back into space? Did you satisfy the ambassadors? I figured when they were hauling away Foromme and his lackeys in shackles, that would have swung things your way."

"Don't know." Rivka picked up a few more things before giving up. She hadn't prioritized her quarters over anything else, but Red had looked like he wanted to talk. However, they had a lot of work to do, and any other conversations would have to wait.

CHAPTER TWENTY-TWO

The Royal City of Khn'Chik, Yoll, Federation Council

After Ankh and Erasmus departed the House of Arbitration with Rivka, Lance Reynolds called the council back into session. He had to resort to banging his gavel, which he detested. It would have put him in a foul mood, except he'd had the pleasure of seeing Foromme, Delegor, and Mastus hauled away.

Anytime self-important ambassadors were put in their places, Lance was the happier for it.

Ankh had stepped up, too. An advocate in a positive way, not a sycophant. That wasn't the Crenellian's way, nor the SIs'. They did what was right because it was right. Despite the outward appearance of being unemotional, they cared deeply about the things Lance Reynolds cared about.

For that, they would always be his friends.

Like Rivka and the High Chancellor.

Thankless jobs. Getting called on the carpet in front of many who wanted to see them disbanded to relieve the pressure on their planets for complying with Federation law.

Already, the Magistrates had worked to end the slave trade. They'd removed much of the embezzlement and outright theft by gaining control of the financial systems, thanks to the Singularity's involvement.

Ankh had put every ambassador on notice that they would be watching. It had been a masterful play.

The Chief Arbiter smiled as he stood.

"Soon, we must stand up and be counted among those who are on the side of law and order, the foundation of a civilized society. But first, some final words from the High Chancellor."

Wyatt strode to the front of the chamber, took his place at the forward lectern, and looked for specific faces, those who would be perfectly happy with anarchy as long as they were in charge. One's anarchy was another's opportunity. In a cesspool, the detritus always rose to the top.

"Esteemed ambassadors and members of the Federation, I bid you greetings. The question before this august body revolves around the use of tools at our Magistrates' command, tools that may not be available to the average law enforcement official. And that's why we need the Magistrates. We need them to abide by the precedents of probable cause and the right against self-incrimination, but once those have been satisfied and gates passed, that is when the Magistrate Corps shines. That is when they find the offenders and bring them to Justice. Offenders that operate on a galactic scale.

"The Magistrates don't enter your worlds to enforce your laws, but should your laws conflict with the Federation's, then your laws will need to change. The Federation Charter signed by your planetary representatives commits to that. There cannot be two sets of laws. That will only serve to confuse your people. With the help of the Singularity, the Magistrate Corps offers to review your laws line by line to highlight those in direct conflict with Federation law. The Magistrate Corps will submit a report to your planetary leadership, through you, to reconcile your laws. We offer this as a courtesy rather than playing both sides against the middle." Wyatt stopped even though it seemed like he had more to say.

The Chief Arbiter saved him by filling the silence. "Thank you, High Chancellor. And thank you, Ambassador Erasmus, wherever you may be at the moment, for your kind offer of technical assistance." Lance knew Ankh had gone to Foromme to help resolve the situation with the pirates. He wanted an update. He was tired of looking at the ambassadors.

"The question is whether the Magistrate Corps continues as they are or if they will be disbanded."

"Oversight!" the Shrillexian ambassador called. Others picked up the shout, but it died quickly under General Reynolds' withering glare.

He glanced at the High Chancellor before putting the question to rest. "The Magistrate Corps has two levels of oversight. First is the High Chancellor's office, and the second is my office. The Magistrates answer solely to the Federation, a terrible and awesome task given us by the Queen and Empress, Bethany Anne. It's our responsibility, and we cannot legislate it away. That is the final word regarding oversight."

"But redress in the case of miscarriage of justice?" the Shrillexian continued.

"Will be handled by our offices as just described. Are you asking for a complaint department, a place where you can complain about being held liable for breaking the law?" Lance countered.

"In case they get it wrong..." The ambassador's voice had lost its fervent pitch.

"Our two offices. Complaints and concerns can be submitted to my executive assistant's secretary once you've received concurrence from the High Chancellor's office." Lance raised his hands to forestall further questions. "Now is the time to stand up and be counted. Those against the rule of law, I mean, those who wish for the Magistrate's Corps to be dissolved, stand up to cast your vote."

The ambassador in the front row, the one Ankh had put in his place, stood, saw that he was the only one, mumbled an expletive, and sat back down.

"If you support the Magistrate Corps, stand up and be counted." Most but not all the ambassadors stood. Lance Reynolds wrote down names on a small notepad. "Abstention wasn't one of the options. Your lack of vote will be considered as a vote against."

"So what of it?" The Shrillexian ambassador shouted, his facial spikes emerging in his fury.

"Nothing. This is a free society. But should you ask for a favor? Well, just don't ask for any favors."

Lance walked to the exit door behind the raised dais and left, not bothering to close out the session.

The High Chancellor smiled at the Chief Arbiter's style

and the respect he had earned, not because of his daughter but because of his own work ethic, his own integrity.

Wyatt faced the crowd. "This special session of the Federation Council is closed. You'll return to your normally scheduled activities on the morrow, and we'll see you back at Red Rock for our regularly scheduled business."

He abandoned the lectern and shook the hand of each Magistrate on his way out. The four followed him, expecting he would update them on Rivka as well as deliver their next steps over an early lunch.

Wyatt Earp, **Crashed on Foromme**

"How long, Ankh?" Rivka insisted.

Ankh stopped what he was doing, removed his hands from within a panel, and stared without blinking. "It'll take what it takes, and it'll happen more quickly if I don't have to answer questions. With Clodagh working on it, it will shave ten percent off the total time."

"Which is? And why only ten percent?"

"She's not as good as me."

"It couldn't have anything to do with you installing a system that she had no idea about, and now she has to learn it while fixing it?"

Ankh didn't reply, which told Rivka she was correct.

She wanted to storm away from him, as was the case in most of her conversations with the Crenellian, but he was right.

As was the case in most of her conversations with him. "We're taking the *Vengeance*," she called over her shoulder.

"Red, Cole, get your suits on. We're putting an end to this bullshit."

Red appeared, with Lindy at his side. "You lost me, Magistrate. There seems to be an endless supply of bullshit, evidenced by what we just left on Yoll."

"Valid observation." She pointed at the overhead. "We're boarding that destroyer."

"I'm all for a good fight," Red replied. In the cargo bay, Lindy started to suit up. Red stopped and stared. "What are you doing?"

"I'm going too. This is what we do. I'm not out of action yet."

Rivka tried to ignore the conversation but couldn't. "What do you say you sit this one out?"

"Is that an order?"

"If I have to make it one," Rivka replied. "No one is doubting your abilities, but I'd like to point out that you already died once today. I think that should be anyone's limit."

Lindy sighed and spoke softly. "I was only mostly dead."

"Clodagh, if you would be so kind as to join us, we're going to need an engineer, just in case they try to sabotage the ship when they realize they're losing."

"What about *Wyatt Earp*? And Alana?"

"Tyler, you have baby duty while the Cole family is beating the fucking shit out of a bunch of pirates."

Clodagh walked through the airlock and into the cargo bay. "Since you put it that way, I'm not sure I can turn you down."

She undid the harness that strapped the baby to her front and carefully handed Alana to the dentist.

"I used to be somebody," Tyler grumbled.

"You still are," Cole said. "I'm trusting my daughter with you while we're in the middle of a shit sandwich. We need to go slap the snot out of those who are preventing us from expediting our repairs and getting the fuck out of here."

"Hear, hear!" Clodagh said while trying to remember how to get into the suit. Lindy explained the finer points, and Clodagh climbed in and powered up.

Each ran through a quick systems check. Lindy accessed the cargo ramp's manual control. With a quick twist and a jerk, it unlocked and slowly lowered to the scorched ground beneath the ship.

Rivka led the way out, stopping to look at the charred booms she had never thought about before. They had served a valuable purpose. She had thought they were cosmetic.

They crawled into the cramped cargo bay of *Destiny's Vengeance*. *Erasmus, if you would do us the honor of delivering us to the top of that destroyer? Bonus points for delivering close to an airlock.*

I love bonus points, Erasmus declared.

Destiny's Vengeance turned invisible before taking off. Erasmus guided the ship smoothly upward.

I have to admit that I remain unimpressed with the betting lines. Ninety of them went unsatisfied, with multiple winners on the lines that closed. Bravo, Magistrate, on not swearing and not resorting to physical violence. I expect your performance should become a class in law schools around the galaxy.

"Was there a video feed of the proceedings?"

I was there, Erasmus replied. *Did you take a violent blow to the head that we didn't hear about?*

Rivka chuckled. "I hear you in my head and think of you as part of the ship and not that you were present in your ambassadorial splendor. Please accept my apologies, Erasmus."

Nothing to apologize for, Rivka. Ankh showed them what he was made of, too. I love him.

"We all do, in our own way." Rivka couldn't see where they were since none of them were tapped into the command deck systems like they were on *Wyatt Earp.* "Could you share the tactical screen, Erasmus? And maybe a little intel on that ship, if you have any?"

The view from the cockpit appeared on their HUDs. They were nearly there.

This is an older ship. You'll find reinforced hull plating around the airlock, but even where the hull armor thins, it will still be more than sufficient to keep your railguns from penetrating.

"I guess we're going to have to open the airlock. Or maybe you can hack into their ship, take over, fly it to the mountains, and crash it in a spectacular fireball."

I've been trying to gain access since we arrived. The ship is old. Its systems are not easily accessible from the outside since it was never designed to be flown remotely.

"At least you can get the airlock open," Rivka said hopefully.

Alas, fair maiden, I cannot.

"You've been spending time with Joseph, haven't you?"

He is interesting, to say the least. Prepare to deploy. You'll drop ten meters and land on top of the airlock. Now, now, now!

Destiny's Vengeance tilted skyward and dumped the four out of the small cargo bay.

They fell feet-first. Rivka never gained her bearings and landed flat on her side. Red and Cole jetted to soft landings. Clodagh activated her jets to the extreme, arresting her fall and sending her upward like a shot and back into the cargo bay. She slammed into the forward bulkhead, shut down the jets, and promptly fell out the back of the ship. She slammed into the outer hull with her knees bent to absorb the shock and held that pose long enough to make sure she was all right.

"Must run in the family," Red said. "If only we had video."

CHAPTER TWENTY-THREE

Pirate Destroyer over Morofite, the Capital City of Planet Mastus

Red accessed the airlock's manual control to find the system locked out. Nothing he could do would open it. Erasmus couldn't get into the system either.

"This is the modern version of a chair blocking the door handle," Rivka said. She walked away from the hatch, looking for an alternate ingress. Less than one hundred meters away, the hull plates were buckled from battle damage.

"Was that from us?" she asked while jogging toward the rents in the outer hull. The others followed. "What do you think?"

"I think the railguns couldn't penetrate all of it, but I'm confident we can cut through that." Red pointed the barrel of his oversized weapon at the gap between two heavy armor plates. He leaned through to make sure he could fit. "I say we breach this bitch right here."

"After you," Rivka said. Cole moved close while Clodagh and Rivka waited.

Red braced himself and started to fire the big gun on auto, drawing a circle on the inner hull. The weapon was smoking when he let up on the trigger. He jumped through the opening and hit the center of his circle with both feet, driving his legs down upon impact.

The plate came free, all but one side. It twisted inward, and Red slid through. Cole jumped through and hit the plate, bending it even more. He slid after Red.

Rivka jumped through next, hit the side of the plate, and slid into a corridor to find Red and Cole running away from the opening. Clodagh came down behind her.

Red reached a corner and fired around it. Cole dove to the far side and opened up.

The suits compensated for the decibels, giving a false reality of what the railguns sounded like inside the upper corridor of the destroyer.

"Bridge is this way," Clodagh said. "And down." She pointed forward. "Makes no sense to put it at the front of the ship since that's where asteroids and enemies make their greatest mark. No. This one, it's in the center of the ship where it's best protected."

They took one step and were pelted by small arms fire.

Rivka aimed at them but didn't fire. Their weapons couldn't hurt her combat armor.

Red suffered no recriminations. When he pulled even with her, he blasted the far end of the corridor where the pirates had appeared. Clodagh waved at a side corridor.

"Cole, we are leaving," Rivka called. He backed down the corridor, which suggested there was more crew in the aft end of the ship. Red fired once more before heading into the cross-corridor. Cole waited until Clodagh hit a ladderwell and started down. He fired forward and aft before assuming a new position at the vertical access. Red pushed his way in after Clodagh, then Rivka.

Cole ran back to the main corridor and found two adventurous souls coming from the forward section. He blasted them without remorse and returned, closing the heavy hatch after he entered and joined the others on their downward climb. Two decks down, Clodagh emerged into another side corridor in the middle of a crew determined not to let her.

She powered into them hard enough to clear the way for Red. He came out and fired, stitching a line across the opposite bulkhead, cutting two crewmen in half. The others fired back with low-grade plasma rifles. Red plinked them one by one, the velocity of the railgun projectile exploding the flesh upon impact. Red offed two with one shot when the round blasted through the first pirate and into a second standing too close behind him.

Red turned his attention to those engaged with Clodagh. They were attempting to penetrate her suit with a plasma cutter. Two men hung from her railgun, and she was too nice to crush them against the ceiling.

Red turned his rifle around and cleared them off Clodagh's weapon with a single axe-like blast, shattering two bodies at once.

A light above told Cole that someone was coming. He aimed up the shaft and vaporized the first body that entered.

Rivka stepped into the corridor and jacked up the

volume of her external speakers. "My name is Rivka Anoa, and you've already lost. Give us control of the ship, and no one else need die."

"Fuck you!" As the last syllable left the pirate's mouth, Red blew his head apart.

"No, fuck you," he clarified. "Anybody else want the big fungu?" Red stormed down the corridor, forcing the less-than-stalwart defenders to run for their lives.

"These guys are putzes. I almost feel bad about killing them." Red cleared a body away from the front of the vault-like hatch leading to the command center. It was secured from the other side.

"I guess they want it the hard way," Clodagh said, handing her rifle to Red. "It appears we have a plasma torch at our disposal."

She fired up the system and started cutting into the door, trying to find the locking mechanism to expedite their access.

Rivka strolled around, unable to check anyone's mind because she had no intention of removing her combat suit. The pirates were on the run, but they were far from harmless.

"Hey!" Red yelled at a face that appeared just long enough to throw a bundle down the corridor. "Incoming!"

The suits compensated for the light and sound, but one could get toppled. Clodagh and Rivka crouched to lower their profiles. Red ran after the thrower. Before he could reach the corner, the bomb exploded, sending metal shrapnel ripping up and down the corridor.

The suits protected them. Clodagh stood and dusted herself off.

"They couldn't hurt us with that," Rivka said.

Clodagh pointed at the plasma torch, which was wrecked and out of action. "Maybe there was a method to their madness."

"Can we get what we want from Engineering?" Rivka wondered.

"I'm sure I can fire the engines. All we want to do is get out from over the city, right?"

"Sounds easy. Once out there, the Bad Company can destroy it."

"I hope we'll be getting off first," Clodagh added.

"We can hope." Rivka winked, a movement that was wasted with the reflective face shield in place. "Cole family to the engine room. Team Rivka will stay here and try to talk some sense into them."

Red joined the small group. "I don't like splitting up. There's no reason to stay here if all we're going to do is fire the engines and then run for it."

"I'd like to think we can get them to surrender. Go on, you two. Make the magic happen. With the futility of their position, they'll have to do something. I've never met a pirate who was suicidal. Their goal is to survive to plunder another day."

Clodagh and Cole headed down the corridor. Cole jumped into the intersection and fired before looking. He sent a couple of extra rounds downrange for good measure and waved for Clodagh to follow. He started jogging, keeping his head down to avoid bouncing his helmet off the overhead piping.

Then he had the grand idea to disable the ship to expedite the crew's surrender. He reached up, grabbed a pipe, and leveraged the weight of the suit and his momentum to pull it free.

It came out of the overhead rack, split, and pulled free, sending black water, the term for sewage, spraying down the corridor behind him.

Coating his wife's suit from head to toe, along with splashing the deck and walls.

"Cole!" she shouted. "You better keep running."

Red watched from the corridor, making sure they were clear to move aft.

"What happened?" Rivka asked.

"Cole sprayed his wife with pirate shit. She's not coming back with us like that."

Rivka didn't try to parse Red's reply. She took the plasma torch wand and used it to beat on the hatch. "Open up!" She stopped hammering on the metal and leaned close to the one small hole Clodagh had opened. "Listen up, those of you who are inside the command center. We are going to move this ship out from over the city one way or another. We're on board, more people will come on board until eventually, we've slaughtered your entire crew, and only you remain. You can try to damage the city further, but the only way to save your lives is to open the hatch. You've been thinking about it, and your restraint in not causing more damage to Morofite is a huge feather in your cap. Now is the time to cash in your chips, make the best out of a bad situation."

"We want your ship and safe passage!" a voice cried from the other side.

"You have to know that's not going to happen. Try again."

Red used a P2P comm channel. "I didn't think you were supposed to antagonize the criminal during a negotiation."

"Not this time. I won't make the mistake of letting them think they have *any* leverage."

Noises beyond the end of the corridor. Scraping. Clanking. Metal on metal. "They're coming," Red said unnecessarily. He aimed his railgun at the intersection, ready for the first bold soul to appear. Rivka stood back to back with him, aiming in the other direction.

A massive metal plate appeared, angled forty-five degrees and nearly filling the space. Red fired. The projectile skipped off the metal with a screech and a scream. Those behind it pushed it farther into the intersection. Red fired incrementally, a round here and there to hold their attention while he waited for the real show to begin.

The plate started to shake. With an abrupt clang, it fell. Behind it, a short-range missile's motor was thrusting it forward. The weapon rocketed down the corridor. It was there before Red could move. It hit him in the chest and threw him into Rivka. He twisted to get out from under it, but the impact detonator had already activated.

The explosion filled the corridor with uncoiling springs that were meant to rip open incoming missiles.

And kill them.

Cole shot anything that moved, including two cleaning bots, on their way to the engine room. Clodagh followed, using her rear-facing video feed to keep an eye on their six o'clock. They moved quickly enough to limit the chase.

Or maybe the pirates were focused on protecting the command deck, ignoring the fact that firing the engines to drive the ship out of the city's airspace was a viable option that had nothing to do with the people flying the destroyer. Clodagh didn't care which direction, and that didn't matter.

Cole smashed through a barrier defended by types who were less pirate and more average crew. They carried ineffective small arms they didn't bother to fire. When faced with the power of an armored warrior storming their position, they lost their nerve and ran. Cole did them the favor of not killing them.

"We're close," Clodagh observed. She could feel the engines' vibrations even though propulsion wasn't active. Ships generated a great deal of power at all times to keep the systems active.

Cole found that the double doors leading to the engine room had been sealed and welded shut.

"Well, now. I guess we can't shoot through these since we don't want to blast anything inside."

"Your premise is correct. I'd prefer we don't blast our way in, but as a last resort, we may have to." *Magistrate, we're at the engine room. They've blocked the door. Will breach and advise soonest.*

They waited a few moments for a reply. "Must be busy with something else," Cole suggested before rearing back and using the full power of the suit to kick the door. The *ka-thump* was deafening. "I'm sure it's worse inside." Their suits compensated, but the crew that had run weren't wearing any hearing protection.

No work-related injury compensation for pirates. A share of the profits. No questions asked.

Cole kicked the door again and again, but it wasn't going to budge.

"Something's wrong. Still not hearing from the Magistrate," Clodagh said, growing more anxious with each extra moment they remained in one place. "Fire it up. Shoot out the welds, and then see if it pops."

Clodagh backed away while Cole lined up the shot, angling slightly to send ricochets down the corridor away from his wife.

He fired and then fired some more, finally resorting to full-auto and stitching a line down the middle of the double door. Cole's aiming point reached the deck, and he retraced his arc to double the number of impacts. He let the barrel cool while he reared back to kick.

This time, the impact bent the door inward. Clodagh pointed at a spot where it was caught—a spot-weld. Cole laid waste to it, and a final kick twisted one side of the door inward. Cole ran, hit it with the suit's shoulder, and barreled through.

The engine room was nothing like that of *Wyatt Earp* or even *War Axe*. It looked more like something of old, a vessel crossing the oceans of Earth. The equipment was oversized and filled the space. The engines hummed and throbbed with life.

Clodagh looked for the system to activate the ship's propulsion. She traced the bank of controls that regulated and maintained the power systems and worked her way around the corner while Cole watched for any crew who might take offense at their presence.

Not that the pirates could do anything without killing themselves. None of the regular crew had demonstrated that level of commitment. They wouldn't be going down with the ship unless it was shot out from under them.

"Aha!" Clodagh declared. "Give me a minute."

At the far end of the engine room was the flow regulation system, sending power to propulsion or not. The system was throttled shut. Clodagh worked the controls to access and override external commands, like those coming from the bridge. She flooded the propulsion system with power.

"Time to get the hell out of here." Clodagh rolled her rifle to the front and started running. Cole ran after her. *Magistrate, the ship is on the move. Are you ready to evacuate? We can meet you topside.*

"We're going back to find them," Cole said, wishing Clodagh to greater speed.

CHAPTER TWENTY-FOUR

Pirate Destroyer over Morofite, the Capital City of Planet Mastus

Rivka crawled out from under Red. Her systems were pinging from multiple failures. Her face shield was cracked, but she was still able to move. She shouted at the corridor from within the privacy of her helmet since the suit's comm systems were down.

Red was nothing but a heavy lump. Rivka surged forward until she was free and stood, even though one leg wasn't fully cooperating.

She fired at the adventurous souls who thought they'd delivered the kill shot, eliminating them without mercy. When the corridor was clear, she turned her attention to Red.

His legs were gone. She looked twice, believing the crack in her face shield had created a misperception of reality. She bent close. The missile's expanding warhead had severed the suit's legs mid-thigh and taken Red's real legs with it. His nanocytes had closed the wounds, barely, but he continued to leak precious blood that carried the nanocytes that would save his life.

Red is down, and I need help, Rivka called to anyone who had a comm chip. *Please.*

She parked her suit and climbed out, snagging the emergency medical kit within it to use on her bodyguard. She used the spray sealant to close the horrific wounds. Red's helmet had been sliced nearly in half but nearly wasn't all the way, and that had saved him.

A vicious wound jagged across the side of his head.

She continued checking him to find that his hands had survived the blast as if he'd been reaching behind him to make sure Rivka was shielded.

"Red. Come on, buddy. Come back to me."

He gasped as his body shocked him back to consciousness. He opened his mouth to speak but closed his eyes instead and screamed like one in mortal agony. Rivka cradled his armor as best she could, but it was too heavy to pick up without her suit on.

She knew what she had to do. There was no treatment for him on the destroyer. She had to carry him out. She stood as Red stopped screaming. He panted until he managed a few intelligible words. "Don't let me die. My boy..."

Rivka lunged for her suit, but rough hands grabbed her.

She continued her rush but passed her suit to catch her captor by surprise. She picked him up and slammed his head into the metal of the corridor's walls. Rivka ducked before jumping to catch a second pirate who had been unable to stop her. He bounced off the wall before coming back toward her. She delivered a throat strike that broke his neck. He toppled.

"FREEZE!" The voice behind her suggested he was too far away to reach. She whirled to find three weapons pointed at her. She glanced at Red. Her eye twitched at being caught between actions.

Clodagh's voice sounded in her head. *Magistrate, the ship is on the move. Are you ready to evacuate? We can meet you topside.*

I need help, Rivka replied, realizing the damage to her suit from the missile had also damaged her chip. She could hear but not transmit. She wondered briefly how violent the blow had been to her head.

"You're the Magistrate. How wondrous that you showed up on our ship," a blustering, overweight fool called from beyond the three holding the weapons. "There is a contract out on you, and it looks like we are going to satisfy it. Half a million credits."

Rivka calmed. Her vision became a single point of focus. She had never seen the individual before. He was a lackey, working for Foromme and trying to make the best of a bad situation.

He called into the bridge, "Jack, get those ships on the horn and let them know we have Magistrate Rivka Anoa in our custody. We require them to retreat to a safe distance to support our unmolested departure from this star system."

"Sir!" someone shouted. "We are accelerating at point-zero-two standard."

"Who gave that order? Make sure we have their attention before we move. Override! Keep us above the city."

"Attempting to change course…"

"I'm going to fucking kill you. All of you," Rivka said, waving her hand to take in the group before her. "And then I'm carrying my friend out of here. Whoever remains on board will die when my ship blows yours out of the sky."

"Is that how the law works nowadays?"

"You have been judged," Rivka said in a low voice.

The pounding of heavy metal signaled the arrival of two warriors in powered combat armor.

"Duck!" Cole shouted. Rivka dropped flat, and an oversized railgun exploded over her head. It was too late to cover her ears. The ringing drowned out all other sounds.

The three holding weapons vaporized from the impacts, and the pirate captain was next. He died ingloriously, his body exploding from the impact. Cole launched himself down the corridor, using the suit's jets to propel him like a torpedo. He caught the doorway and jerked himself to a stop, then pulled himself inside, aimed, and blasted the three within.

"This bitch is going down," Cole growled. He returned to the corridor to find Clodagh struggling to pick Red up.

"We'll get him. You lead us out," Cole told his wife. She set Red down, and as an afterthought, she picked up the two sections of Red's suit that had been blasted off. Her rifle was slung under her arm just in case.

Rivka climbed into her suit, yelling as she did, "I have no comm. Shuttle bay to get out of here. We can't climb a ladder."

Can't climb a ladder carrying a man clinging to life, wrapped in the wreckage of his combat suit.

Clodagh had a general idea of the ship's layout. They

needed to go forward. "Follow me," she said after giving Red to Rivka and Cole. They made a saddle with their arms, locking gloved hands together, Red sitting with his arms on their shoulders. Tears streamed down his face.

"We got you, Red," Cole told him. Rivka couldn't say a word. She wouldn't know what to say if she could speak besides telling Clodagh to hurry up.

Clodagh hatcheted an arm toward the first ramp and raced down it, picking off one individual unlucky enough to be coming up while they went down. She might have let him go, but he carried a hand blaster. That signed his death warrant.

They ran down, hit the next deck, and doubled back to take the next ramp down. And the next. Three levels. Clodagh left the ramp at a dead run. Rivka and Cole struggled to keep up.

Vengeance, *pick us up at the shuttle bay. We'll be there in ten seconds.*

Erasmus replied, *The ship is accelerating at an inconsistent pace. We will be unable to dock.*

"Well, fuck," Clodagh mumbled. She didn't slow down. Shuttle bay first, then she'd figure out how to get off the ship. It was a *shuttle* bay, after all.

She blasted through the hatch without slowing down to find only one shuttle—and the pirate crew was boarding it. Clodagh switched to external speakers. "We'll be taking that ship."

Someone had the audacity to fire their weapon. Clodagh didn't want to kill all of them. She didn't want to kill any of them.

She ran into the group, pushing aside those who didn't

see fit to give her space. "Get the fuck out!" She climbed through the back and bodily tossed two out, then ripped out two rows of seats and threw them after the group she'd kicked off the ship. The pilot looked torn. "It's your lucky day. You get to fly us off this pig."

Cole and Rivka lumbered in and laid Red on the deck. He was out, his complexion graying.

"Get us out of here!" Rivka shouted, hoping to be heard through her broken face shield.

"Door won't open," the pilot called from the front.

"I got this," Cole replied. "Button up and take off. I'll be right behind you."

Once Cole was out, the shuttle hatch closed and sealed.

"Fuck off!" Cole yelled at the crew, torn between trying to storm the shuttle or running back into the ship. He ran two steps toward them, shattering their resolve. They bolted.

He sprinted toward the shuttle bay activation panel to find that it had been jury-rigged, probably more than once. Below it was the manual release and a lever. He popped the release and started cranking. The door moved agonizingly slowly. The wind whistled across the opening as it got wider.

Cole put all of his suit's strength and dexterity into spinning the wheel to open the door. He glanced up, and again, and again. It was like watching a pot of water on the stove. Would it ever boil?

Would the door open in time?

The lever screeched and came free of the fitting. The doors stopped moving. Cole ran to the opening and gripped one door, then leaned into it to push it on its tracks. He roared with the effort, driving his suit and himself to the extreme level of their capabilities.

The door rolled and then gained momentum. He heaved, and the shuttle bay door broke free and ran to the end of the track. The city was behind them as the ship increased speed. Cole waved at the shuttle to go, but it was already accelerating toward the opening. It flew out and away. Cole jumped, activating his jets to fly after the ship, but intra-atmospheric, he couldn't maintain horizontal flight. He started to drop. They were barely a thousand meters off the deck.

The destroyer continued away from them. Cole activated his rear video just in time to see the ship head into the side of a mountain. The hull crumpled in slow motion as explosions highlighted the death of subsystems and munitions cooking off within. The engines were the last to impact the granite peak, ending the ship's life in a spectacular fireball.

The shuttle raced toward Morofite. Cole oriented himself vertically to ease his impact with the ground.

With a heavy thump, he hit, but he was still five hundred meters up.

Destiny's Vengeance materialized beneath his feet.

"Red's injured," Cole reported.

"We know. We're on our way," Erasmus replied.

CHAPTER TWENTY-FIVE

Wyatt Earp, **Crashed on Foromme**

Lindy waited impatiently in the entry to the cargo bay. The ramp was down, and the pirate shuttle was coming in hot. On board, they carried an injured Red. No one had articulated the extent of his injuries, but Lindy expected them to be bad, considering the urgency in Clodagh's voice.

The shuttle flared and landed with its stern facing *Wyatt Earp*. The ramp popped, and Rivka and Clodagh ran out with Red cradled between them.

Lindy gasped and suddenly found she couldn't breathe. She clutched her stomach as she started to see spots and dropped to her knees before falling over.

The shuttle took off and raced skyward.

A millisecond later, it disappeared in a small fireball as *Destiny's Vengeance* hit it with a single round from its plasma cannon.

Ankh waited at the controls of the Pod-doc. Tyler was torn between helping Lindy and dealing with Red. Sahved stood nearby, holding Alana while taking in the chaos of a body torn asunder.

Rivka yelled at Tyler to look after Lindy, but he couldn't hear her. Clodagh could, though.

"Lindy first. We'll see to Red."

They put him on his face so they could access the back of the suit, having to use the power of their suits to get past the damage to undo the fastenings. In the end, they each took a side and pulled it apart.

Cole ran in, ready to help, but Rivka had already picked him up and was carrying him to the Pod-doc.

Clodagh showed that she still carried Red's legs.

"Throw them in with him!" Tyler shouted. It was easier to rejuvenate that flesh than build new legs from scratch. The Pod-doc would reattach them and make the repairs. Ankh took care of the final programming, and they closed the lid. He activated the system.

The panel showed a minimum of three hours. Ankh took one last look before walking back into the ship to continue making repairs to bring the ship back online. Rivka parked her suit and climbed out. She hurried to where Tyler was working with Lindy.

"That's not the kind of shock someone in the advanced stage of pregnancy needs to get."

"Did she just faint?"

Tyler looked at the Pod-doc. "How long?"

"At least three hours."

"I think we need to get her looked at sooner than that. It feels like the baby is jonesing to get out in this world."

"Jonesing?" Rivka wondered, unsure of what he meant.

"Ready to come. Maybe right now."

Rivka jumped up. "Clevarious! We need *Potemkin's* Pod-doc right fucking now!"

"With the demise of the destroyer, they are on their way, Magistrate. ETA is five minutes."

"Have them spooled up and ready to go. We'll be carrying Lindy aboard the instant they land."

Tyler cradled Lindy's head in his lap. She started to sweat. There was little they could do to help her.

Joseph and Petricia joined them. Joseph's red eyes unfocused for a moment before he fixed Tyler with an unnerving stare. "The baby is coming, and right now. You need to do a c-section."

"A what?" Tyler looked between Rivka, Joseph, and Lindy. "I don't think I can."

"I will help. I've done plenty in my days as a rancher."

"She's a human," Tyler countered.

"And she has no choice if you want the baby to live. Der'ayd'nil says that he needs us to do this. He is ready."

"The baby talked with you?"

Joseph nodded. "We must hurry." The urgency in his voice suggested there was no other option. Rivka helped Tyler pick Lindy up, and they headed for the guest quarters they'd taken to calling the birthing room.

For good reason.

I will contact Potemkin and ask their doctor to join us as soon as they land, Clevarious said.

Petricia waited behind to escort the *Potemkin's* doctor.

Into the corridor, four doors down, and onto the bed. Medical equipment had already been pre-staged. No scalpels or clamps, but there were sutures.

CRAIG MARTELLE & MICHAEL ANDERLE

Joseph removed a small knife from his pocket and opened it.

"You're going to use that?" Tyler held his hand over Lindy's bare abdomen.

"Nanos. She'll be fine." Joseph felt for the baby and selected a spot where he could cut through the skin and open the womb below. He traced a line the length of his hand, then added a little bit to it. The baby's shoulder and wing appeared, both looking small and extremely fragile. Tyler reached in to wrap his fingers under the neck to support it while pinning the wings tightly to the baby's body.

He rotated the body enough to bring the head out first, then the rest of the body slid through.

"Water!" he called. Rivka ran for the galley. They removed the placenta and cut the umbilical cord, tying it off from the baby. The rest was dumped into a bucket that had seen much bodily waste in its life. Tyler took the first suture and started stitching. "Is there any way you could have cut a bigger hole in this poor lady?"

"Probably," Joseph replied. "But I was in a hurry."

Tyler stopped stitching while he laughed. "We're getting pretty good at the weird stuff, aren't we?"

Joseph smiled. "I've been a master of weird for four centuries, my good man."

A knock on the door signaled the arrival of *Potemkin*'s doctor. Petricia ushered him in, and the doctor checked the baby.

"Good. You can take over," Tyler said.

"No, no. Looks like you're doing just fine."

"But I'm a dentist," Tyler countered.

"Not today, you aren't. The baby doesn't have any teeth." He snorted at his joke, and Joseph joined him.

Cole leaned through the doorway, holding Alana to show her the newest addition to the family. Sahved watched over Cole's shoulder.

"What a fucking day," Cole mumbled with a sigh.

"I could use a beer or six," Tyler said. Cole saluted by lifting his baby to his brow.

Normal overhead lighting replaced the emergency lights as power surged back into the ship. The air handling system started cycling fresh air into the spaces.

"I'm a mom," Lindy said softly, watching the clock countdown on the Pod-doc's panel. "And you're a dad," she told the closed lid.

The machine seemed to stall before renewing its count and cycling to completion. The cover popped and opened. Red had his eyes closed and appeared to be sleeping.

"Red?" Lindy put her hand on a chest that slowly rose and fell with each breath.

He slowly opened his eyes while pulling in a great lungful of air. "What have we here?" he asked with a smile.

"You almost died," Lindy blurted.

"But I didn't, and you didn't. Now look at us. What are we going to call our son?"

"He told Joseph that his name was Der'ayd'nil."

Red looked confused. "That sounds like Lindy and Red backwards."

"No shit!" The light went on behind Lindy's eyes.

Rivka joined them. "It's good to see you in one piece, big guy."

"You seem to keep saving my ass," Red told her as she helped him out of the Pod-doc. He swayed on unsteady legs. Lindy wouldn't let him hold his son while he wobbled. He staggered to a nearby chair and sat.

He cradled his swaddled son. Lindy showed him how to support the baby's head. He unswaddled his son to see the wings. "I'll be damned. Wings. Already an angel, huh?"

Lindy sat next to him.

Rivka touched them both gently on the shoulder. "Welcome to the family. I'll leave you two alone. We're headed to space and then back to Yoll. I guess we have some unfinished Magistrate business."

"And us, too," Joseph interrupted. "I think we'll remain on Yoll to open an AGB franchise. We volunteered to be Terry Henry's people on the ground, as it may be. My brother offered his place to us. He is looking at taking an extended vacation on Torregidor."

"The green women? Say it isn't so."

"I cannot because it is so. I fear that I may have suggested it," Joseph admitted.

"We'll see how that turns out," Rivka replied, heading to the bridge.

Once there, she found Clodagh with a baby travel restraint bolted to the bulkhead. Alana gurgled within.

"I remember the good old days. Seems like they weren't that long ago when we rode free, no seatbelts."

"Those days sucked." Clodagh smiled at the Magistrate.

"Maybe just a little. I wouldn't change it for anything."

Sahved turned his seat at the back of the bridge, close to

the baby carrier. "You need me on your crew," the Yemilo-rian said.

"I've always needed you, Sahved. As an investigator, and even more so now to help Chaz and Dennicron..." Rivka's voice trailed off. "How are they?"

"Ankh and Erasmus are working on them to the exclusion of all else," Sahved replied.

"I need them to be all right," Rivka said. She looked at the front screen, but it wouldn't stay in focus. "Let me know when we've arrived. I'll be in my quarters."

Rivka bowed her head and walked out. She made it ten steps into the corridor before she leaned against the bulkhead and slid down it to sit on the floor. Tiny Man Titan barked from the bridge, just once, a happy bark. The Pod-doc had fixed him up as good as new because the explosion had almost cost his life. No one knew that. Tyler hadn't shared it with anyone because he didn't want to cause anyone more stress, but he had put Titan into the Pod-doc before most of the others to make sure he survived.

Triage. Worst cases first.

So close to losing everything. Rivka closed her eyes and fought the tidal wave that threatened to consume her.

Floyd! came the little girl's cry as she bounced down the corridor. Rivka started to scramble since Floyd wasn't slowing down. The wombat jumped and hit Rivka mid-chest, toppling both of them. Floyd rolled and came back to settle in Rivka's lap.

"My good girl didn't get hurt during a nuclear explosion. Who knew wombats were so tough?"

Floyd knew, she answered.

"Yes, you did. You defended yourself against those creatures at the Forbes Spaceport. A nuclear explosion is nothing."

Nothing! Floyd cried happily.

"I'll tell you a secret, little girl. I was ready to be sad because of all the pain our people suffered today. All of us. This was a hard day, Floyd, maybe the hardest of my life. We never stopped getting hurdles put in front of us."

Lindy shouted so loudly it nearly shook the ship. "For fuck's sake, just sit down to pee!"

"I gotta see what that's about." Rivka jumped to her feet, refreshed from her temporary loss of focus, and ran down the corridor toward Lindy and Red's quarters.

"Sit down to pee? What the hell is wrong with you? Things don't work that way because I'm a man! I'll stand, even when I'm on my death bed."

Rivka stayed to the side; she didn't want to look. "Patient not recovered yet?"

"He's wobbling all over the place," Lindy replied. She looked back into their room and threw her hands up in frustration. "I'm not cleaning that bathroom."

"Ah, marital bliss. Where's Dery?"

"That kid sleeps like a champ. Through the worst of Red's bullshit antics."

"You love me," Red called from inside the room.

"I do," Lindy admitted. She smiled and softly patted her belly. "Two-week gestation. You should try it sometime."

"I'm pretty sure no." Rivka shook her head. "I'll live vicariously through you. Wings? A citizen of the Singularity from a planet without computers. This is going to be interesting."

"Ankh promised to train him on the finer points of cyberspace."

"Very interesting." Rivka headed for her quarters with a smile on her face. In minutes, her attitude had changed. The past was best left in the past. The future held a visit to Yoll and the departure of their short-term companions Joseph and Petricia. She skipped her quarters and went to theirs, finding them packing their meager belongings and ready to go.

"Are you going to keep Red's yacht?" Rivka asked.

"It's already on Yoll and is quite the status symbol for business owners of our stature," Joseph replied.

"Is Red okay with it?"

"It's only going to cost me free meals for the rest of his life. I know that could be a long time, but there's zero down and no interest." Joseph smiled. The discordance of passing through the Gate flowed through the ship and was gone just as quickly.

"We'll be over Yoll. Next stop, wherever the High Chancellor wants us to land, or wherever Ground Control tells us to go."

CHAPTER TWENTY-SIX

The Royal City of Khn'Chik, Yoll, Office of the High Chancellor

"By calling you before them, the ambassadors helped solidify the Magistrates' role in the Federation. After you left, the council called for an expansion of the Corps," Wyatt said.

Grainger nodded along with Rivka. Jael, Chi, and Buster didn't look pleased.

Buster raised his hand, saw that no one else was ready to speak, and started talking. "What does that look like? Do we recruit, or do you recruit? How do they get trained? Rivka was a special case, but not just anyone is already an expert in Federation law." He pointed at everyone but Rivka.

"I'll recruit with the assistance of my brother," Wyatt proclaimed. "I'll look at their records, and he'll look at their minds. We'll probably start with the Dip Corps and the Spy Corps, where we might find the right temperament and possibly someone trained well enough in the law. We shall see."

"No secrets. No subterfuge." Rivka took in the office. Joseph and Petricia were also there, along with the entirety of the Magistrate Corps, less her trainees Chaz and Dennicron, who were still down hard. Ankh was working to restore them to their former selves. He would not tell her their prospects. All she could do was wait. "A selfless purpose. That's the requirement. I look forward to seeing our compatriots and having a reduced caseload."

Grainger scoffed. "You will always get the hardest cases, Rivka, because General Lance Reynolds wouldn't have it any other way."

"Nor I," Wyatt added. "Nothing about the abilities of any of you, but Rivka's telepathy is an extra tool that helps us resolve cases with abject finality."

"And she's good with the law, too," Grainger remarked. "Anything else, High Chancellor?"

"I'll be taking a little vacation at my brother's urging. This business with the council has been trying. I'm tired of having to watch my own back when I can have an emerald beauty walking on it instead."

"Get the hot stone treatment. Maybe wax," Jael offered.

"Probably not." Wyatt shook his head. He looked at Rivka. "Did you ever get your other cat from General Reynolds?"

"You have to know that people don't have cats or own cats. The cats choose who they want to clean their litter boxes."

"Get your cat before you leave Yoll, Rivka."

"Maybe I'll task Red with getting her. Little Hamlet is so cute."

"Red on cat recovery duty? I don't see it. Maybe Groenwyn."

"She's still on Azfelius. We're headed there next, assuming the galaxy isn't coming unhinged, of course, and can spare me for a few days."

"Get your cat, and then get your people." Wyatt reached into his desk and pulled out a bottle of champagne. "For Red and Lindy. I hear congratulations are in order."

Rivka accepted the gift and stood to go. "I have to run, High Chancellor. Thank you for your support throughout this. Today was a hard day, really hard. Yesterday wasn't much better either, but I'm glad it's over. We have work to do."

They hugged and shook hands. Rivka opened the door to find Red waiting right there, as he would always be. He leaned against the desk. His legs were working better with each passing moment, but he wasn't up to full speed yet.

Aurora and Ryleigh, I have a mission for you. Head over to General Reynolds' office and collect Hamlet. It's time to reunite the cats.

Rivka smiled at her solution. *Wyatt Earp* was parked on the lawn in front of the Federation's main governmental building, cloaked to prevent security from getting twisted up about their presence.

"Master Vered!" Wyatt called. He took the champagne from Rivka and gave it to him directly. "Congratulations."

Red beamed. "I have a son."

"Yes, you do. We look forward to following his progress through life. When will you teach him to shoot?"

"The same time we teach him to fight," Red replied.

Rivka nodded at him, and with one last wave at the High Chancellor and her peers, they headed out.

Red tried to stay in front of her but failed because he couldn't walk as fast as he wanted to. Rivka stayed beside him. "Don't sweat it, Red. We're on Yoll, and all the bad guys are in prison."

"You said that pirate admitted there was a half-million-credit price on your head. Makes the bounty on me seem trivial in comparison."

"When the one dropping the contract gets bagged and tagged, the contract is meaningless. The one on me will die a quick death. I wanted to thank you for shielding me from that missile."

"It knocked me over. There was nothing else I could do."

"Except hold me behind you while you took the full brunt of the warhead. Sorry, but the supply officer says you owe him for the damage to a suit. I'll take it out of your pay."

"Hey!"

Rivka winked at him. They continued to the ship, making only small talk. *Open up. We're here.*

The side hatch popped, and they hurried inside before too many people saw it.

Ankh stood in the corridor with his blank expression and stared at the Magistrate without blinking. "Come with me." He walked toward Engineering, which was the de facto embassy of the Singularity.

Inside the door, Rivka stopped.

Chaz's and Dennicron's torsos were on small pedestals. The lower halves of their bodies lay on a workbench.

Chaz waved.

"You're alive," Rivka noted.

"Obviously," Chaz replied. "Dennicron and I agree that was the singularly most unpleasant experience of our lives. We do not wish to repeat it. We are working on design upgrades for the other SCAMPs.

"Good call," Rivka replied, still puzzled by the disassembly.

"Ah. We need new parts, but the old BHGs are intact."

"BHGs?"

"Brain housing groups. We have lost no capacity or memory. We are as good as new."

"Just no legs." Rivka gestured at the workbench.

"For now." Chaz and Dennicron nodded at each other.

"Thanks, Ankh and Erasmus. This universe needs you far more than it needs me."

Ankh stared at her until it became uncomfortable.

"We disagree."

THE END

JUDGE, JURY, & EXECUTIONER, BOOK 12

If you like this book, please leave a review. I love reviews since they tell other readers that this book is worth their time and money. I hope you feel that way now that you've finished the latest installment. Please drop me a line and let me know you like Rivka's adventures and want them to continue. This is my new favorite series. I hope you agree.

Don't stop now! Keep turning the pages as Craig hits his *Author Notes* with thoughts about this book and the good stuff that happens in the *Kurtherian Gambit* Universe.

Your favorite legal eagle will return! I guarantee it:).

AUTHOR NOTES - CRAIG MARTELLE

WRITTEN JULY 2021

Here we are, halfway through 2021 and this is the third Judge, Jury, & Executioner story to hit this year. I don't know if I'll get a fourth one done before year's end. I have a few other books and series in the pipeline.

One of the biggest life changes is that we have added a new dog to our lives. It took an act of Congress to get him to Alaska from California because Canada was closed for casual travelers to pass through. So Stanley, a six-year-old pit bull had to train as a service dog, get officially certified, and then fly in the cabin of a commercial plane with an individual who rates a service animal companion. This effort took four months and a great deal of effort, but he is finally here and has been here since May 30th.

For the first few weeks, we spent a great deal of time figuring each other out, but for the past month, we have our routine and it is solid. I know when he needs to go out.

We have our two-acre yard that is backed up against a ten-acre forest where we're the only ones who go in there. We have a half-mile trail set up and walk it twice a day in addition to our walks around the neighborhood. We're spending a solid 2 ½ to 3 hours a day outside. Because of burning more calories than I'm taking in, I've lost fifteen pounds since the beginning of the year. I'm only two pounds from my goal and I feel like I can get well past that. I think the weight I was when I retired from the Marines might be an optimal weight. The question is, will I be able to maintain it? That's the forever challenge but for right now, Stanley is doing right by me.

He also loves it up here, but he's never seen snow. That will be coming soon enough. And then the extreme cold. Where Phyllis had hair as thick as a sea otter's, Stanley's is thin and not densely packed. We'll see if he grows it when temperatures plummet. I expect he'll be wearing a sweater all winter and boots when he goes out onto the snow and ice. He'll get used to all of it quickly enough. He's easy going.

Rivka! In my continual effort to paint most bureaucrats as the universe's main antagonist, The Interview continues that theme. Those who sit in judgment of others while not doing anything themselves. They deserve our disdain.

But the stalwart crew from *Wyatt Earp* does what they do, save the day while making the galaxy a better place, by dealing with one scumbag at a time.

I've been through this book twice since I wrote it because I think it is some of the smoothest flowing prose yet. The dialogue engages at a better level than usual. I wish I could capture this magic and bottle it, adding a little to my coffee each morning before starting my writing day.

I have to admit that I'm only able to write for about three hours a day. The majority of my day is spent in author philanthropy. I run conferences for authors and meet with a great number of authors regarding all things publishing. The conferences take a great deal of effort, Vegas with 2000 attendees. Madrid next summer with a cap of 300. And then there's a drive across America. I'll meet with 500 people at fifteen sites over sixteen days. I won't get any writing done during that time as I drive from Las Vegas to St. Petersburg, Florida.

That's it – back to the grind. I have three new series that will publish this fall. A solo trilogy called *Battleship: Leviathan* that I'm wrapping up right now. The first book will hit the market for 99 cents and should be available for pre-order any day now. If you liked *Superdreadnought* and/or *Metal Legion*, *Battleship: Leviathan* will be right for you. We'll publish those volumes one month apart so you'll have all three by the beginning of December.

I have a series called *Zenophobia*, where the first book of a trilogy will publish in October. I've written the first book and Brad Torgersen will write books two and three. You should see the whole series before year's end :).

A series called *Glory*, pure military science fiction, the aliens coming for Earth. This one is co-written with Ira Heinichen, but we have meticulously gone through each and every word and plot point to make sure this one is the best it can be. I think you'll be gripped and stoked from the second you start reading.

I also have a new series called *Not Enough*, a coming-of-age fantasy that I'm co-writing with Eden Wolfe. This is a little out of my main genres, but it's a damn fine story. Also, another one where we have meticulously gone through each and every word to give you the very best stories we can. The second book is almost finished. I think we'll publish book one around the end of October.

I guess that's four new series coming this fall. Next up will be *A Fatal Bragg*, Ian Bragg's fourth thriller. I want to have that book finished by September 3rd. During my drive across America, I'll finish up Tommy D's sixth book – *Family Reunion*. I'm a third of the way finished but I have to get these other two books done first. I'll focus on Tommy's book in September and I bet I'll have it done in short order there. And then we'll see if the 14th book in *Judge, Jury, & Executioner* is right or the second book in the *Rick Banik* thrillers, a book I've been promising for years. And the fourth book in the *Cygnus Space Opera* series.

All kinds of stuff that needs to be written. I'll get there. There is enough time because I have no new commitments for 2022 and that takes some of the pressure off.

Peace, fellow humans.

Please join my Newsletter (craigmartelle.com—please, please, please sign up!), or you can follow me on Facebook.

If you liked this story, you might like some of my other books. You can join my mailing list by dropping by my website www.craigmartelle.com or if you have any comments, shoot me a note at craig@craigmartelle.com. I am always happy to hear from people who've read my work. I try to answer every email I receive.

If you liked the story, please write a short review for me on Amazon. I greatly appreciate any kind words; even one or two sentences go a long way. The number of reviews an eBook receives greatly improves how well an eBook does on Amazon.

Amazon – www.amazon.com/author/craigmartelle

BookBub – https://www.bookbub.com/authors/craig-martelle

Facebook – www.facebook.com/authorcraigmartelle

My web page – https://craigmartelle.com

That's it—break's over, back to writing the next book.

BOOKS BY CRAIG MARTELLE

The Expanding Universe—science fiction anthologies

Krimson Empire (co-written with Julia Huni)—a galactic race for justice

Zenophobia (#)—a space archaeological adventure

End Times Alaska (#)—a Permuted Press publication—a post-apocalyptic survivalist adventure

Nightwalker (a Frank Roderus series)—A post-apocalyptic western adventure

End Days (#) (co-written with E.E. Isherwood)—a post-apocalyptic adventure

Successful Indie Author (#)—a non-fiction series to help self-published authors

Monster Case Files (co-written with Kathryn Hearst)—A Warner twins mystery adventure

Rick Banik (#)—Spy & terrorism action adventure

Ian Bragg Thrillers—a man with a conscience who kills bad guys for money

Published exclusively by Craig Martelle, Inc

The Dragon's Call by Angelique Anderson & Craig A. Price, Jr.—an epic fantasy quest

A Couples Travel—a non-fiction travel series

For a complete list of Craig's books, stop by his website —https://craigmartelle.com

BOOKS BY MICHAEL ANDERLE

Sign up for the LMBPN email list to be notified of new releases and special deals!

https://lmbpn.com/email/

For a complete list of books by Michael Anderle, please visit:

www.lmbpn.com/ma-books/